The Kissing of the Shrew

A Survivors Short Story and Prologue

Part I

"I desire that we be better strangers."
As You Like It, *William Shakespeare*

"Are you afraid to die?"

"No."

Lieutenant Colonel Benedict Draven wasn't surprised by the soldier's answer. In as much as Benedict had seen of the young man's conduct on the battlefield, Neil Wraxall wanted to die. "You behaved rather recklessly at Sabugal."

This was understatement. Major Wraxall had behaved like a lunatic, cutting down the enemy even after they were clearly in retreat and the order to stand down had been given.

"I had nothing to lose."

"You have your rank. I could bring you up on charges for conduct unbecoming an officer."

The major's hollow blue eyes didn't blink. "Yes, sir."

"I won't do it, Major. Do you know why?" Benedict stood, resting his hands on the table where maps and missives from General Wellesley were strewn about. Portugal's April

11

rain had finally abated, but the wind whipped against the walls of his tent with determination.

"No, sir."

"I have a mission for you. A suicide mission, truth be told."

Wraxall's expression didn't change. He looked utterly and completely uninterested. Had they been in a drawing room, rather than an army encampment, Benedict would have called it ennui. And still Benedict wished Wraxall's eyes would narrow and his nostrils flare in outrage. Benedict had felt outrage when Wellesley had delivered the orders from the King. But outrage or not, the orders were clear— assemble a troop of men to carry out impossible missions. Draven had been instructed to find the best, the brightest, and—most importantly—the expendable.

Benedict had added his own criterion.

He'd sat on the orders for the past fortnight until he'd woken early one morning with the knowledge of what he must do clear in his mind. He would recruit men who were survivors. Men who could, against all the odds, emerge alive from the treacherous missions they were given.

On that Portuguese battlefield Major Neil Wraxall had proved he was a survivor.

"We're losing the war," Draven said. "These are desperate times. Bonaparte must be defeated at all costs."

"Yes, sir."

Draven fisted his hands, wishing he could scream at the man, shake him. Wraxall should be cursing him for sending him to his death. Instead the man appeared as resigned as an elderly mule when hitched to a cart on market day.

He lifted a packet of papers closed with red wax, a *D* inside two circles pressed into the crimson seal. "These are your orders. You will be in command of twenty-nine men. I have already selected a dozen of those. If you choose to accept the assignment, I want the names of those you recommend."

Wraxall held out his hand, accepting the pages.

"We need men with special skills. I've already tapped Ewan Mostyn. He's as strong as an ox. You want him at your back in a fight. And he's smart. He knows when to attack and when to hold back. Rafe Beaumont is another. He's a bit of a rake, which works for us. He can ferret information out of wives of the enemy. Lord Jasper Grantham is a tracker. He can find anyone and anything." He gestured to the papers. "It's all there and more. I've found you a sharpshooter, a strategist, a negotiator. You fill in the remaining roles."

"Yes, sir."

Draven gave Wraxall a hard look. "You don't have to accept this assignment."

"No, sir."

"But you will anyway."

Wraxall made no answer.

"Then you're a damn fool, but if you're determined to kill yourself, you might as well do it for a good cause." Draven shuffled papers and stacked them. "I'll want your recommendations in two days. Right now, go back to your tent and sleep. That's an order, Major."

"Yes, sir."

The major bowed then retreated through the tent flaps. Draven sank into his chair, head in his hands. Wraxall wouldn't sleep, any more than Draven had slept since receiving those orders. It was a vile thing, sending men to their deaths. Vile and necessary, thanks to the bloody war and bloody Napoleon Bonaparte.

The tent flaps rustled and Draven pushed his fingers against his burning eyes. His batman must have been waiting for Wraxall to depart so he might press Benedict to eat or sleep. Benedict wanted neither at the moment. He simply wanted a few moments of peace.

"Go away, Ward," he said, voice muffled behind his hands. "I told you not to come back for an hour."

No answer.

Perhaps Wraxall had forgotten something and returned. Benedict dropped his hands, but the man before him was neither his batman nor Major Wraxall.

It wasn't a man at all.

Draven would have jumped to his feet if the female hadn't pointed a pistol at him.

"Sit," she said in accented English. "And keep your hands where I can see them."

Draven nodded. "Very well." The pistol shook slightly, indicating her hands trembled. If the thing was loaded, he'd rather she wasn't pointing it at his heart. "What is it you want?"

Her dark gaze met his with a steadiness and determination he recognized quickly enough, having seen it all his life on the faces of generals and commanding officers.

"What I want—no, no—what I need," she said coolly, "is a husband."

***

Catarina didn't trust the soldier in front of her. By the same token, she had little choice but to trust him. Her time was up. Little as she liked it, this man was her only hope.

"I beg your pardon, miss," he said, one eyebrow arching upward. "I don't think I heard you correctly."

She jerked her chin up. "You heard me."

"You need a husband," he said slowly. He was more handsome in close proximity than he'd appeared on horseback and from a distance. She'd chosen him not for good looks but because he was in command. He was large and strong—a man who could stand up to her father.

But now she saw he was not quite so large as he'd seemed when mounted. He was probably not even six feet. But she had not been wrong about his commanding presence. Even sitting and at the other end of the barrel of her pistol, he appeared calm and in control. His blue eyes, eyes that had crinkled slightly with confusion, met hers levelly and without any concern or anger. Only his red hair seemed immune to regulation. It jutted about his head in wild swirls and spikes. Catarina had the urge to tamp it down with her fingers.

"I see." He began to stand, but she shook her head and raised the pistol higher. The soldier lowered himself again. Slowly. "Miss—?"

When she didn't give her name, his expression turned exasperated, but only for a moment. "Miss, must we have this conversation with a pistol between us?"

"Yes," she said.

"I'd rather—"

She waved the pistol. "I have no time to argue. I need a husband. Please."

"Yes, as you said. Help me to understand. Do you mean…ah"—he ran a hand through that wild hair, and she understood why it stuck up—"*marido*?" His Portuguese accent was horrendous but she was not one to judge. She doubted her English was much better.

"Husband. That is what I said."

"Did one of my men—" He seemed to reconsider. "Has one of my men been too familiar?"

"Familiar?" She knew the word. Unlike the rest of the people in the provincial town she'd had the misfortune to be born into, Catarina read. She read in four languages, including English. *Familiar* meant something or someone one saw every day, such as the path to the market. These English had only come to the area recently. They had come to fight the French, who were now in retreat. They were not familiar. "How do you mean?" she asked.

He looked a bit sheepish, which rather intrigued her. "Perhaps I did not make myself clear. Has one of my men…ah…caused you trouble?"

She frowned. She'd had to skirt his men in order to gain entry to the camp, but that had not been much trouble. "No."

"Has one accosted you?"

She considered.

"Attacked?" he said, clarifying.

"Oh! No."

"Then perhaps one of them visited you in the village and did not pay for—er, services rendered."

She narrowed her eyes. Not paid? Her father was the mayor of the village, not a merchant. And then it struck her what the soldier meant, and she straightened indignantly. She must have swung the pistol about as well because the man flinched and jerked to one side.

"I am not a prostitute."

He held both of his hands up. "I did not mean to imply that you were."

"My English is not so perfect when I talk, but I understand. You did more than imply, *senhor*."

"And you, miss, have more than tried my patience." He stood, and even when she waved the pistol at him, he did not take his seat again. "Go ahead and shoot me. Put me out of my misery, I beg you, for I fail to see how any of this relates to me." He came around the table and stalked toward her. Had she thought he was short? He seemed a giant in that moment as the space between them rapidly diminished. She could not back away. If she did, he would have the upper hand. And she did have the pistol, after all.

"Stop!" she said, brandishing her weapon. To her surprise, he halted. "Do not come any closer."

"Is that pistol even loaded?" he asked.

"Yes." But she'd hesitated, and he'd seen it. His brows lifted with skepticism.

"Very well then, shoot me."

"I would rather not, *senhor*. You are more valuable to me alive."

"You think to take me as your prisoner? Whom do you work for? The French?" He moved closer. "I assure you, I will never be taken alive."

"I do not work for anyone—French or English. And I do not wish to kill you. I need you alive so you can marry me."

He was close enough to touch the pistol now, but her words had stopped him in his tracks. "Say again?"

"Do you not understand English? You will come with me now and be my husband."

He stared at her as though understanding for the first time. "You want *me* to marry *you*?"

She cursed in her native Portuguese. Perhaps she had made the wrong choice after all. The man was not nearly as clever as she had thought him. She closed her eyes in frustration, and that was her mistake. The next thing she knew she was flat on her back, her wrist imprisoned in one his hands, rendering the pistol unusable.

The soldier straddled her, his face dark and dangerous in the shadows. She bucked and struggled, but he simply grasped her other hand and held her in place easily. His broad shoulders were obviously not the result of a padded uniform but actual muscles.

"Let me go!"

"Not likely. I think we shall begin our conversation again. This time on my terms and with civility."

"I was civil. I said *please*."

His mouth turned up at one corner, and in that moment, she almost forgot she wanted him to get off her. She would have rather he kissed her. A strange thought to enter her mind since he was at least a dozen years older than she. But he did not seem such an old man at the moment. He seemed strong and virile—too strong, she thought as she tried, again and in vain, to push him off.

"Yes, you did. But perhaps we might begin with introductions. Lieutenant Colonel Draven of the 16th Light Dragoons. And you are?"

She did not see the harm in telling him. She would have had to give her name during the wedding. "Catarina Ana Marciá Neves."

"And is that your real name?"

"Yes."

"Who sent you?"

He still thought her a spy for the French. "No one. I came on my own. I told you, I need a husband."

His grip on her wrist loosened. "Are you with child?"

Her instinct was to immediately deny it, but the release of pressure from her wrists gave her another idea. She raised her hands, ramming them into his chest. If he hadn't been balancing precariously above her, the push would have been completely ineffective. Instead, it left him off balance and while he struggled to keep from toppling back she slithered from between his legs, crawled to her knees, and pushed off for flight.

She was back on the floor in only one step. He'd caught her ankle and dragged her back. She tried to kick him. He swore and grasped her about the waist, locking her arms beneath his grip. Still kicking and fighting, he carried her across the tent and set her down, none too gently in a chair. She tried to jump up again, but he pinned her arms to the armrests.

"Miss Neves, what did I say about civility?"

"Let me go!"

"Oh, no. *You* came into my tent. *You* threatened me with a pistol. Now it is *my* turn for some answers."

He dragged her, still trapped in the chair, toward a trunk, which he then flung open. He reached in and yanked out what appeared to be tack for a horse and used it to bind her wrists to the chair's arms. When he attempted to secure her ankles to the legs of the chair, she almost landed a kick to his nose. He managed to dodge it and grasped her leg in a firm grip. "That was unwise."

She gasped as his hand slid under her skirt to caress the bare flesh of her calf beneath her dress. "Do not touch me."

He raised a brow. "What, no stockings?"

She tried to shake his grip off. "And where would I acquire them? This town is still living in the sixteenth century. I did not give you leave to touch me!"

He eyed her warily. "Never let it be said I did not treat a woman with respect. I will release you if you give me your word you will sit still and allow me to bind you."

She shook her head. Her long, dark hair had fallen into her eyes. She must look as much a peasant as she felt. "And when I am bound, how am I to fight you should you take liberties?"

He nodded as though considering the point. "Very well, I give you my word, as a gentleman, I will not touch you."

"You are a gentleman?" she asked.

"I am not titled, but my father owned land and can trace his ancestry back over four hundred years. I am also an officer of His Majesty the King of England. I would not behave dishonorably."

She blew out a breath. She knew enough of these English soldiers to know they often behaved dishonorably. The rumor was that a girl in a village a day's ride from here had been accosted by a group of English soldiers, and now all the women in Catarina's village were to stay indoors and not go anywhere without a male escort.

She'd disregarded that rule entirely in coming here. And she reminded herself that she'd come because she'd seen this officer and known instinctively that she could trust him. It was too late to turn back. She had no choice but to trust her instincts.

"Very well. I agree."

He released her leg, and she found the removal of his touch and the warmth of his skin on hers more of a loss than she'd expected. Perhaps her mother was right, and she was a wanton woman who needed to marry sooner rather than later. While the soldier tied her ankles, Catarina said a prayer to the Blessed Mother, asking for forgiveness for enjoying the man's touch.

When she was bound, he stepped back, giving her space. She supposed the gesture was to make her feel less threatened. It did not work. He was such a presence in the tent that she could not help but feel overwhelmed by him. Even the tent, which was larger than her little stone and tile-roofed cottage, seemed small when he stood.

He drew the pistol, *her* pistol, from his pocket and studied it. Then he looked at her and back at the pistol. "If you have actually fired this antique, you're braver than I am. It must be sixty years old."

"Eighty," she corrected. "It was my grandfather's."

"And you planned to fire it and kill both of us?" He examined it closer then made a sound of disgust. "No, of course you weren't. It isn't even loaded or primed." He looked up at her, his blue eyes narrowed in anger. "You've made quite the fool of me."

"That was not my intention. If I had come here with no weapon, you would not have listened."

"Wouldn't I? You know me so well then?"

She only knew what she had heard about the English soldiers. They were proud and haughty and took what they wanted. She had seen him and thought he looked powerful enough to serve her purposes but also fair and honest. She'd watched him for several days and he always treated his men with dignity.

But she had never considered asking him if he would marry her without the pistol pointed at him,. Why would he, a powerful English soldier, want to marry her, a Portuguese peasant? She wasn't even beautiful—not like the pale, flaxen beauties who resided in England. She was dark with coarse curly hair and what her mother liked to call a *strong personality*. She was not dainty or demure. She was not quiet or obedient. No wonder her father wanted to be rid of her.

She lifted her chin. "Very well, *senhor*. If I had asked you to marry me, would you have said yes?"

"The name is Draven. Lieutenant Colonel Draven."

Draven. It sounded odd to her ears, but she liked it nonetheless.

"And to answer your question, Miss Neves, no. I am not looking for a wife at present."

"And I am not looking for a husband. I would not have asked you to remain my husband. I do not even think the marriage would be considered legal in your country."

"No doubt it wouldn't. You are a Catholic, I presume."

"And you are a heathen, but I do not hold that against you."

To her surprise, he laughed. His face looked younger when he laughed, even more handsome. His cheeks reddened slightly and his eyes looked even bluer. "That is something then. Tell me, Miss Neves, why are you in such desperate need of a husband?"

She sighed. "My father is the mayor of our town."

"The little one on the other side of the hill?"

"Yes."

"I met him. He seemed a good man. Has he treated you ill?"

She tried to wave a hand, but she couldn't as it was tied to the chair. "Nothing like that, *Senhor* Draven. It is that he has had the misfortune to be given seven daughters, and I am the eldest."

"Seven? Gad, one would think he would have stopped after four or five."

"He is a man with much...how do you say? Optimism?"

"Yes, obviously." He crossed his arms over his broad chest. "And so he must marry you off in order to make a good match for your sisters."

"Yes. It is the same in your country?"

"The older girls do generally marry before the younger."

"Yes, well, the men of the town are eager to marry my two next younger sisters, Ana and Luisa. They are both quiet and shy and very beautiful."

"And no one is vying for your hand?"

"I scare them off."

He laughed again, but this time she was somewhat annoyed. "I am happy to amuse you, *senhor*! But I do not find it amusing. My father is also not amused, and he has made arrangements to marry me in two days' time."

"And you do not like his choice?"

"The man is ancient! He must be fifty."

"Ah, only ten years my senior then."

She was genuinely surprised. He did not look forty. Or perhaps *Senhor* Guerra was older than she had thought.

"I will not marry him."

"And you think me a better alternative?"

"No! I do not want to marry you, either. But I want to escape, and I can think of no better way. If you marry me, I will have the protection of your name. I need but a year's time to save money so I might travel to Lisbon or perhaps farther—Paris or London."

"You wouldn't be safe in London."

"That is not your concern, *senhor*."

"It is if I marry you."

She held her breath. "*Will* you marry me?"

Part II

"If I be waspish, best beware my sting."
The Taming of the Shrew, *William Shakespeare*

He actually considered saying *yes*. If he'd been a super-stitious man, he might have suspected her of witchcraft. After all, she'd certainly beguiled him with those large brown eyes and that soft mouth. And now the look on her face was one of pure desperation. He would have been a man of little honor indeed if he had not wanted to help her.

But she was no child. Both her figure and her mind proved to him she was very much a woman. If he'd had to guess, he would have put her age at somewhere between one and twenty and five and twenty. She was certainly old enough to stand up to her father and reject any unacceptable marriage prospects he might offer her.

"No," he said, with a stab of regret. She was beautiful and lush and the part of him that was male was drawn to her. But he was also a soldier with a duty to his country. He couldn't take care of a wife, and he did not believe for a moment she planned to stay behind when the British army moved out. She'd follow him back to England, and how would he explain her to his family? What if, after this business with Napoleon had ended, he wanted to retire and marry for love? How would he explain a Portuguese peasant woman?

Her eyes widened. "No?" she said, her voice edged with just enough steel to give him pause.

"I cannot marry you." He crossed to her and began to free her from the bindings. Now that he knew the pistol was useless, she was really no threat. "I do apologize, but you will simply have to return home to your father and explain to him—"

She jumped to her feet, causing him to stumble back. Perhaps untying her had been hasty.

"Do you think I have not tried that?" She sputtered a stream of words in Portuguese. His understanding of the language was rudimentary, but he could have sworn he heard *stupid man.* "You tie me up and ask me to tell you my story and then you send me on my way? No compassion!"

He straightened. "I have compassion. I have compassion for hungry dogs and injured horses, but I don't marry them either."

Her eyes grew larger. "Do you call me a dog?"

"No!" This had gone horribly wrong somehow. "You misunderstand."

"Yes. I see that now." The direct way she looked at him told him she meant she had misunderstood more than his comment. "I will leave you in peace."

With that, she whirled on her heel and swept out of the tent, looking more like the Queen of Spain than a barefoot peasant.

Christ! The woman didn't even have shoes on! He had to go after her. But when he emerged from his tent, he stepped into darkness. A few low fires burned but most of the men had gone to sleep. The sentries kept watch—little good they had done since she'd slipped past them—but the camp was quiet and all but deserted.

Catarina Neves had disappeared.

A day later Wellesley gave the order to move out. At first light the men and horses marched north, away from Sabugal and toward yet another battle with the French. To his annoyance, Draven hadn't forgotten about the woman. Every time he turned he seemed to catch sight of her, but what he took for black hair was a horse's tail and a woman's skirts was the flapping of a tent.

After a long day of marching, he was finally tired enough—or perhaps far enough away—to forget her. Major

Wraxall had given him a list of names, and Benedict had spent the evening discussing the list with Ward, his batman and a trusted friend. Wraxall had chosen well and carefully. Benedict couldn't help but notice the major had not selected any men with children or wives.

So Wraxall knew what he was in for. He knew he would most likely not ever return home to England. It was a sacrifice thousands of men had made in this war, but Benedict hated to see another make it nonetheless.

"Is there anything else, sir?" Ward asked.

"No. You are dismissed."

Alone, Benedict started to shed his coat. The ride today had been long and tomorrow would be equally arduous. He should sleep, but he couldn't seem to settle. Instead of removing his coat, he paced the floor and considered the orders he would send before the end of the month—orders to the men of the suicide troop. Orders to meet him on the border of Spain and France to receive the details of their first mission.

His legs had grown stiff in the saddle, but still restless, Benedict decided to make a tour of the camp and then turn in for the night. He left his tent and shoved his hands in his pockets against the chill of the night. He strolled confidently between the tents and campfires. He nodded at his men, stopping at times to exchange a few brief words.

Finally, he came to the edge of the camp and stood staring out into the rocky landscape and the distant mountains. The night was still young, but the moon had risen early. It was a full moon and sat low in the sky, appearing so close Benedict felt like he could reach out and touch it. Just as he was about to return to his tent, he spotted a furtive movement a few yards away. Two figures, visible in the moonlight, emerged from the crowd of tents and started away from the camp.

Benedict waited for the sentries to call out to them, but the sentries were not at their posts. He'd have a word with them. But as he watched the two figures move away, their shapes became more distinct. One was most certainly a man, a soldier. The other was a woman.

And he was willing to wager all he possessed that he knew the woman.

"Bloody hell," he swore. He moved quickly now that the stiffness had eased from his muscles. His legs ate up the ground dividing the couple and himself so that it was only a few moments before he was close enough to call out. "Halt!" he shouted.

The soldier skidded to a stop, clearly used to following orders. The woman only peered over her shoulder with a look of annoyance.

He'd *known*. He'd *known* it would be her.

She tugged at the soldier—just a boy, really, barely old enough to need a razor—urging him forward.

"Miss Neves," Benedict said before she could persuade the lad to behave as stupidly as she. "If you wish to see this lad in the stocks or worse, then by all means, continue luring him from camp."

Now she too halted and gave him a look of exasperation. "*You!*"

"My thoughts exactly. You should be back in Sabugal."

She tossed her head. "I have an aunt who lives nearby."

"Do you, now?"

The lad straightened. "Sir, I can explain. I was not deserting—"

Benedict waved a hand for silence. "Oh, I know exactly what is happening here, and I will give you ten seconds to march back to camp and go directly to bed."

"But, sir! I cannot leave the lady—"

"Ten, nine—"

The lad looked from Miss Neves to Benedict. "Sir!"

"The clock is ticking, soldier. Eight, seven…"

With an apologetic look, the boy took off running back into camp.

The woman gave a long, loud sigh. Then she turned her glare on Benedict. "Are you following me?"

He should take pity on her. Clearly, she was daft. "Need I remind you, Miss Neves, this is my regiment. *You* are the one who does not belong." And in more ways than one. In a camp full of soldiers and the usual spattering of camp followers, she was young and bold and, in the silvery moonlight, impossibly beautiful. Her hair had been pulled back and away from her face, but she'd left it down so it hung in long, dark waves about her shoulders. Her face was pale, her eyes larger than he remembered. And she seemed smaller as well. She wore a dark peasant blouse and a long dark skirt, cinched about her small waist with some sort of scarf.

She was weary, most likely from walking these past days and surviving only on what food she could gather or beg from the soldiers. If she'd gone to these lengths, she was more desperate than he'd thought. "Quite obviously, you are following me."

She gestured in the distance, toward what he assumed was the location of a small village. "I told you, my aunt—"

"I don't believe a word of it. There is no aunt. You have followed the soldiers in the hopes you might persuade one of the more gullible to marry you."

She stabbed her hands on her hips. "And what is the harm if the man agrees? I would have brought him back after the ceremony."

"He does not have permission to marry."

"No one need know he had even left the camp. I went to much trouble to make sure!" She closed her mouth abruptly, seeming to realize she had said something incriminating.

"What trouble?" Benedict narrowed his eyes then looked about. "Where are the sentries?"

"They are unharmed, although I cannot vouch for the ache in their heads tomorrow."

Benedict closed his eyes in frustration. He could see her hanged for this. She'd singlehandedly ensured the camp had weakened defenses. What if the enemy was nearby, waiting for a chance to attack? "We could win the war in a fortnight if I could but set you on the French," he grumbled. "They would never see it coming."

"Try it, and I will gut you like a fish."

He opened his eyes and saw she'd moved to a crouching stance and held a knife out in front of her. Benedict raised a brow. "This again?"

"I assure you this knife works perfectly. It may be old, but it is wickedly sharp."

Benedict put his hands on his hips, affecting boredom. In truth, this was the most entertainment he'd had in months—perhaps years. "Yes, but do you know how to use it?"

"Come a little closer, and I will give you a demonstration." She shifted her weight, keeping on the balls of her feet. Someone had given her a tip or two, quite possibly one of his men. But Benedict had been a soldier when she was still in swaddling clothes. She was no threat to him.

"Very well." He started toward her. Her eyes widened in surprise. She hadn't expected him to take her up on the offer, but she was braver than he'd expected and she held her ground.

"I don't want to hurt you," she said as he came within striking range.

"Don't worry. You won't."

Now she moved backward, suddenly on the defensive. "If you leave me in peace, I promise to go straight to my aunt's house. You won't see me again."

He advanced. She retreated.

"I don't believe you."

They circled each other now, she brandishing the knife and he with his arms hanging loosely at his sides.

"I cannot take the risk that I will come across you again and lose one of my men to your schemes."

"Schemes? I do not know that word, but I do not like it." She was light on her feet, moving just out of reach every time he thought he had a chance to take hold of her.

"You shouldn't. To be called *scheming* is not a compliment."

"You insult me? Then I shall do likewise, *old man*."

His brows shot up. Old? At forty he was in better shape than most of the youths he commanded. And he had the wisdom to complement the strength. Yet the insult stung. He was not as young as he had been.

"Old, am I? I will show you exactly how old and feeble I am." He reversed directions, taking her off guard. As he'd expected, she swung the knife at him. He ducked and moved agilely behind her, kicking her feet out from under her. He'd expected her to go down with a thud, but at the last moment she rolled.

She lost the knife. It thumped on the rocky ground between them, and Benedict reached out with the toe of his boot and flipped the knife into his hand.

She gasped. "How did you—"

And then she must have realized he had her knife and she stood defenseless. She whirled and started to run, but she had to skirt some of the larger rocks and he easily caught up to her and grasped her around her slender waist.

She fought him, kicking and attempting to bite through the thick wool of his coat. With a curse, he sheathed the dagger and struggled to hold her still. Leaning close to speak in her ear, where he knew she could hear him, he said low, "Do not make me tie you up again."

She stilled then, and Benedict noted several details, all of them quite unwillingly. Firstly, she smelled irresistible. He could not describe it, but later when he was in a market in Spain, he would think her scent akin to the mixture of cinnamon and cloves. She was rich and mysterious and he could have breathed her in all night.

Secondly, she was not quite so small and slender as he had thought. Beneath the modest peasant clothing, her body was rounded, firm, and lush. He had to resist the urge to run his hands over the bounty of her flesh.

Thirdly, she was terrified. This last point made acting the gentleman a good deal easier. He would never have known it from her behavior, but touching her, he could feel how she trembled and shook. He considered that it might be out of anger or from the cool night air, but Benedict could not believe that even a hardened soldier would not have felt some fear in her position.

"I won't hurt you," he said. He didn't know why he said the words. He did not want to comfort her. He wanted to throttle her. But though his brain told his arms to release her, his arms had ideas of their own.

"Then let me go," she said, finally stilling, though still tense in his embrace. He could not see her face, but he could imagine the pleading in the large brown eyes and the determined set of her full mouth.

"And if I let you go, how can I be certain you will not be back husband hunting?"

She tensed then relaxed. "I will not."

"You are lying." If he hadn't been holding her, he would not have known, but her body had given her away. She'd had to steel herself to make the lie sound believable.

"I am not."

"Miss Neves," he said against her ear, the scent of her swirling about him until he was all but dizzy with it. "Catarina, let us be honest with each other."

She tensed and before she could speak he made a tutting noise.

She blew out a breath. "I promise *you* will never see me again."

"Not good enough."

"Then what do you want? If I say I will give up, you will know I am lying."

She was a problem that would not simply go away. He'd been in the army long enough to recognize the stubborn quandaries that turned up again and again. One must deal with them directly or never be free.

Slowly and carefully, he released all but her wrist. That he held with an iron grip. "Come back to my quarters," he said. "We will make a battle plan."

***

Catarina felt almost at home when she was once again in Draven's tent. Perhaps because it was familiar. Or perhaps because it smelled of him—the mingled scents of horse and gunpowder and man. And when Draven sat her on his cot and draped a rough blanket about her shoulders, she did not argue. She was bone weary.

"Would you like tea?" he asked.

She had heard about the English and their tea. She had never had tea, but even in her poor village, coffee from the colonies was available. Truth be told, she would have preferred a few sips of port wine. It would warm her faster than any other beverage she could imagine. "Thank you," she finally answered. She was not certain the last time she had eaten or when she would eat again, and she was in no position to be choosy.

She was vaguely aware of him moving in and out of the tent. She struggled to keep her eyes open, but the blanket on her shoulders seemed to push her down. And she was already so weary. She'd been following the soldiers for two days with little rest and less sustenance. And now all her work, all her efforts, were for nothing. She would be forced to return to her family and marry *Senhor* Guerra.

And if she had thought Guerra angry before, he would be furious now.

She did not remember closing her eyes, but when she opened them it was to call out in pain. She wrenched her arm away and sitting, cradled it close. For a moment she was completely disoriented, and then she heard his voice.

"Miss Neves, what is wrong? Is your arm injured?"

She held it tighter, swiping at the tears that had come to her eyes. "I am fine."

"The hell you are. I barely touched your arm, and you jumped as though you'd been burned. Let me see."

"No!" Her sleeves, long and loose, concealed the damage that had been done. She had not looked at it in two days, but she could imagine the flesh was mottled with bruises.

He took a deep breath and stood surveying her with eyes as cool and blue as frozen lake. He looked at her with the same calculation he might an opposing army. He was still dressed in his uniform, his attire impeccable. Only his hair, tousled and spiky, refused to be tamed. The tent walls flapped, and for the first time she heard the sound of raindrops on the canvas.

He looked up. "It started about two hours ago."

"I fell asleep?" She could not believe she had slept for over two hours.

"You were asleep within minutes, and I concluded anyone that exhausted should not be disturbed. And now you shall be able to rest further. We stay here until the rain abates. I would not have woken you, but I must tend to my horse. I did not want you to wake alone."

She nodded. "Thank you, *senhor*. That was kind."

He raised a brow. "I have been called many things, but *kind* is not one of them. I assure you, you are still very much a prisoner. I have a man standing guard outside. He will stop you should you attempt to flee."

She shrugged. "And where would I go?"

"I shudder to think, madam. When I return, we shall have tea and discuss that arm." He nodded to the arm she still cradled, and then he was gone.

Catarina sat on the cot for a long while, hopelessness washing over her in waves. She had always been clever—even her father had said so—but she did not think that trait would save her now. She had tried and failed to secure a husband. She could not keep traveling with the British army. She would either starve or have to become a prostitute, and neither option seemed terribly appealing. She could run off to another village or go to Lisbon, but she knew the fates that waited for a young woman without a guardian in those scenarios. She would end up dead—or worse.

If she had any money, she might be able to flee to a convent. But then if she'd had any coin, she would not be in this position right now. Her only hope had been to marry and to use her husband's name to escape her father's plan to marry her to *Senhor* Guerra. If her new "husband" had given her a bit of coin that would have helped, but Catarina had been earning her keep from the age of five. She could cook, sew, take in washing, tend the garden, and look after the family's goats and chickens. She'd often been praised for her embroidery. Perhaps she could sell some of it to bring in additional funds and eventually escape.

And she would probably do all of that and more, but as the wife of *Senhor* Guerra. His children were already grown and married, with the exception of the youngest daughter who kept house for him. But even that youngest daughter was only a couple years younger than Catarina herself. No doubt her father would not have agreed to the match if he hadn't been desperate to rid himself of one of his seven daughters, and what a stroke of fortune that *Senhor* Guerra would take the most willful and disobedient of the lot, Catarina.

She did not want to resign herself to her fate, but what other choice did she have? She had tried and failed and no doubt she would be beaten soundly for it.

She rose to try and work some of the stiffness from her legs and shoulders. Other than the table, cot, and a trunk Catarina presumed was filled with clothing, this Draven did not have many possessions with him. Not that she would have looked at them if he had—well, not taken much more than a quick peek.

She found the chamber pot behind a tall screen she had thought simply for decoration. She used it then spotted a mirror dangling from one of the tent poles. It was a small mirror such as a man might use for shaving. She was too short to see herself in it, so she lifted it down and then gasped at her appearance. She looked almost wild with her hair in tangled curls about her face and her eyes too large in her pale face.

The effort of taking the mirror down reminded her of the bruising on her arm, and she loosened the simple tie holding the bodice together and lowered the neckline over her bruised shoulder. She wore a shift underneath, but with her arm exposed she could almost discern the bruising. Unfortunately, there was not enough light behind the screen, and she moved around the screen and into the light of the lamp in the tent to see better.

She winced at the sight that greeted her. Her upper arm was a palette of blacks, blues, greens, and mottled yellows. It actually looked as bad as it felt. The other arm was also bruised, but she did not think quite as badly as this one. She was about to raise the sleeve so she could lower the opposite one when she heard a quick intake of breath.

Catarina looked up and met the angry gaze of Draven, standing in the tent's opening, water dripping from his hat and shoulders onto the rug. Catarina hastily yanked her sleeve up, but Draven moved too quickly. He was beside her in an instant, snatching the sleeve back down.

"*Senhor!*" Catarina protested.

"Who did this to you?" he asked, the heat of his fury in sharp contrast to the cold raindrops falling on her arm. "Who?"

"Let me go!"

He cupped her chin and tilted it up, his touch strangely gentle. She could feel how he all but vibrated with tension. "Tell me who did this to you."

"Release me."

"Tell. Me."

Catarina narrowed her gaze, frustration pouring through her. "The man who would be my husband."

Part III

"In time the savage bull doth bear the yoke."
Much Ado about Nothing, *William Shakespeare*

Benedict released her abruptly, grimacing when she stumbled backward slightly. He resisted the urge to grab her arm to steady her. She had obviously been grabbed there once too often already.

He looked at her bruised arm again as she hastened to cover the injury. He'd thought—feared—that one of his men had abused her. He could see now that the bruising was recent but not fresh.

"Your betrothed did this?"

She tied the strings of her bodice with quick, practiced movements. "I told you I would not marry him. I told you I wanted to escape."

"I thought—"

Her dark eyes narrowed again. "You thought I was a silly girl who considered her betrothed not handsome

49

enough. No, *Senhor* Draven, it is not so silly to wish to survive to my old age."

"And if your father knew—"

She sighed as though he was a child who did not understand the ways of the world.

"So he knows and does not care."

"When I returned home after your refusal of me that night, who do you think sent for *Senhor* Guerra?" She looked away from him, her mouth set in a hard line. "I am to be sold and tamed, broken like you might break a horse. Now you see why I acted so rashly."

"And if you were to marry another man you would be safe?"

She shrugged. "I am not without resources and skills. I will use the protection of my husband's name to bide my time, save my coins, and leave for a better life in Lisbon or perhaps a convent."

He couldn't help it. He laughed aloud.

She shot him a dangerous glare. "How wonderful you find me so amusing. I would not wish for your pity."

"Catarina," he said, moving toward her. "You would make an awful nun."

She stiffened. "I do not know your customs, *senhor*, but in my country, we are not so…familiar."

"You may call me Benedict."

She shook her head. "I told you, it is improper."

"Even among husbands and wives?"

Her mouth closed, then opened, then closed.

"You understood me correctly," he said. "I will marry you." He looked about the tent for a coat or covering he could spare to protect her from the rain. "And I suppose we had better go tonight. Will there be a priest in the village, do you think?"

"Why?" she said, her voice low. He glanced at her. She hadn't moved at all.

"We cannot marry without a priest," he quipped.

She merely looked at him, his attempt at levity having fallen flat.

"You need protection. As a gentleman, I cannot, in good conscience, leave you unprotected."

"But before—"

"I didn't know the circumstances before. Now I do. You are certain you will be safe if you return home?"

"No," she answered, "but I could stay with my aunt for the time being. I did not lie when I said she lives in the village."

That was something then. "Good. Then we'll marry, and I'll leave you in her care."

He fought the feeling of a fist squeezing his lungs. How could he marry this woman? He did not even know her. Benedict opened a trunk and pulled out a coat for her. He would not be marrying her in truth, he told himself. The marriage would not be legal in England. And he would never see her again. After they exchanged vows, he could forget her.

He would have to forget her. Bonaparte and his French army demanded it.

***

Catarina walked through the next several hours as though in a dream. Benedict Draven, the man who would be her husband, had readied his own horse then borrowed one for her and led her into the little town. She'd showed him her aunt's house, and they'd knocked on the door until poor Tia Alda had called out, asking who had disturbed her. She'd opened the door when Catarina answered and dragged the girl inside.

It took Catarina another few minutes to persuade Tia Alda to also admit Benedict Draven.

There had been more arguing when Catarina had revealed her plan to Tia Alda. Alda was her father's sister and not keen to anger her brother. Benedict Draven had been patient through Tia Alda's arguments and Catarina's rebuttals, but when the rain had begun to ease, he'd cleared his throat. "General Wellesley will take advantage of a lull in the storm to break camp. If we are to do this, it must be now."

Catarina had translated, and Tia Alda gave a huge sigh then threw on her shawl, shoved her feet into her crude shoes, and led them to the church. The priest had already been awake, which saved time, but Catarina had to argue with him to convince him to conduct the ceremony.

"What seems to be the problem?" Benedict Draven had asked, glancing at his pocket watch.

"He fears for your mortal soul, *senhor*," Catarina told him. "You are not Catholic. Would you be willing to convert?"

Benedict Draven merely raised a brow. "Tell him if it eases his conscience, I am willing to make a donation to the church." He withdrew a purse heavy with coins and held it out.

After that the priest decided sprinkling holy water on Benedict Draven and assigning him several prayers would be enough of a penance.

And then Catarina had blinked and she was married. She knelt in silence as the priest said the final words of the ceremony. Benedict Draven rose, Tia Alda wept softly, and the priest patted the pocket of his robe where he'd secreted the purse.

"The rain has ceased," Draven announced to no one in particular. "I must return to camp."

Catarina stood, her legs unsteady. She knew Benedict Draven did not consider the vows he'd spoken binding. She knew his country would not consider the marriage legal. Perhaps her country would not either. She knew she would never see him again.

And yet she could not help but feel a connection to the man.

He was her husband. The two were now one in the eyes of God. Did it really matter if no one else considered them joined together? They'd spoken vows in a church in the sight of the Almighty.

Her eyes lifted to the cross with the crucified Christ looking down at her with an expression of both pain and mercy.

"Thank you, Father," Benedict Draven said with a nod. Then to Catarina, "I will see you to your aunt's house before I return."

She'd nodded mutely and began to follow her aunt out of the church. Draven was close behind, and she felt him place a protective hand on the small of her back as they walked. For some reason, his touch made her tremble.

She was a married woman now. She belonged to Benedict Draven. There was relief in that thought. Her father could not give her to *Senhor* Guerra. She was safe from him, safe from other men too. Draven and the British would leave, and she would have new freedom and independence. Perhaps in time she could see something of the world.

On the way back to Tia Alda's home, she glanced at her new husband several times. But he kept his own council, his face stoic. Was he really so unaffected by the events of the evening?

All too quickly they arrived at Tia Alda's home. She, of course, invited the couple in for port to celebrate. Catarina translated.

"Tell her thank you, but I must go."

Tia Alda had a few words to say about that, but finally Catarina shooed her inside, and she and Benedict Draven were left alone. Catarina felt suddenly shy. She was uncertain what to do with her hands, and she clenched them before her so she would not fidget and pluck at her skirts.

Finally, Benedict Draven spoke. "I am sorry to leave so abruptly."

"I understand," she said. "And I thank you. I cannot repay you enough."

He held up a hand. "I do not want repayment. I want you to be safe. Stay here. No more running after the army."

She nodded, looking down at her clasped hands. He held out a handkerchief. She glanced at it then up at his face. "A token of remembrance?" She smiled. "For me?"

He looked surprised at her words. "Yes, well, I gave the priest my purse, but I wrapped some coins in here for you."

Catarina felt cold seep into her veins. "You do not need to give me any money."

"I want you to have something. If only so you are not wholly reliant on your father."

She didn't want to take it, but she did not have the luxury of refusing. Married or not, if she was a burden to her father, he would try to find a way to make her another man's responsibility. Draven's coins would buy her time until her younger sisters married or she could save enough to run away to Lisbon.

She reached out. "Thank you."

He placed the handkerchief in her hand, but when she closed her fingers on it, he didn't release her. He lifted his other hand and held both of her hands in his warm ones.

Catarina looked up at him, her heart beating wildly in her chest as though it were some caged thing eager to be free.

"Despite everything, I am glad I met you, Catarina Neves."

"And I you, Benedict Draven." Her voice shook slightly, and she prayed he had not heard the quaver.

"May I—" he began then shook his head. "I shouldn't."

"No!" she stammered before he could release her hands. "What is it?"

"Would it be impertinent to ask for a kiss?"

She was not certain of the meaning of *impertinent*, but if it would keep him from kissing her, she hated the word.

"No." She shook her head. "There is no impertinent."

"Then I may kiss you?"

Please. Her voice did not seem to work, so she merely nodded her head. He leaned down so very slowly she thought he might have changed his mind. And then she felt the barest brush of his lips over hers. Her skin tingled where he touched her—her hands, her lips. Her heart continued its rapid fluttering, and her eyes slid closed.

His mouth swept over hers once, then again, so lightly she was not even certain it constituted a kiss. And suddenly she very much wanted a kiss from her husband. She would have nothing else from him save a few coins and a handkerchief. A kiss to remember him by did not seem too much to ask.

Tentatively at first, she leaned into him, pressing her lips against his with the barest pressure. His hands tightened on hers, but he did not pull away. Imitating his earlier actions, she passed her lips over his. The heat from the friction she caused made her sigh, and it was on that sigh that he swept her into his arms and brought his mouth down upon hers.

Catarina had never been kissed. She'd never been held tenderly in a man's arms. Never felt the all-consuming need engendered by passion. Now all the new sensations rushed at her with a suddenness she could hardly understand much less make sense of. So she did the only thing she could.

She kissed him back, her lips moving against his, her tongue making shy advances to meet with his.

The world around them seemed to fade away. She no longer smelled the flowers in Tia Alda's window box or the damp soil from the rains. She didn't feel the cool night swishing her skirts against her legs or the hard cobblestones beneath her thin, ragged shoes. She only knew Benedict's warm body pressed to hers, his skilled lips teasing hers into doing things she had never even imagined, and the scent of him—all masculine and foreign and delicious.

And then with a groan he placed his hands on her waist and gently separated from her. Catarina might have swayed if he hadn't been holding on to her. Gradually, she opened her eyes and blinked at him.

"Let me remember you like this," he said, his voice low and husky. He raised her hand, kissed it, and then with a stiff bow, walked away and into the night. Catarina might have followed. She knew he would go to the nearby stable and fetch the horses. She would have time to catch him, time to beg him to take her with him.

Time to plead for one last kiss.

Instead, she clutched the handkerchief more tightly in her hands then raised it to her nose, inhaling the scent of him. For though she might wish differently, this was all she would ever have.

***

He shouldn't have kissed her.

Benedict repeated the refrain at least a hundred times before he reached camp. The ride back to camp seemed longer and colder than the ride into the village. But everything was cold after that kiss.

Why had he done it?

Well, he knew why he'd done it. She was a beautiful woman and saying the vows in the church, no matter how dubious their legality, had made him think of her as his. How could he walk away from her without one kiss, without one taste of her?

And now he'd spend the rest of the night wishing he hadn't had that taste. He'd probably spend the rest of the week thinking about her, imaging her lush body in his arms and her soft skin beneath his hands. If he'd known she would kiss him back—and that she would kiss him so eagerly and so absolutely without guile—he would have…still kissed her.

Damn. How was he supposed to leave her now? How was he supposed to ride away for glory and honor when that sweet, warm kiss was waiting for him? How—

"Colonel Draven, sir!" Ward rushed up to him as Benedict entered camp. Just before he could turn around again and ride back to Catarina. Benedict looked down at his batman, noting the frenzy of activity around him. The men were packing up belongings and gulping down hastily prepared meals.

"Ward." Benedict nodded.

"General Wellesley has given the order to march, sir. We are to leave in about an hour as the roads may be drier by then."

Benedict already felt Catarina Neves slipping away. "Very good, Ward. Would you see to this horse while I make sure Majeed is taken care of?"

Ward gave the horse Catarina had ridden a puzzled look. "Of course, sir." He took the animal's reins and walked him back toward the paddock.

Benedict made to follow, but he spared one last look over his shoulder at the little town. The sun was peeking over the horizon, washing the tiled roofs with golden light. Catarina Neves slept under one of those roofs, and today he would ride away, quite possibly to his death at the hands of an enemy soldier.

But as he watched the sun's rays chase the shadows away, there was one fact Benedict knew to be true. If he survived this war, somewhere and somehow, he would see Catarina Neves again.

The Claiming of the Shrew

One

"But when I came, alas, to wive,
With hey, ho, the wind and the rain"
Twelfth Night, *William Shakespeare*

Catarina Ana Marciá Neves ran into the London rain storm without so much as a cloak or an umbrella. She didn't care. She was glad for the rain that washed the hot tears away. If anyone were to see them—if *he* were to see them, she'd be shamed.

She swiped at her eyes and looked fruitlessly for one of those conveyances that transported people for a fee. She didn't know why she was crying. Of course, he had another woman. What had she expected? She hadn't seen him for five years. And though they were married in God's eyes, this country did not recognize the union. She had supposed Benedict Draven had considered himself wed, but clearly she had been wrong.

About a great many things.

Oh, why could she not find one of those carriages for hire?

"Catarina!"

She spun around in time to see her husband exit the door to his lodgings and barrel into the storm. He was the sort of man who barreled or shouldered or plowed into most things—war and marriage chiefly among them. He had broad shoulders and a wide chest and the unruliest red hair she'd ever seen, and unless her eyes had deceived her, that red hair was not yet streaked with gray. It was too dark outside to see anything but shadows now.

She gave him her back. "Go away."

"You didn't come all the way from Portugal to tell me to go away," he replied, speaking loudly to be heard over the pouring rain.

"I did not come from Portugal at all." It gave her a small measure of pleasure to point out his mistake. "Leave me alone, adulterer!" She lifted her valise and took a few steps.

"I am not an adulterer. The woman you saw in my flat is not my lover."

She gave him a scathing look over her shoulder. "No decent woman would go to the home of a man unchaperoned."

"Catarina, come inside and let me explain."

"No, thank you."

He frowned at her. "We haven't seen each other for five years, and I come home to find you in my parlor. Now you plan to leave without even saying more than a dozen words to me?"

"Go speak to your harlot!"

He rolled his eyes and seemed to reach for patience. "You can't stand in the rain all night." His voice was oh so reasonable.

"I do not plan to. I am seeking a hacking or hackly...I forget the name." She waved a hand.

"A hackney. Come inside, and I'll have my man flag one. In this weather, it might be some time before one passes."

"I will not." She set the valise on the wet walkway. "There is nothing for me to say to you, at any rate. I only came to tell you that I want an annulment."

Even in the dim light she saw the shock on his face. His ruddy complexion paled, and his mouth opened and closed uselessly. He took a step back from her, as though she had struck him.

Good. She wanted to wound him.

"Why?" he asked, voice barely audible in the downpour.

"I want to marry someone else, of course."

He didn't speak, and she watched as water cascaded down his forehead and across his face. His unruly hair lay flat for once, finally tamed.

"I have all the papers, *senhor*," she said, hoping they hadn't become wet along with the rest of the items in her valise. "I need your signature before I send them to the Holy Father."

"I'm not even Catholic."

She nodded. "That may help my petition. That and the fact that you never intended to—" Even with the cold rain pounding down on her, she felt her cheeks heat. "Never intended to produce children with me."

His eyes locked on hers, and she was the first to look away.

And that's when she saw the hackney. She raised her hand and the driver veered toward her.

Her husband grasped her hand and lowered it, turning her to face him at the same time. "Catarina, don't go. Come inside and talk this over with me."

His voice was deep and compelling, and even in the cold, his hand was warm and comforting. But she could not give in to his charms. Slowly, she drew her hand away.

"I cannot stay. You may find me at Mivart's."

"I see." His shoulders straightened at the mention of the exclusive hotel. Now he would know she was not the same impoverished girl he'd known, a girl who had not even been able to afford shoes.

"Where to, gov?" The hackney's driver directed his question to her husband, of course.

"Mivart's in Mayfair. I can see to the door." He opened the door for her and helped her inside, his hand colder now than it had been earlier. A moment later he set her valise on the straw lining the floor.

"Thank you, *senhor*."

"I have…business to attend to, but I will call on you at my earliest convenience. Perhaps the day after tomorrow."

"Fine." She gave a pointed look at the door, but he didn't close it. Instead he continued to stare at her, almost as though he thought she might be a spirit.

"Me 'orse shouldn't stand long in this weather," the driver called.

"You're right," Draven said. "Good night, Catarina." And he shut the door.

Catarina did not cry on the ride back to the hotel. She didn't know what to feel. When Draven had walked into his receiving room with the woman, Catarina had been angry. But then when he'd said she was not his lover, Catarina had wanted to believe him. She wanted to believe his reaction to her request for an annulment was one of shock and dismay. She wanted to believe he did not want to let her go.

But she was no longer a child, and she could not afford to hold on to such childish fantasies. For years she'd prayed and hoped and yearned that he would come for her. If he'd wanted her, he would have. She had mistaken his reaction tonight. He probably cared only for the inconvenience she caused him.

She was barely inside the doors of the hotel when Juan Carlos stepped out from behind the chair where he'd been lurking. His face blushed red with anger and his mustache quivered with impatience. "You are late," he said in Spanish. He took her arm then abruptly dropped it, looking down at his damp hands. "What happened to you?" His gaze flew to her face. "You look like a street rat."

"I was caught in the storm," she answered in his language. She continued walking, heading for the staircase. "If you do not mind, I would like to change before I catch cold." She lifted the hem of her heavy skirts.

His dark eyes dropped to her valise. "Did he sign the papers?"

"No," she said simply. "Not yet."

"What do you mean, 'not yet'?" He followed her up the staircase. "You said this would be simple."

"It will be simple, but it will also take more than a quarter hour. Benedict Draven is not the sort of man who acts without thinking."

"Then he will sign tomorrow?" They reached the landing and she turned in the direction of the room she shared with Ines.

"He said he would call on me here the day after tomorrow."

Juan Carlos made a sound of disgust. Catarina paused outside her room. "Do not fret, *senhor*. You will have control of my business soon enough."

"Nonsense," he said, reddening further. "I think only of your happiness and your marriage to my son."

She gave him a hard look. "You think only of your own finances."

"I am helping you, my dear."

"I hardly consider blackmail a charitable endeavor. *Buenas noches*."

She opened the door and Ines was immediately before her. Her younger sister had obviously been waiting on the other side and had probably heard the conversation with Juan

Carlos. That was no matter. Ines knew all of her secrets, scant as they were.

"It seemed you were away forever. Oh!" Ines immediately began unbuttoning Catarina's spencer. She was relieved as her own hands were too cold to manage. "You are wet to the bone." She tugged the spencer off and turned Catarina around to begin unfastening her dress. Catarina felt as though she were the younger sister, though she was eight years older than Ines, who was barely eighteen.

"The weather is very bad." Catarina stepped out of her gown and Ines started on her stays. "Cold and damp and wet."

"I miss home." By *home* Ines meant Portugal, not Barcelona, where the two had lived for the past three years.

"I do too." But not as much as she would have thought. Catarina had liked the bustling city of Barcelona, and she found much in London to like as well. She might have wished to see the sun a bit more often than she had since arriving in England, but this was the land of knights and round tables. She found it enchanting. "Did Tigrino eat?"

"A little. He still hides under the bed and swats at the chamber maids' feet when they walk by." That sounded like her ill-tempered cat.

"I can do the rest," Catarina said when Ines had loosened her stays. "Would you send for hot water?"

While Ines rang for footmen to bring hot water for a bath, Catarina stripped out of her wet stockings and chemise and wrapped a large blanket around her shivering body. She stood near the fire until she could feel her fingers and toes again.

"I am guessing your husband did not sign or Juan Carlos would have sounded happier."

"I only spoke with Benedict Draven briefly," Catarina said. "I waited for him at his home, but he did not return alone." She gave her sister a meaningful look.

Ines furrowed her brow. "Why should that matter?"

Catarina wondered if she had ever been so innocent. "He had a woman with him."

"His wife?"

Catarina had never even considered that possibility. Thankfully so. "No. He claims she is not his lover."

"Do you believe him?"

Catarina shrugged. She had no reason not to believe her husband. To her knowledge, he had never lied to her before. He had always treated her with dignity, honor, and respect. "I lost my temper."

"*Oh.*"

Her sister's tone was one of horror.

"It was not *so* bad."

Ines pursed her lips, looking dubious.

"We argued in the rain and—"

"And then he kissed you!"

Catarina rolled her eyes. Ines was in love with love. She supposed that was why her father had tried to marry the girl when she'd been fourteen. If Catarina hadn't convinced her sister to run away with her, the girl would have a house full of babies by now, like four of her other sisters did. Perhaps five were married by now as Beatriz was sixteen already. Ines had been the only one of her six sisters who was anything like Catarina, though to be fair Joana had been only six when Catarina had left home and her personality still developing. But like all the others, Joana had shown signs of being shy and obedient and utterly subservient. It was difficult to be otherwise when one's father was a tyrant who demanded submission and subservience from the women in his household.

Only Ines had shown a spark of rebellion. It wasn't the stubborn, pig-headed rebellion her father said Catarina possessed. Ines was a dreamer and a romantic. She was also overly idealistic, which in itself did not recommend her to

Catarina, except that she was willing to fight for her ideals. When she saw injustice, she challenged it.

Thank the Holy Mother Catarina had been able to spirit the girl away or she would have had her spirit crushed by whatever old man her father chose for Ines's husband.

Her father hadn't been able to touch Catarina by then. After twenty years of enduring her father's control in every aspect of her life—from what she wore to what she ate to when she spoke—she had escaped. She had married and left her father's house to live with Tia Alda, but after she'd convinced Ines to leave home, she thought it wise to leave her aunt's house. She'd always wanted to go to Lisbon, and that was where she and Ines had first set up shop.

"He did not kiss me," Catarina said.

"Oh." Ines looked disappointed. No doubt she wanted to hear about the kiss in detail. Her favorite story about Colonel Draven was when he'd kissed Catarina after their wedding. Catarina had made the mistake of telling her sister about the kiss and regretted it ever since. She'd made it sound too perfect, too magical, too…everything. Now even she doubted if it could have ever been as wonderful as it was in her memory.

But then again, she'd thought her husband could not possibly be as handsome as she remembered him, and tonight that had proven untrue. If nothing else, he was more attractive to her. He wasn't handsome, not in the way some of the boys she'd flirted with in her village had been. But he drew her nonetheless. It was more in the way he carried himself, the way he spoke, the way she felt when he looked at her.

"I told him I wanted an annulment, and he agreed to come and sign the papers the day after tomorrow."

"Just like that?"

"Just like that."

"But he is supposed to fight for you. He is supposed to save you from Juan Carlos."

"I do not need saving from Juan Carlos. Marriage to his son will not be so bad."

Ines's expression turned stricken. "But all you have worked for will be taken away. You will be his property, and you always said you never wanted to be a man's property."

Catarina blew out a breath. She should learn to stop talking so much. "I was foolish to say so. I was already a man's property."

"Not really. *Senhor* Draven made no demands on you. You were free and independent."

She was forgotten, which was not quite the same thing. "Yes, but those days are over. I have no one to blame but myself."

"How can you blame yourself? It is not your fault you were attacked!"

"Ines, hush!"

"No one can understand Portuguese here."

"We cannot be too careful. If you expose me, you do Juan Carlos's work for him."

"Good. Then he cannot force you to marry Miguel."

"I would rather marry his son than dangle on a scaffold."

"You wouldn't—"

Ines was interrupted by a knock on the door, which turned out to be the footmen carrying water and a standing tub. Catarina went to the dressing room, as she wore only a blanket, and Ines directed them to place the tub behind a screen and fill it. When they were finished, Catarina discarded the blanket and poured the water over herself, warming her skin and washing away the mud and dirt splashed on her from the rains.

By the time she was in her night rail again, she hoped Ines had fallen asleep. But Ines, as usual, was full of energy. "Tell me how he looked. What did his house look like? What did the woman look like? Or do you not wish to discuss her?"

"I do not wish to discuss any of it," Catarina said. She was exhausted, having barely slept the night before because she'd been worried about seeing Draven today. And now after seeing him, she didn't think she'd sleep very well tonight. "I am tired."

"But you haven't eaten any supper. I sent for soup and a vegetable tart. It's waiting on the table." She indicated a small table in the corner of the room with a plate under a dome on top.

"I will eat tomorrow. I am too tired tonight."

Ines gave her a look of incredulity. "May I eat it then?"

"Yes."

And Ines scampered away to have her second dinner of the night. Catarina did not know how the girl stayed so thin when she ate so much. It seemed no matter how many times Catarina skipped a meal, her hips stayed round. But she was honestly not hungry tonight. Her stomach roiled, and she didn't know if it was because she wouldn't see Benedict tomorrow or because she *would* see him the day after.

At some point Tigrino curled up at her feet, and Catarina fell into a light sleep. Her thoughts were fraught with worry. How could she escape Juan Carlos and his son Miguel? How could she keep her business? And what would she say when she saw Benedict again? Finally, she dreamed, her mind returning to its favorite subject—that first, and only, kiss.

Two

"Marriage is a matter of more worth
Than to be dealt in by attorneyship."
Henry VI Part I, *William Shakespeare*

He should never have kissed her all those years ago. He hadn't needed to. He could have left her with money and a farewell handshake.

But he'd wanted to kiss her. How could he be expected to resist when she had such lush, red lips? He had to leave her the same hour he'd married her. Perhaps the kiss had been selfish, but he'd wanted something for himself.

But two days later, as Draven made his way to Mivart's hotel, he wished he'd had some compassion on his future self. How many nights had he lain awake, nervous about the battle to come, remembering that kiss? That kiss had sustained him on those endless nights when he hadn't known if he would live or die the next day. That kiss had given him solace when he'd issued orders to his men, orders he knew would mean certain death for many of them. That kiss had given him strength when he'd written letters of condolence to wives and mothers. That kiss had tormented him when he'd returned to London and tried to remember what it was like to exist without the constant threat of attack.

And that kiss had taunted him when he'd returned to Portugal, just to look in on Catarina—nothing more—and found she had left her small village and the home of her aunt years before. Even her own father did not know whether she lived or where she had gone.

So he'd returned to his life in London. He'd retired from the army and had promptly been asked to take a position in the Foreign Office. He mostly acted in an advisory capacity, but the threat of foreign spies or plots was ever-present, and he was often called upon to ferret them out.

Fortunately, he kept in contact with the surviving men of his troop, and their respective skills were useful when he needed them. His men were a loyal lot, more like his sons or younger brothers now than subordinates. Not that he ever let them know he saw them as equals. Still, he enjoyed watching their new endeavors. Recently, he'd funded Ewan Mostyn's boxing studio and spent his free afternoons there, watching the large man teach the art of pugilism. Other days and nights he spent at the Draven Club, where his men often whiled away their free hours.

In short, Benedict had done what he could to forget Catarina Neves. He'd resigned himself to the fact that all he would have to remember her by was that kiss.

Until two nights ago.

Two nights ago, she'd walked back into his life in very much the same way she'd entered it the first time. And Benedict had thought of her every single waking moment thereafter.

Now he was here. Now he would see her again.

Now he would officially and properly sever their relationship. If one could call it that.

He should have been overjoyed to have that last loose end from his time in Portugal tied, but as he stepped into Mivart's sumptuous lobby, joy was the last emotion coursing through him. He felt…annoyed. He had not set a time for their meeting and did not expect that she would be waiting for him. He approached the desk where the concierge stood and was immediately greeted by an older gentleman with thinning white hair and a long nose. "How may I serve you, sir?"

"I'm here to see a guest, a Miss Catarina Neves."

The concierge gave Benedict a long look before opening his guest register and perusing the contents. "And is the lady expecting you?"

"Yes."

"Hummm."

Benedict shifted impatiently as the man flipped back and forth between pages.

"Hemmm."

"What does that mean?"

The concierge looked up at him. "Sir?"

"Why are you dithering? Just give me her room number." He hadn't planned on going to her room. It didn't seem appropriate, but now he did not wish to sit in the lobby with this man *hemmming* his disapproval.

Besides Benedict was her husband. If he couldn't go to her room, no one could.

"I don't seem to have a Miss Neves on my guest registry. Perhaps you have mistaken her place of lodging."

"No. This is it. Her surname is N-E-V-E—" Then the thought occurred to him that perhaps she used his surname. In her eyes, they were wed. "Hold. Try Draven. Catarina Draven."

"You are here to see Miss Draven?" Clearly the man knew her since he did not need to consult his book. "May I ask your name, sir?"

"Colonel Benedict Draven. Her husband."

The man's eyes widened. "*You* are her husband?"

Benedict knew he was older than Catarina. He was probably too old for her, but he wasn't some feeble, doddering ancient. "I am. Is that a problem?"

"No. I—No. I'll have Barrows here escort you."

"I don't need an escort."

"It's our policy, Colonel. Barrows!"

Barrows was a young man with spectacles and wavy brown hair. He loped more than walked, but Draven made sure to keep up. He wasn't too old to climb a flight of stairs. Barrows stopped in front of a door and bowed, palm up. "Here you are, sir."

"Colonel."

"Here you are, Colonel."

"Thank you."

Barrows cleared his throat and wiggled his hand. Benedict blew out a breath and dropped a halfpence into the outstretched palm. Now the hotel staff could call him old *and* miserly.

Barrows looked at the coin and wrinkled his nose. "Colonel."

When he was gone, Benedict knocked on the door. It opened a moment later and a young woman stood on the other side. Benedict had been expecting Catarina, and for a moment he worried Barrows had led him to the wrong room.

This woman's skin was lighter, her face narrower, and her form thinner. Upon seeing him, her eyes widened and her mouth formed an O.

"Is Catarina Nev—Draven here?"

The woman said nothing, merely stared at him.

"I asked if—"

The door closed in his face.

Benedict rocked back on his heels. What was he to do now? Knock again? Would Barrows have taken him to the wrong room? Benedict was about to knock again, but the door opened. The same woman stood there. Now she was breathing rapidly, as though she had run a great distance while he'd been standing in the corridor. "Colonel Draven?" she asked, her accent almost certainly Portuguese.

"Yes. And you are?"

"Ines Neves. The sister of Catarina. Come in, please."

Anxious as he was to see Catarina, Benedict was the son of a gentleman. He bowed respectfully. "A pleasure to make your acquaintance, Miss Neves."

She blushed and giggled then stepped out of the way, giving him a view of a comfortable chamber fitted with chairs, a table, and a couch settled near a hearth. The door to the bed chamber was closed, but he didn't need to wonder if Catarina was in bed. She was seated in one of the chairs, still arranging her skirts, as though she'd hurriedly moved there. A glance at the table showed him a slip of fabric had been thrown over the work being done there. Letters? Sewing? He didn't know why women felt obliged to give men the impression they spent all day sitting about doing nothing.

Their eyes met, and Catarina rose. She wore a deep yellow gown with a wide neck that showed her lovely collarbone. Though it was not cut low, Benedict was aware of heat rising in his cheeks at the sight of her neck and upper chest. He dared not look any lower.

"*Senhor*. You have come, as you promised."

"I'm a man of my word." He moved forward, entering the parlor.

"You have met my sister?"

He looked back at Ines for a moment, but it was Catarina who held his gaze. The younger sister said something in Portuguese. He knew a bit of the language, but he wasn't paying enough attention to translate. Then the younger sister exited to the bed chamber and he and Catarina were alone.

They looked at each other for a long time. Finally, Catarina said, "I will ring for tea."

"There's no need."

"I know your customs. It is appropriate to serve a caller tea."

"I'm your husband. I think we can dispense with the social customs."

Her dark eyes flashed fire before she quickly lowered her lashes. There was the temper he knew so well. She was attempting to control it for the moment.

With a savage yank, she pulled the bell summoning a servant. "So now you wish to acknowledge me as your wife."

"I've never denied you."

"Nor did you claim me. Do you know how long I waited for you to return?" Her brows rose in challenge.

She'd waited for him to return? He hadn't known that. He'd always assumed she'd used their marriage to escape. Had she felt something for him? Perhaps he wasn't the only one who'd been affected by that kiss.

"If you waited—"

A knock on the door interrupted them, and Ines hurried out of the bed chamber to answer. Benedict fell silent as the young woman ordered tea and cakes before slipping back behind the door, where she was most certainly eaves-dropping.

"Please sit down," Catarina said, indicating the couch across from her. "If I must look up at you for any length of time, my neck will ache."

"I thought we were following convention."

Her brow creased in a way he found quite adorable.

"I cannot sit until you do, Mrs. Draven," he explained.

She gave him a withering look but took her seat. He followed, sitting on the couch she'd offered him. They sat in silence for a moment, the sound of the crackling fire the only respite. She was so lovely. When he'd first met her, there'd been something wild and fierce about her beauty. Now she looked perfectly polished and sophisticated. Only her eyes gave a hint that she was that same untamed woman he'd married all those years ago.

The moment dragged on, as she too looked at him. He wondered if she wished he were young and dashing. He cleared his throat and she shifted restlessly. And then they spoke at once. "You look beautiful," he said at the same time she said, "I need an annulment."

Silence descended like a shroud. He'd known an annulment was what she wanted. He'd come willing to grant it to her. After all, the marriage wasn't valid. He'd never considered it so, but he understood that her religion was important to her. She considered the marriage valid and could not in good conscience marry another man without annulling it.

"You have papers for me to sign?" he asked.

Her eyes widened. "Yes." She might have been surprised at his easy acquiescence, but she didn't let that forestall her. She jumped to her feet, forcing him to rise as well, and collected a sheaf of papers that had been sitting on a side table. "I do not have a pen," she said, looking about distractedly.

"We can send a servant for one. Let me see them." He held out his hand. She gave them and took her seat again. He sat as well, looking over the request to the Pope for the granting of the annulment.

But he could hardly focus on the words. His eyes kept returning to Catarina. She sat nervously pleating her skirt. Was she nervous he would not sign or nervous he would?

"You said you want to marry someone else."

Her chin jerked up. "Yes."

"Who is it?"

"No one you know, *senhor*."

"Why don't you ever call me Benedict?"

She blinked at him, her long lashes a veil. "I suppose because I don't feel I really know you, *sen*—Benedict."

She didn't know him, and he didn't know her. Well, he knew she had a temper. He knew she could be impulsive and stubborn and determined.

He knew her lips were like silk when he kissed them.

He'd come willing to grant the annulment. He *should* grant the annulment. She was young and at the very beginning of her life. He had already lived what felt like two lifetimes. She'd only married him because she'd been desperate to escape the abusive man her father had promised her to, and his name would give her protection.

She hadn't wanted him. She did not want him. What could she possibly want in a man old enough to be her father?

But how would he ever know if there could be something more than desperation between them if he granted the annulment?

And was he hoping to be humiliated? That was exactly what would happen when she laughed at the very suggestion of giving their marriage a chance.

Not that he was entertaining that suggestion.

Was he?

"And you know this man you plan to marry?"

"I…I fail to see how that is any of your concern."

Benedict narrowed his eyes. "That's an unusual response."

"Is it?"

"It would have been easier to say you know him well or you love him. Why refuse to discuss it?" Why did he care? Why not sign the papers and let her go?

She rose, the skin of her neck coloring. "Because it is not your concern." The flush rose from her neck to her chin and her cheeks.

"I'm your current husband. I think my successor is my concern."

"I knew you would make this difficult!" She extended her arms wide. "Please just sign the papers!"

He raised a brow at her show of temper. She wanted this badly, but something was not right. He had the same sensation now that he'd often felt when a battle did not end in his favor. In battle there was a point when he realized he'd been flanked or the reserves would arrive too late or his enemy had a better position. At that moment, he felt a wave of dizziness. It wasn't enough to unseat him from his horse or make him stumble, but it was enough to disconcert him.

Benedict felt dizzyingly disconcerted now.

"I still don't have a pen," he drawled.

Her expression turned from anger to fury, and he wondered if she would throw something at him. He also wondered if she could possibly look more ravishing than she did at this very moment. But before she could reach for the closest object, a tap sounded on the door. Catarina smiled in triumph.

"Our tea. And very soon, a pen."

The Claiming of the Shrew | 91

She lifted her skirts, but Benedict held up a hand. "Allow me." He strode toward the door and opened it.

But a servant with a tea tray did not wait outside. Instead, a man a few years his senior stood there. "You must be Colonel Benedict," he said. Benedict immediately recognized the Spanish accent.

"I am. And just who the hell are you?"

Three

"I am as vigilant as a cat to steal cream."
Henry IV Part I, *William Shakespeare*

Catarina closed her eyes. Of course, Juan Carlos had to interrupt now. Now Benedict Draven would have even more questions. And more reason not to sign the annulment papers.

And if he didn't sign them, what then? She was lost, and she refused to believe Benedict Draven could help her. She'd believed that once before. She'd thought he was her knight in shining armor—the hero who would ride in and save her.

He'd never come.

"I am Juan Carlos de la Fuente. I have been wanting to meet you, Colonel."

Benedict looked over his shoulder, his gaze meeting hers. She could read his thoughts perfectly. *This is the man you wish to marry?*

"Juan Carlos—"

But before she could find a pretext on which to send him away, Juan Carlos shouldered his way into the room. "Have

93

you signed the papers already?" he asked, his greed evident to her by the way he rubbed his fingers together, almost as though he was already counting the money.

"No, we have not. Why don't you come back later, so we might discuss it privately?"

Juan Carlos moved away from the door, and Benedict slammed it shut.

The older man turned to face Benedict. "Why have you not signed the papers?"

The look on her husband's face made Catarina flinch. "Who the devil do you think you are?" His voice was low and menacing.

Juan Carlos's chest puffed up. "I am the business partner of Catarina."

Benedict arched a brow at the use of her Christian name. "And what business would that be?"

Juan Carlos opened his mouth in astonishment. "*Señor,* how—"

"It's Colonel, and I was just reacquainting myself with my wife before you interrupted."

"I am not an interruption. She will soon marry my son Miguel. I should be present now to insure nothing inappropriate occurs."

Catarina rubbed a hand over her eyes. She did not see how this meeting could have gone any worse.

That was the moment Tigrino chose to wake from his nap and saunter across the carpet.

"Mrs. Draven is my wife. Your presence here is the only thing inappropriate, Mr. de la Fuente."

"Oh, now you wish to protect her?" Juan Carlos all but shouted. Catarina moved slowly toward Tigrino, attempting to block his path and encourage him to move away from the men.

"Where were you in Barcelona? I was the only man protecting her there."

Catarina's chin jerked up, Tigrino forgotten. "I beg your pardon, *senhor*! I did not need your protection then any more than I need his"—she jerked a thumb at Benedict—"now. You care nothing for me. It is my lace you care for."

"What—" But before Benedict could ask for clarification Tigrino stopped in front of Juan Carlos and hissed.

"Stupid cat!"

As though he understood the insult, Tigrino made a sound somewhere between a growl and a menacing whine.

"Get him away before I kick him."

"Don't be ridiculous." Benedict moved forward and bent to scoop Tigrino in his arms.

"No!" Catarina and Juan Carlos said in unison. But it was too late. Benedict lifted the cat into his arms, cradling it almost like a baby. Catarina flinched then her jaw dropped as Benedict scratched behind the cat's ears and Tigrino began purr loudly.

"It's just a cat," Benedict said. "Your shouting probably woke him from his nap."

"How are you doing that?" Juan Carlos asked. "How do you know that cat?"

"I don't know the cat."

Another knock sounded on the door. "That must be the tea," Catarina said, relieved. She started for the door, taking Juan Carlos's arm as she passed him. "Go back to your room," she said quietly in Spanish. "I will call on you when this is done."

"I do not like to leave you with him."

"I did not ask your permission." She opened the door and smiled at the maid pushing the tea tray. "Come in." She pushed Juan Carlos toward the door. "You go out."

She stood in the doorway, blocking Juan Carlos from reentry until the tea had been readied. She placed a coin in the maid's hand as the servant left then closed the door and returned to the sitting area. Benedict had retaken his seat on the couch, the cat on his lap.

She scowled at Tigrino as she passed, but the cat only rolled over to give Benedict better access to his belly. Strange. Tigrino didn't like anyone but her. In fact, he had a bad habit of biting everyone who tried to pet him. Sometimes he even allowed the petting for a minute before attacking. Everyone who knew Tigrino, including Ines, kept away.

"What's his name?" Benedict asked.

"Tigrino," she said, lifting the tea pot before realizing she didn't even know how he took his tea. "How do you take it?"

"Black. The name makes sense. He has black and brown tiger stripes. Here we call that coloring a tabby cat."

She nodded and handed him the tea cup and a plate with a small cake then prepared her own tea. She had started drinking tea when she finally had enough money to afford it. She'd heard the English always drank tea, and there had been a time when she'd been desperate to be as English as possible.

That was when she still believed Benedict would return to her.

She'd heard Englishwomen took their tea with a bit of cream and sugar, and that's what she added now. He waited until she sat to give her an expectant look.

"I apologize for Juan Carlos."

"I wanted explanations, not apologies."

"I do not see why it matters. You have come to annul our marriage. My acquaintances are of no concern to you."

"I wish to be certain you will be taken care of without me."

She gaped at him. "Why? You have never cared before!"

"That's not true."

Oh, why did Tigrino not bite him already?

"I gave you money after our marriage, and I came back to look for you."

The sharp barb that had been on her tongue melted away. The hand holding her tea cup shook so the cup rattled on the saucer. "You came to look for me?"

"I went to your aunt's house, but I was told she had passed away. I'm sorry for that."

"Thank you."

"And so I found your father. *Senhor* Neves told me you had run away, and he did not know where you had gone. He said you kidnapped your sister as well." He gave the closed bed chamber door a meaningful glance.

That liar! Her father knew exactly where she'd gone and that Ines left home willingly. The tea felt like sand in her mouth, and she set it on the tray before she spilled it. "He lies."

"I thought that a distinct possibility, but what could I do? I couldn't force him to tell me where you'd gone."

He'd come for her. Like she'd always wanted. But he'd been too late.

"I assume you went to Barcelona."

"Lisbon first, where I worked for a seamstress from Barcelona. When she returned to her country, Ines and I went with her." Maria had been like a mother to her, and if she had lived, Juan Carlos would never have had the chance to sink his claws into Catarina and Ines.

"Why did you not send me some word as to where you were going?"

She blinked at him. "I had no idea how to reach you, not to mention, I did not think you would care."

"Of course, I cared."

Of course? He'd never given her the slightest indication that he cared one way or the other whether she lived or died.

Except for that kiss. She supposed that was some indication of interest.

"If you cared so much, why did you not come for me sooner?"

He rose, jostling the snoozing Tigrino who tossed his head and began licking his ruffled fur.

"How could I come sooner? I was fighting in a war. I was responsible for men's lives. I couldn't simply leave my posting to check on you."

Now she stood too. "You might have written."

He opened then closed his mouth, seeming to have no response to that criticism. "I suppose I didn't know that you could read."

"If I could not, I would have found someone to read it to me."

He let out a sigh. "You're right. I could have written."

She moved to the edge of her chair, interested in the look on his face. So many emotions seemed to cross it, and she couldn't recognize any of them. She didn't know him well enough. One thing she did know was that no man had ever admitted she, a mere woman, was right and he, the man, was wrong.

"Why did you not write, truly?" she asked, her voice quieter.

"I don't know." He turned away when he said it, and she couldn't see his face. But she had to wonder whether he did not know or whether he did not want to say. He turned back to her, and this time she saw determination. "But I won't make that mistake again."

"How do you mean?"

"I mean, we married in haste, which I understand was necessary, but I should have never walked away."

Her heart seemed to clench in her chest. "How could you have stayed? And you said I could not go with you."

"That was my thinking at the time, and I've had five years to regret it. I don't want to regret what I do here today."

"I do not understand you."

"Then let me be clear." He took a step closer, and she realized he was almost touching her as he looked down at her. "I will not sign those annulment papers. Not today. Not tomorrow. Perhaps not ever."

***

She uttered a curse in Portuguese that he thought translated into something like *bastard*. Perhaps he should have been surprised, but he'd known she was no lady.

He rather liked that she was not a lady. He'd never liked ladies very much.

"Call me whatever you like," he said with a wave of his hand. "I won't argue that I'm a fool. I'm too old for you, and far too set in my ways to take on a wife." And yet, he wanted to try. He wanted her. He wanted her far too much to give her away to another. Truth be told, he'd never stopped wanting her. Seeing her two nights ago suddenly made what had only been a wish, a reality.

He wouldn't force this marriage on her, but he would ask her to give it—give him—a chance. And if, in the end, an annulment was the right course, this delay would give him time to find out more about Juan Carlos and his son. He didn't like the man and didn't want Catarina under his control.

"Why are you doing this?" she all but spat.

"That's the question I have for you, actually. Why do you want an annulment now? Surely you can't be that eager to live under Mr. de la Fuente's thumb."

"You have no idea what I want."

"I agree," he said, reaching for her arm. At his touch, she jumped. He withdrew, not wanting to scare her.

"You agree?" Her neck and face had turned red, and her bosom rose and fell beneath her modest yellow—or was it gold?—her yellow-gold dress. He had remembered her as truly lovely, but his memory was nothing compared to seeing her in the flesh. She was older now and had grown into a lovely woman, leaving only traces of the peasant girl he'd known before. "What does that mean? You agree?"

His agreement had disconcerted her. She was obviously used to having to deal with difficult men. He wasn't difficult.

But he was stubborn. And he did intend to have his way.

"It means that I do *not* know you well. I know you not at all."

He reached for her arm again, lowering his hand when she flinched back. "I want to know you better. And I can't give you an annulment until I feel confident that it's the right thing for you. For both of us."

He'd expected her to argue, to issue him a scathing rebuke for, ostensibly, telling her he knew better than she. He didn't think he knew better; he didn't think he knew anything. Who was this Juan Carlos? Why had she come all the way to London to ask for an annulment when she might have simply written to him? He had too many questions, and he wanted answers.

But instead of arguing, her shoulders sagged as though she had been tense and could finally relax. "I know what is best for me," she said, but it sounded rehearsed.

"Then humor me. Clearly, I am not as decisive as you."

She gave him a small smile. "Juan Carlos will not like it."

"And who is this Juan Carlos? Why does he have a say?"

"He is a business partner. Nothing more." But she averted her eyes. "Let me handle Juan Carlos."

He inclined his head.

She clasped her hands. "What next? How do you propose to, as you say, get to know me better?"

He liked the sound of that. "I suppose you and I will have to spend more time together."

"How much time together? How much time do you need to spend with me until you grant the annulment?"

"I suppose it depends. Why don't we go for a walk in the park tomorrow and take it from there?"

"A walk?" She looked as though the concept was foreign to her. "In the park? It is cold."

"Wear a cloak. I will come for you about four," he said, bowing.

"Very well. I will meet you downstairs."

He offered his hand, and she looked at it as though he held poison. "It's customary to give me your hand before I depart," he said.

"Why?"

"So I might kiss it."

She looked down at her gloved hands then slowly raised one. He took it, wrapping his fingers about her slim wrist. Keeping his eyes on hers, he lifted her hand to his mouth and pressed his lips to the fabric of the glove. The glove smelled faintly of cinnamon and something sweet he couldn't quite identify. He inhaled, trying to capture the scent so he could recall it later tonight or tomorrow when he thought of her.

"Is it also—what is the word you used?—customary to hold the lady's hand for so long?"

"Customary?" he said, his lips moving against the glove. "You and I can make our own customs, Mrs. Draven."

She frowned, watching him closely as though trying to make sense of him. Finally, he released her hand.

"Until tomorrow." He lifted his hat from the couch, brushed the cat hair from it, and started for the door. The cat, seeing where he was headed, jumped down and followed, uttering a plaintive meow.

"Tigrino, no," Catarina said, followed by something in Portuguese. She bent to lift the cat. The feline allowed it but struggled to be free almost as soon as she had him in her arms. "I do not understand it," she said in English now. "He does not like anyone."

Benedict reached the door and looked back. "Everyone likes me."

She arched a brow. "Oh, really?"

He nodded. "Even you."

And he left her sputtering in Portuguese as he walked away. Benedict couldn't remember the last time his smile had been so wide.

Four

"O, how ripe in show Thy lips,
those kissing cherries, tempting grow!"
A Midsummer Night's Dream, *William Shakespeare*

Catarina paced the lobby, glancing over her shoulder every few minutes. She'd managed to evade Juan Carlos and Miguel, sneaking down without their knowledge. Ines had promised to say Catarina was in bed and not feeling well if either of the men came looking for her before she returned.

But, oh, how she wished Benedict would hurry.

She walked the length of the carpet again, turned, and there he was. Her steps faltered at the sight of him. His unruly red hair was contained under a tall hat. She imagined if he removed it, his hair would fly in all directions, but with the hat in place he looked quite tame. He'd dressed in black trousers, a black coat, and a gray waistcoat. His white cravat was tied simply but with style.

He looked as handsome as she had ever seen him, especially when his blue eyes locked on her. "There you are," he said, as though he'd been looking for her all his life. She felt her face warm. Men often flattered her, but she was not used to the sort of genuine pleasure she saw on Benedict's face. His gaze swept down over the deep pink dress and white satin cloak with a cream velvet lining she'd chosen for the afternoon. It was not as fine an ensemble as the ladies in London probably wore, but it complemented her olive skin and dark hair. She'd paired it with a fashionable bonnet—at least she hoped it was fashionable in London—and wore her most comfortable walking boots as she was not certain whether Benedict's suggestion they go for a walk meant literal walking. The few Englishmen she'd met in Portugal and Spain did seem rather keen on long walks, so she rather guessed Benedict had spoken literally.

"As promised." She took his proffered arm. "Shall we depart?"

He looked about. "Do I have you all to myself? I was certain the formidable *Señor* de la Fuente would insist on accompanying us."

She smiled tightly, wanting to say that if they did not hurry, Juan Carlos would do just that and more. Instead, she tried to lighten her tone. "I think you and I can manage one outing on our own, yes?"

He led her outside where he had one of the carriages for hire waiting. He assisted her inside and then climbed in and seated himself across from her. "Hyde Park," he called when they were both settled.

The carriage jerked to a start and Catarina peered out the window. She hadn't seen much of London, save the rainy night she had gone to Benedict's flat. Then she'd had such high hopes, but as usual, Benedict had disappointed her.

"I wonder if you really mean for us to walk," she said, watching the throngs of people stroll on the sides of the street. Lisbon had been bustling and Barcelona was also quite populous. But she had never seen so many people in one place as she had since arriving in London.

"I do mean for us to walk," he said. "But I don't want to tire you before we reach the park."

"We drive so that we might walk?"

He smiled, his eyes crinkling. "When you put it that way, it does seem rather foolish." He crossed his arms over his broad chest. "I confess I also thought we would not be alone. It's easier to navigate a small party through Town in a carriage than on foot." When she said nothing, he gave her a more pointed look. "How did you escape your chaperone?"

She jerked her chin. "I do not need to escape Juan Carlos. I told you. He is my business partner. Not my chaperone."

"That is what you said." He seemed inclined to speak more on the matter, then leaned back, apparently content to wait.

In truth, Juan Carlos was furious that the annulment papers hadn't been signed yet, and he'd threatened to go to Benedict himself and demand the colonel sign immediately. To that suggestion, Catarina had merely said, "Go ahead." Her easy acquiescence had given the man pause the way no objection would have. He'd given her a shrewd look and seemed to reconsider. Catarina hadn't mentioned this outing. She'd put Juan Carlos off by saying Benedict was thinking the matter over and would contact her when he'd made some decisions.

That meant the party of four had to remain in London for the time being. Ines was perfectly happy with that arrangement as Juan Carlos had taken her to shop and see some of the famous sights. Miguel was probably happy as well. Catarina hadn't seen her so-called betrothed since she stepped off the ship. He had probably found a brothel and ensconced himself there. But Juan Carlos was no fool, and he kept close watch on Catarina, which meant her escape today was fortunate.

She would probably not be so fortunate again. She needed to either convince Benedict to sign the papers or tell him the truth. She didn't particularly care for either option.

The hired carriage finally stopped at a great green expanse, and Catarina felt her eyes widen. She'd thought London a warren of busy streets and limestone buildings. This pretty park was an oasis in that desert.

"Do you like it?" Benedict asked.

"I did not expect it to be so large."

He opened the carriage and stepped out then handed her down. After paying the driver, he took her arm and led her toward the verdant walks. They did not have the park to themselves. Not by any means. Men rode on horseback along a path that was also traveled by open carriages carrying the most exquisitely dressed women. Catarina wished she could take a look at one of those women's handkerchiefs. She was willing to bet the workmanship was superb.

Benedict led her toward the path where people were walking, pausing frequently to speak with others they knew. In the spring and summer, the path was probably lined with flowers, but this late into the fall most of the flowers were dead. The grass was still green and the leaves on the trees were turning vibrant shades of yellow, red, and orange. It was a chilly day, and she was glad the sun was out, else it would have been too cold to enjoy walking outside.

"Warm enough?" Benedict asked, as though he read her mind.

"Yes." She was not used to a man like him, a man who seemed to care about her comfort and her well-being. This was why she'd married him. Well, she'd married him to escape the arranged marriage her father had ordered her into with the abusive *Senhor* Guerra, but Benedict's character was why she'd chosen him as her savior. He was strong and powerful enough to gainsay her father. But she'd also observed him with his men. He was fair and, if not kind, concerned for their welfare.

"It seems everyone in London had the same idea we did," she said. Even here at a park they could not seem to escape the crowds. And what fashionable crowds. The women were dressed so elegantly and the men impeccably. The horses were of the finest stock, those pulling the carriages inevitably matched pairs. Grooms and footmen in livery rode alongside or on the carriages, giving the occupants even more prestige. "Are the parks always so busy?"

"No. I daresay at other times of the day and in other areas of the park, you'd find much more solitude. This is the hour everyone comes to ride and walk. Well, everyone fashionable, that is."

"I did not think you cared much for the fashionable set." But perhaps she didn't know him as well as she thought.

"I don't. But I thought you might enjoy seeing the lady's dresses and the spectacle of it all. You can't see this anywhere else in the world, except perhaps Paris."

Catarina did enjoy the dresses and the fashions. As a lacemaker, she was particularly interested in the lace the ladies wore, but she was unable in this sort of venue to see any real details. And so, as they walked, she found her gaze more often drawn to the lovely foliage. The park seemed to burn with a thousand hues of fall colors as the sun began its slow descent into evening.

"Colonel." A man on horseback passed them, tipping his hat to her and then to Benedict.

Benedict tipped his hat as well. "Major."

They walked on. "Do you know him?"

"Not really. We both served in the war and have a passing acquaintance. As you surmised, this isn't really my set."

"Your set?"

He smiled at her, his blue eyes crinkling at the corners, and her heart sped up slightly. "These are not my friends."

"Who are your friends?"

"Mostly other soldiers. I still do some work for the Foreign Office, and I dine on occasion with the undersecretaries as well as ministers and diplomats. But most of the time I enjoy the company of men I've served with. I suppose once a soldier, always a soldier."

She noted he did not mention any women acquaintances. Catarina would have liked to ask about the woman who had been at his flat the other night, but before she could, a carriage coming toward them slowed. Inside two ladies, one older and one younger, peered out at him.

"Colonel, how lovely to see you out and about," the older woman said with a toothy smile.

"Mrs. Buford-Smythe, how good to see you as well. And is this your daughter?"

"This is my second born, Miss Eliza Buford-Smythe."

He gave the pretty blond a slight bow then turned to Catarina. "Madam, I don't believe you have met my wife, Mrs. Draven."

The woman's jaw dropped and her eyes bulged. "Your—I seem to have heard incorrectly, Colonel. I thought you said *wife*."

"I did. Mrs. Draven has been recently in Barcelona, but she is in London now for a time."

The two Buford-Smyth women blinked in silence. Finally, the mother cleared her throat. "I did not realize you were married, Colonel. You never said anything."

"A man must have a few secrets, Mrs. Buford-Smythe." He tipped his hat again. "Good afternoon, madam. Miss Buford-Smythe."

They walked on. When they were out of earshot, Catarina gave him a little jab in the side. "Why did you tell her we were married? It was obvious she had you in mind for her daughter." As they'd stood talking to the two women the thought that perhaps quite a few mothers had Benedict on the list of eligible men for their daughters occurred to her. Jealousy had bubbled up, much as it had when she'd seen the woman with him that night she'd waited in his flat.

"She's a notorious gossip," he said. "Telling her we're married saves me the trouble of telling everyone else."

Catarina froze, and Benedict was forced to look back at her. "What is it?"

"You *want* everyone to know we are married?"

"Of course. Why else would I bring you here? You didn't think I merely wanted to parade you about as though you were some sort of medal on my sleeve?"

The thought hadn't occurred to her until he said it. They began to walk again.

"I may be an old man, but I'm not so vain as to use you to convince everyone I am still strong and virile."

"I doubt anyone would think otherwise. You are not old."

"Old enough to be your father."

"You would have been a very young father then." But she did not wish to move away from the topic of the reason for their visit to the park. "I do not understand why you want everyone to know we are married. I am seeking an annulment."

"And I am not. I thought I made that clear."

"But why?" She stopped again and waited until he faced her. "You said I am not a medal to you, a prize to show off, and you say you think you are too old for me. Why do you want to remain married to me?"

He leaned close to her, so close she thought he might actually kiss her. "Because you still need me. And I'm not so much the fool as to pretend I don't need you. Shall we walk on?"

She stumbled after him, not certain what to make of his statement. He needed her? And how could he possibly know the trouble she was in?

"Colonel Draven!" A man on a white horse waved then directed the beast toward them. Even Catarina, who knew nothing of horses, could tell the creature was magnificent. The animal reminded her of Benedict's horse in Portugal. This beast all but pranced toward them.

"It's good to see you here, sir." Handing the reins to a groom who rode beside him, the man dismounted and shook Benedict's hand. "I haven't yet had a chance to congratulate you on that business at the Ashmont ball. But Jasper certainly came out the better for it."

"All in a night's work, my lord."

The man, who had lovely green eyes and honey-colored hair, scowled. "Don't you start with that. Call me Duncombe, as you always did. Better yet, call me Phineas." The man still smiled at Benedict, but his eyes had slid to her. He was plainly curious about her but far too deferential to ask about her. Benedict didn't keep him waiting.

"Mrs. Catarina Draven, this is the Lord Phineas, brother of the Duke of Mayne. He served under me in the war and was, without doubt, the best strategist on the Continent."

Lord Phineas bowed. "Mrs. Draven. How good to meet you. The colonel never talks about his family. Are you married to his older brother or his younger?"

Catarina looked from Benedict to the Lord Phineas, uncertain how to answer. Benedict only smiled as though he were enjoying this.

"Actually, my lord—or is it your lord?"

He waved a hand. "It doesn't matter. Every time I hear the courtesy I think one of my brothers is behind me. I'm much more apt to answer to Duncombe or Phin. You're not English."

"No. I am from Portugal."

"Ah. That's the accent." He nodded, his manner friendly. She imagined the ladies thought him quite charming, especially with that pretty hair that was just a bit too long to be respectable. "Lovely country, Portugal. Is that where you met the colonel's brother?"

"Actually, I have not met any of the Draven family." She glanced at Benedict, still uncertain whether he wanted to claim her. He gave her a nod. "I am the colonel's wife," she said, warmth at the idea of being wanted seeping into her. No one had ever wanted her before—not her father, not the man he'd promised her to, and not Miguel de la Fuente. Benedict wanted her. He wanted everyone to know she was his.

Lord Phineas blinked and stared at her, obviously taking time to digest what he'd heard. He glanced at Benedict, but when her husband merely looked back at him, the man burst out laughing.

The response took Catarina by surprise. She didn't know why her marriage should be amusing. But Lord Phineas clapped Benedict on the shoulder, seeming genuinely happy. "Good for you, sir. I'm surprised the Foreign Office didn't ask you to do espionage. You can obviously keep a secret." Then his smile faded and his yes narrowed. "Or am I the only one who doesn't know?"

"Grantham knows," Benedict said. "No one else. Catarina has been in Spain these past few years. We've only recently been reunited."

"That explains all then. I would invite you to dinner or the theater, but I know you hate that sort of thing."

Catarina's hopes rose and then plunged. How she would have loved a night at the theater.

Benedict looked at her then back at his friend. "I could make an exception."

Lord Phineas's brows lifted. "Good. Then I'll arrange it. In the meantime, I will see you at the club." He turned to Catarina. "I look forward to coming to know you better, Mrs. Draven. Truly, it was a pleasure."

"For me as well, sir lordship."

And with a bow, he mounted his horse as though it was the most natural thing in the world. Then he saluted and continued his ride.

"I don't know about you," Benedict said after a moment of silence, "but I've had quite enough of the social scene. Shall we walk for a bit in the direction away from the crowd?"

She did not mind at all. It felt as though a thousand eyes were on her. Catarina's heart kicked when Benedict led her toward the trees. They were by no means thick, especially as their leaves were beginning to fall, but among them she and Benedict would be much more alone than they had been.

Would he kiss her again? Would she allow it? There was nothing improper about it. After all, they were married in the eyes of God, if not in the eyes of this country.

But they walked for some time without Benedict making any move to kiss her. Perhaps he did not want her after all. Perhaps he had merely wanted to scare away persistent mothers of daughters.

As they walked, they discussed ordinary things like the changing seasons and how the weather in London differed from that in Portugal and Spain. He told her a bit about his work for the government, which he claimed was usually quite tedious. Walking with him like this, speaking with him about such mundane matters was like something out of a dream. For so long she'd imagined what it would be like to see him again, but she had never thought it would be so ordinary. And yet, being this close to him, feeling his arm under her hand, was not ordinary at all. Her senses were acutely aware of him—his scent, the sound of his voice, the warmth of his body. All of these elements served to remind her that her desperation to escape *Senhor* Guerra was not the only reason she'd wanted to marry Benedict Draven. She'd been attracted to him the first time she saw him.

Of course, she'd been a silly young girl then. She had found many men attractive. She was not so innocent or so undiscerning now. She knew what qualities made a man desirable, and appearance was far down the list. She admired men who were honest, responsible, loyal, honorable, and unselfish. She didn't know if Benedict Draven had all of these qualities, but he'd showed several of them in the little time she had spent with him.

Not that it mattered what a wonderful man he was. She was with him to obtain his agreement to annul their marriage. After that, she'd never see him again.

"Shall we stop here for a moment?" he asked.

Lost in her thoughts, she hadn't paid much attention to the path they'd walked. Now she looked about and saw they were quite alone. He was pointing to a stone bench covered in leaves. "Let me clear this for you."

She shook her head. "The stone will be too cold. I do not mind standing."

He cleared the bench anyway with a sweep of his hand. "Now that we're alone, I wanted to ask. What's the real reason you came to London?"

***

Despite her protests about the bench being too cold, she sank onto it. She looked so small there, sitting all alone. With all the colored leaves about her, she made a stark contrast wrapped in her white cloak. Strange, he'd always remembered her as alive and vibrant. Where had the spark that had driven him mad when he'd first met her disappeared? He'd seen glimpses of it, but it was merely flickering as though on the verge of being extinguished.

"I told you. I want an annulment."

"To marry Juan Carlos?" He'd intentionally misspoke to provoke her. It worked. Her eyes flashed annoyance.

"His son, Miguel."

"You've fallen in love with him."

"Yes."

"What made you fall in love with him?"

She stared at him. "W-what do you mean?"

"What about him do you love?"

"I…" Her eyes skittered left and right, and she swallowed convulsively. Quite obviously, the question had taken her completely off guard.

"It's a simple question, Catarina. You love him so much that you came all the way to London, found me, and agreed to meet with me twice now, even though I have said I don't plan on granting the annulment. It should be easy to explain why you love him so much."

"It is not your concern."

He put a foot on the bench and rested an arm on his knee, leaning down close to her. "Ah, avoidance. The refuge of those with something—or everything—to hide."

"I have nothing to hide—"

"Who is Juan Carlos?"

"I told you—"

"What does he hold over you?"

"Nothing!"

"Then why do you look scared in his presence?" His questions were rapid-fire, designed to make her speak without thinking.

"I am not scared in his presence." There was the spark he loved.

"Then why do his bidding? Is he blackmailing you?"

She rose. "I do not have to answer these questions. You said you wanted to spend time with me before you would grant the annulment. That does not mean you can harass me with questions and...what is the word?—*insinuations*."

He hadn't thought it would be easy to get the answers he sought. He liked her all the more for that. She started to walk away—in the wrong direction if she meant to return to the hotel—so he called out. "You're right. In fact, there's only one question I really want answered."

He thought for a moment she would keep walking. She took three more steps before she slowed, them turned. "What question?"

"If kissing you now will be as memorable as it was the first time."

Her cheeks turned pink, and he wondered how he could ever have thought the leaves around them outshone her. Her dark eyes lifted and settled on his face. "I do not know how to answer that question."

"I do." He walked to her, telling himself if she showed any signs of reluctance, he would keep his distance. He would take her back to the hotel, if that was what she wanted. But she didn't move except to reach behind her, grasping a tree trunk with one hand.

Benedict stopped mere inches away from her. He wanted to touch her, to hold her, but now that she was here and the moment upon him, he hesitated. How could she see him as anything other than an old man? Except he didn't feel like an old man. He just felt like a man who was attracted to a woman.

He removed his gloves, tucked them into his coat pocket, then leaned forward and placed a hand on the trunk, just above her head. For a long moment, he looked down at her. She looked right back up at him, her eyes bright, her lips parted, her breath coming quickly. She wanted this too.

She wanted *him*.

He dropped his hand to touch her hair. It was soft and thick, and he let his hand skate over it until he reached her cheek. As soon as he touched her flesh, she closed her eyes, turning her face toward his palm. Benedict let his fingers drift down her silky skin until they reached her jaw. Then he slid his hand back and cupped her neck gently.

"I want to kiss you."

She opened her eyes.

"May I kiss you?"

"Please," she whispered.

His mouth lowered to meet hers. The moment his lips touched hers, he felt the spark of heat and the punch of arousal. There hadn't been another woman in so long that he'd almost forgotten what this was like.

Almost.

Catarina must have felt the heat between them too because she made a soft sound low in her throat and lifted her arms to wrap around his neck. Benedict forced himself to keep his hold on her light even as he deepened the kiss, pressing his mouth to hers more firmly, exploring the shape of her and the feel of her lips.

Finally, she parted her lips and Benedict had the urge to slip inside her sweet mouth and take the kiss even further. But he was already sinking. Holding her was like jumping into the surf and allowing the waves to wash over you until suddenly you looked about and had no idea where you were or how you could ever get back to where you'd begun.

He pulled back, slowly, and her eyes opened. They were as unfocused as he felt.

"Well?" she whispered.

"I'm definitely not ready to give you that annulment."

Five

*"For what is wedlock forced but a hell,
An age of discord and continual strife?"*
Henry VI Part I, *William Shakespeare*

She wanted more. She wanted him to kiss her again and kiss her longer and touch her and do so, so much more. But he was drawing away, and she had to squeeze her hands into fists to stop herself from dragging him back. The force of her longing for him was so strong she thought she might draw blood at the effort it took to restrain herself.

His words finally penetrated the wool around her brain, and she scowled. Not at him, but at life. *Her* life. At the mistakes she'd made to end up here. Why was she torturing herself by kissing him? Why was she pretending this could be any more than a brief diversion?

"You must sign the annulment," she murmured.

"So you may marry Miguel." He raised his brows as he said it, looking dubious.

She nodded.

127

At the moment she couldn't even remember Miguel's face, much less think about marrying the man. He'd never kissed her. She didn't even know if he wanted to, although knowing how low Miguel's standards were, she assumed he would kiss anyone and anything with a pulse.

"Because you love him."

"Yes."

"You're lying. I don't know why, but I know it as sure as I know my own name."

She was lying, but what good would it do to tell him he was correct? He couldn't help her. No one could help her. So she didn't answer. She didn't like lying to Benedict.

"Can you accept that I have my reasons and grant me what I ask?"

He pulled his gloves back on, a gesture that saddened her as it seemed to indicate even more clearly he would not be kissing her any more today. "I can't, no. I'm not usually a difficult man, and it's not my intention to make you unhappy. But..." He looked away, staring blankly at the trees and, if she had to guess, seeing nothing.

"But?" she prompted, curious to know what he would say.

"But you're mine," he finally said, then seemed startled by his own admission. His eyes flicked to hers. "I mean, you're my responsibility."

"I have no wish to be your responsibility. It would be easier for you if you signed the papers."

"If you want me to sign them so much, tell me what I want to know."

She pressed her lips together.

"So we are at a stalemate."

"What do we do now?"

"Dig in, I suppose. Eventually, one side will run out of supplies or be forced to retreat or"—he lifted his brows—"surrender."

"You must know I will never surrender."

"You should know I *have* never surrendered." He held out his arm. "You're beginning to shiver, and the sun is going down. I'll take you back to the hotel."

She thought about what he said as they rode back to Mivart's. They could both dig in, as though they were opposing armies, but he had all the advantages. He could draw this out as long as he liked, while she had Juan Carlos demanding progress. She would have to tell Juan Carlos something or risk him doing something unpleasant.

"You haven't yet told me what you were doing in Barcelona," Benedict said from the seat across from her. "The last I heard you had plans that would lead you to Lisbon. Why did you go with a seamstress to Barcelona?"

"Because she was a very good seamstress. I knew I could learn much from her."

"And did you?" He held up a hand. "Don't answer. You can tell me tomorrow."

"Tomorrow?"

"Yes. I want to see you tomorrow. I don't know what we'll do yet. Do you like the theater?"

"I have no idea."

"Or perhaps a musi—you've never been to the theater?" His look was incredulous, and she felt, once again, like that peasant girl she once was.

"No."

"Then I must take you. I'll come for you tomorrow evening."

"Benedict, we cannot keep on like this."

"Juan Carlos won't allow it?"

"No, he will not."

He leaned forward, almost conspiratorially. "Then tell me the hold he has over you."

She looked away, staring out the window at the passing buildings and not really seeing them. When the hired carriage stopped before Mivart's, Benedict helped her down again. But before she could sweep past him and sneak upstairs, he took her arm. "I can help you," he murmured close to her ear. "If you'll allow me."

And then he released her, and she was stepping into the lobby. Her whole body thrummed. She could still feel the light pressure of his hand on her arm and the caress of his breath on her cheek as she made her way toward the stairs. She was shivering and hot and wished she could go back to him.

The bubble of pleasure she felt from being with Benedict popped when Juan Carlos stepped in front of her. "Where the hell have you been?"

"Juan Carlos!" She jumped, feeling guilty. She was supposed to be in bed, too ill to come out of her room.

"Your sister said you were ill. I knew she was lying."

Catarina was immediately on guard. "Do not blame Ines. I told her to lie. If you are angry, blame me."

"Oh, I will blame you. But I would rather not have this conversation in public. Go up to your room."

Catarina didn't wait for him to say more. She took the stairs quickly, so quickly that she was out of breath by the time she reached her door. She didn't have the key with her and tapped on the door lightly. "Ines, it is me."

The door opened immediately, Ines's sweet face pale with concern. "You were gone for so long."

"Sorry." Catarina closed the door and locked it. "I lost track of time. Did Juan Carlos come to see me?"

Ines nodded. "I told him you were ill, but I do not think he believed me."

"I met him in the lobby."

"Oh, Catarina! What are we to do?" Her hands flew to her cheeks, her eyes wide.

"Not panic." She removed her bonnet and spencer. "He cannot fault me for meeting my husband and asking for the annulment."

"Did he agree?"

Catarina sighed, and Ines's hands slid to cover her face. "We are surely doomed!"

A key turned in the lock, and Catarina grabbed her sister's shoulder. "Get into the bed chamber and lock the door. Do not come out no matter what."

"But—"

"Go!" Catarina scooped Tigrino into her arms and handed the unhappy cat to Ines. "Hurry!"

The door opened just as Ines and Tigrino disappeared into the bed chamber. She knew it would be Juan Carlos. She and Ines had one key to the room and he had the other. What she did not expect was that he would have Miguel with him.

At least she thought it was Miguel. The short, dark-haired man looked awful—bloodshot eyes, disheveled hair, bloody nose.

"What happened, Miguel?" she asked.

Juan Carlos waved a hand. "Do not worry about him. I want to know where you were."

"I was at the park with my husband, doing as you asked of me."

"Did he sign the papers?"

"Not yet."

"Not yet!" he roared. He grasped her arm, his rough, pinching grip so much different than Benedict's had been only a few minutes before. "You do not try hard enough."

"I am!"

"Oh really?" He looked her up and down, causing her to shrink back. She didn't like his eyes on her. "If you are trying so hard, where are the papers?"

She pointed to the other side of the room.

"Exactly. How can he sign them if you do not even bring them?"

She opened her mouth then closed it again. Nothing she said at this point would help matters. She would only anger Juan Carlos further. He bore down on her, and she refused to shrink away from him, so she stood her ground until he towered over her.

"Have you forgotten that I know your secret? Have you forgotten that one word from me and you will hang?"

"We both know that is not your wish."

Behind Juan Carlos, Miguel slid to the floor, and she leaned to the side, giving Miguel a concerned look. Juan Carlos turned. "Stand up!" he bellowed. Miguel jumped to his feet.

"I think you need an incentive." He gestured to Miguel. "Grab her."

Miguel stumbled toward Catarina. She didn't try to escape when he took her arm. Miguel was a puppy whereas his father a snarling wolf.

"Miguel wants to marry me as little as I want to marry him. Why not just draw up contracts and we will be business part—"

Juan Carlos raised a fist and both she and Miguel flinched back. "I will not share with the likes of you, even if I could trust you. As it is, you would sign a contract one day and kill me the next." He wagged a finger at her. "You will marry Miguel, and all your property goes to me."

"And what makes you think that even if I marry your son, I won't kill you?" she asked, her voice icy. "All of my property does you no good if you are dead."

"That's a problem I will consider after you say your vows. But first you need to say them." He moved forward, grasping her by the throat and pushing her backward until her knees collided with the couch. She fell back, but before she could scramble up, Juan Carlos grabbed her hands.

"Let me go!"

"Miguel, take her."

Miguel had followed them slowly, and now he stood at the end of the couch, looking perplexed. Catarina understood exactly what Juan Carlos had in mind—rape. But Miguel was either too drunk or too stupid to understand. "Miguel, take her!"

"Where, Papa?" he said, words slurred.

Juan Carlos swore. "Exercise your husbandly rights with her."

Miguel's eyes opened wider and his gaze snapped to Catarina.

"No, Miguel. No."

Miguel looked at his father. The son, for all his faults, was not violent.

"Take her," Juan Carlos all but growled.

Miguel reached for the placket of his breeches, and Catarina began to struggle and kick. Juan Carlos's hands were sweaty, and she was able to wriggle out of his grip. She rolled off the couch and tried to run, but her foot caught on the hem of her skirt, and she fell. Juan Carlos grabbed her ankle then put a hand on her back, pushing her down. She kicked and fought, but she couldn't manage to free herself.

The bed chamber door opened, and Ines peeked out. Catarina's heart froze. She shook her head. "Get inside and lock the door," she hissed while Juan Carlos berated his son. Her momentary stillness had given the men an advantage. She felt the hem of her dress lift and cool air on her bare bottom.

"No!" she yelled.

"Are you a boy or a man?" Juan Carlos taunted. "Take her."

She tried to crawl away and was prevented by the weight of Miguel who had come down on top of her. She felt his soft hands on her thighs, inching them apart. "Miguel, no!"

He fumbled with his breeches, moved into position, and she squeezed her eyes shut, waiting for the invasion.

But it didn't come.

"Do it!" Juan Carlos said from above them.

She turned her head and looked up at him. He stood over them, sweat pouring down his face. But the more Miguel fumbled, the more she realized he couldn't perform. He was impotent from either anxiety or too much drink—or perhaps both. He made a half-hearted jab at her with his limp member and then put his head on her back.

"I can't," he muttered. "Too tired."

Juan Carlos had words for his son. He called him names Catarina had not ever heard before, but she didn't wait to see if the father would cajole his son into finally performing. Instead, she wriggled out from under Miguel and fled to the bed chamber door. Ines opened it the moment she reached it, and then she was inside, panting for breath against the wood as Ines slid the lock into place.

***

Benedict sat in his private room at the club that bore his name. Porter, the Master of the House, had brought him a light repast and a full pot of tea. He sipped the tea and stared into the fire, wishing he had brandy. But if he started drinking brandy, he might not stop.

Benedict needed all his wits about him.

He heard the *step-thump-step-thump* of Porter's wooden leg as the man moved down the corridor and glanced at the door even before the man opened it. Porter didn't knock. When you had known each other for over twenty-five years and been through as much as he and Porter, knocking was an unnecessary formality.

"Is there anything else, Colonel?" Porter asked, peeking inside and showing only his face and silver hair.

"Did you send for FitzRoy?"

"He hasn't arrived yet. I'll send him up as soon as he does."

"Of course, you will. My apologies."

Porter stepped inside and closed the door. The reason for this became immediately clear. "Benedict, are you unwell?" Porter would have never referred to Benedict by his Christian name in public. "Is there anything I can do for you?"

"You're a good man, Porter, but you've done enough for a lifetime." He would have added he wished Porter would simply retire or—hell—content himself to be waited on at the club. But to say as much would only insult Porter, who thought it an honor to serve Benedict and the Survivors. Benedict couldn't say why. Logically, he knew it wasn't his fault Porter had lost a leg. Porter had been his batman when he'd fought in India for the British East India Company under Wellesley. A group of the enemy had sneaked into camp one night and ambushed the sleeping men. Porter's leg had been gravely injured. It later developed gangrene and had to be amputated.

But Porter had refused to return home. He'd stayed at Benedict's side and was there for the victory celebrations. Benedict had not allowed Porter to accompany him to the Continent when Wellesley asked him to fight the French with him. Instead, he'd taken on Ward. But when Benedict had returned from the fighting, he'd sought Porter out at the coffee house where he worked, enticing him to run the club he wanted to open as a refuge for the men who'd survived his suicide troop.

"A man can always do more," Porter said. It seemed to be his motto.

"Why don't you go visit your sister, Porter?"

Porter's nose wrinkled ever so slightly. "I will see her at Christmastime, as usual. That is soon enough."

"Is she still trying to see you married?"

"She will never give up until she has inflicted the institution of matrimony on everyone of her acquaintance."

Benedict sat forward. "Do you really think so little of marriage?"

Porter gave him a long look. "I think it is perfectly fine for some men." Quite suddenly, Porter cocked his head. "Ah, perhaps that is Mr. FitzRoy now. Excuse me." He left quickly, and Benedict listened to the quick *step-thump* as he retreated.

The man had the hearing of a cat. Benedict hadn't heard a sound. But just a moment later, Porter tapped on the door and admitted Colin FitzRoy.

"Mr. FitzRoy is here, Colonel."

"Take a seat, FitzRoy. That will be all, Porter." He looked at FitzRoy. "Unless you are hungry?"

"I've dined."

Porter retreated again, and when they were alone, Benedict lifted the tea pot. "Tea?"

"Thank you."

While he poured and served, Benedict studied FitzRoy. He'd been known as The Pretender when he'd served under Benedict. It wasn't immediately apparent as to the reason. Colin was of medium height and build with curly dark hair and light green eyes. The eyes had turned the head of more than one woman. The hair probably had too. He had the look of one of the romantic poets.

Or perhaps that was the look he cultivated tonight, because Colin FitzRoy could disguise himself as practically anyone he chose. When the troop needed information and there was no woman for Rafe Beaumont to seduce, Colin went to work. His French was flawless, as was his German, Spanish, and Portuguese. He might have other languages as well, but Draven couldn't remember. There was a rumor that FitzRoy had an uncle or great-uncle who had scandalized the family by becoming an actor. Perhaps that was where Colin had inherited his ability to masquerade as practically any man—or woman—he'd ever seen.

"You didn't call me here to drink tea," Colin said.

"I need your help. It's a personal matter."

One of Colin's dark brows rose.

"This isn't an order. This isn't official work, you understand," Benedict went on.

Colin waved a hand. "I understand."

"This would be a personal favor to me. I hate to even ask it of you."

"Sir, forgive me, but just tell me what it is. If we go on this way, one or both of us will be forced to say something embarrassing or emotional."

Benedict lifted his tea cup to hide his smile. He'd forgotten how much FitzRoy hated displays of emotion.

"It's a personal matter," Colin went on, summing up. "I understand. I know how to keep my mouth shut. I'll help in any way I can."

"I need you to get me information on a man named Juan Carlos de la Fuente. He and his son Miguel are staying at Mivart's. They are traveling with two ladies, an Ines Neves and a Catarina Draven, formerly Neves."

Colin's gaze flicked to Draven's, but that was the only indication that he'd taken note of Catarina's surname. "Is the party Spanish or Portuguese?" he asked.

"The ladies are Portuguese, but I'd like you to disguise yourself as a Spaniard. Talk to this Juan Carlos or his son. Find out what they do, their business here, their interest in…Mrs. Draven."

This time Colin didn't react at all to what must be his first indication Benedict had a wife. Colin gave a curt nod. "Anything else?"

"I feel I should tell you—"

"You don't *have* to tell me anything."

"I know your skill, and you'll find out anyway. Better to hear it from me. Catarina is my wife. It was a marriage of convenience that took place years ago. She's in London to arrange an annulment."

"She's a Catholic," Colin said, showing that he understood the matter perfectly.

"Don't involve her if you can avoid it, but find out why she wants the annulment, if you can. See if Juan Carlos has a reason to want this marriage annulled."

"Anything else?" Colin asked again.

Benedict took a deep breath. "I feel as though I should ask how your wife fares."

FitzRoy's light eyes turned dark. "Don't."

"Understood. You will report back when you have information?"

"Count on it. I'll take my leave then."

"You have my permission."

And he was gone.

Benedict sat for a moment, sipping his tea. FitzRoy hadn't even touched his. He was a good man, but Benedict couldn't save them all.

At the moment, he wasn't even certain he could save himself. He couldn't seem to stop thinking of the kiss he'd shared with Catarina. It had fired his blood like nothing else he could remember. He still wanted her, and if he was not mistaken, she still wanted him.

Now there was nothing to do but wait.

Six

"Hover through the fog and filthy air."
Macbeth, *William Shakespeare*

"Are you certain we should do this?" Ines asked for at least the fifth time in the last hour.

"Do we have any other choice?" Catarina shot back. "I won't stay here to be raped and abused or risk the same happening to you."

"But what if Colonel Draven won't take us in?"

"He will." At least Catarina hoped he would.

"What if he lied, and he does have a mistress living with him?"

"Then I toss her out." She might toss Draven out too if she found a woman at his house.

The two sisters were locked in the bed chamber, whispering by candle light. They'd stayed inside the room all day, refusing to come out to eat, for fear it was a trick by Juan Carlos. Catarina had pushed a note and a couple coins under the door for a maid, asking her to have the letter sent to Colonel Draven.

In it, Catarina had claimed her sister was ill, and she must stay home from the theater to tend her. She had been careful to say nothing of her plan, lest Juan Carlos intercept the letter. She had no doubt he was keeping a careful watch on the room.

"What do you think Juan Carlos will do if he catches us?" Ines whispered.

Just then Tigrino pawed at the base of the door, rattling it, and both women jumped. When their hearts had slowed to a gallop, Catarina took her sister's hand. "He won't catch us. Now, lay back and try to sleep for a while. I'll wake you when it's time."

Ines rested her head on the pillow and closed her eyes. Tigrino, annoyed at being held captive in the room all day, jumped on the bed, and began to clean himself, his back to Catarina. Catarina stroked her sister's forehead until Ines fell into a restless sleep. Then she stood and paced the room, listening for the sound of the outer door and Juan Carlos's footsteps.

Sometime after midnight she heard the key in the lock and hurried to blow out the candle still burning in the bed chamber. She hardly dared breathe as the footsteps came closer to the bed chamber door. She saw Tigrino's silhouette as he sat up, his ears twitching. The latch on the bed chamber door rattled but would not lift. Catarina listened as Juan Carlos moved around the sitting room and then finally departed, closing the outer door softly behind him.

And still she and Tigrino listened. She heard nothing more. Indeed, even the city outside seemed to have quieted, though it never went completely silent. Finally, Tigrino curled into a ball on the bed. Catarina went to wake her sister.

It was just before dawn when Catarina, her sister, and the cat in his latched basket crept out of Mivart's. Ines carried the basket and Catarina carried two valises, stuffed with as much as they could manage. She and Ines had to leave several dresses behind, but there was no question that her bobbins and thread were more important. She could buy new dresses but not if she couldn't make lace.

A footman snored softly in his chair by the hotel's door and somewhere below a plate clinked. Silently, Catarina pushed the hotel's door open and stepped into a gray fog that swirled through the still dark streets. She led Ines away from the hotel, across the street and out of view of the front door—not that anyone could have seen anything in this fog, even if the sun had been shining in a cloudless sky. Catarina paused, setting the heavy valises down and resting her arms. "I don't know how we'll find a hired carriage in this."

"Perhaps we could walk."

Catarina bit her lip, not wanting to admit she did not know London well enough to discern in which direction to walk. But they couldn't stand here. The longer they waited, the more they risked. Once Juan Carlos realized they were gone, he would go on a rampage to find them. Catarina had to have Ines safely inside Benedict's residence before that happened. But how was she to walk blindly about London carrying two heavy valises and leading her younger sister and a cat?

"Which way?" Ines asked.

Catarina sighed. Anywhere else was better than here. "This way?" She lifted the valises and began walking away from Mivart's. Maybe once the sun came up and the fog burned off, she would be able to locate a landmark or recognize a street. She'd worn her warmest cloak but hadn't thought to wear mittens, and her hands were already cold. It wouldn't be long before the damp seeped through her cloak and she was shivering.

A dark man-sized shape stepped out in front of them, and Catarina halted. Why hadn't she thought to bring anything she could use for a weapon?

"Do you need assistance?" the man asked.

Catarina took a step back, colliding with Ines. "No."

"Are you certain? The streets are dangerous at night." The light from a lantern blinded Catarina for a moment. He must have raised the shutter. She squinted and saw the man had lifted the lantern higher so she might see his face. He looked far less threatening than he'd seemed in the dark. He had a mop of curly dark hair and pale eyes that looked out at her with a despondent expression.

"Perhaps you could direct us to Jermyn Street." Her voice shook slightly, but she hoped he'd attribute that to the cold.

"Of course, but you're not thinking of walking?"

"Is it far?" Ines asked.

"Far enough in this fog and with the baggage you carry. Would you allow me to find you a hackney?"

Catarina put a hand on Ines's shoulder. "That would be very kind of you, sir."

"Stay here," he said. "I'll return in a few minutes." His lantern disappeared into the fog, and Catarina and Ines huddled together for warmth.

"What a nice man," Ines murmured.

"Yes, but why is he being so nice to us? What does he want in return?" She had learned early in life not to trust men.

Ines huffed out a breath. "Why do you always suspect people of the worst intentions?"

Because in her experience people usually did have the worst intentions. "It seems suspicious. Why is he out here in the middle of the night?"

"*We're* out here in the middle of the night."

"Shh!" Catarina heard footsteps approaching and then spotted the faint beam of light bobbing closer.

"Mrs. Draven? Are you still there?"

Catarina opened her mouth to reply when she realized she hadn't told the man her identity. Ines must have realized it too because she gasped. "Don't say a word," Catarina hissed. "Here!" she called so the man could hear.

"I've found you a hackney. Follow me."

"Thank you." She lifted one valise and motioned for Ines to take the other. It was a heavy load for the slight girl, but it would only be for a moment. The man waited until they were in the beam of light then turned to lead them to the hackney—if there really was a hackney.

As soon as his back was turned, Catarina swung her valise high and hit him hard in the back. He doubled over with a loud "oof!," and she moved to the side and smashed him in the face. The lantern shattered on the ground and the light went out.

"Drop the valise and run, Ines!" she said in Portuguese. Ines ran in the opposite direction, and Catarina followed, dropping her valise too. Ines still had Tigrino's basket, and she clutched it to her chest as she tried to pick up speed.

"Wait!" The man called after them in Portuguese. "I'm here to help."

Catarina slowed then shook her head and continued running. So he knew Portuguese. Juan Carlos might have hired him.

"I work for Benedict Draven!" he said. "Isn't that where you want to go? His flat on Jermyn Street?"

Catarina stopped. "Wait." She panted. "Ines!" She turned, watching as the man gained his feet. "How do I know you're telling the truth?"

"It's no mistake I'm here," he said, voice pinched with pain. "Colonel Draven asked me to try and speak with a man named Juan Carlos de la Fuente and find out why he's in London. I had no luck last night and decided to stay close in case I saw him this morning."

"Don't come any closer. Who are you?"

"Colin FitzRoy."

"That means nothing to me."

"I'm one of the Survivors, one of his men."

One of Benedict's soldiers then. Hadn't Benedict said this afternoon that he kept in contact with his men? But how did she know this man was telling the truth?

"You don't have to believe me," he said, "but at least let me escort you to Draven. He'll kill me if anything happens to you. Not to mention, you're running in the wrong direction."

Catarina took a breath, considering. The man hadn't come any closer. If he truly had malevolent intentions, would he wait this long to act on them?

Tigrino gave a plaintive wail, and Ines whispered. "I trust him."

Catarina almost rolled her eyes. Ines trusted everyone.

"I really do have a hackney—if the jarvey hasn't driven away by now. It's cold. Let me take you to Draven's."

"Very well," she said. "But be forewarned that I have a pistol, and I'm not afraid to use it." She wasn't lying. Her grandfather's pistol was in her valise. She didn't have powder or shot for it, and as far as she knew it hadn't been fired for fifty years, but she found it a useful item to brandish every so often.

"Point taken. My lantern has gone out." To his credit, he didn't mention her part in that problem. "You'll have to follow closely." He bent and lifted the abandoned valises. "I'll carry these for you."

Catarina moved closer and held out her hand. "I prefer to carry my own, thank you."

He handed her one. "Just don't hit me in the head with it."

She wasn't making any promises.

Colin FitzRoy, however, seemed inclined to keep his. Catarina was almost ready to bolt again when they finally came across a line of three or four hackneys on a side street. She would never have found them on her own. FitzRoy called out to the jarvey who answered sleepily, then FitzRoy told the man to stay put as he stowed the luggage himself and handed Ines and Catarina into the carriage.

When he climbed in, Catarina scowled. "What do you think you're doing, sir?"

"Taking you to Draven." He pulled the door closed and knocked on the roof. Since she'd heard him give the address, and it seemed to be the correct one, she didn't say anything further. FitzRoy did not break the silence. He sat slumped on his side, occasionally rubbing his head where she had hit him.

Ines took Catarina's hand in hers. "All will be well. You'll see."

Catarina didn't have Ines's optimism. What would Benedict do when she turned up unannounced on his doorstep with her sister, running from a man who would now have no reason not to ruin her? Benedict would probably *beg* her to sign the annulment papers. He had not asked for, nor did he deserve, the problems she brought with her. It was one thing for him to help her five years ago. It was quite another to expect him to continue saving her when she was a grown, independent woman. She should never have asked him to marry her in the first place.

She couldn't go back and undo the past, but she could certainly control the way she treated him in the future.

The carriage lurched to a halt, and Catarina peered out the grimy window. Benedict's windows were dark. Sunrise was probably less than an hour away, but if he'd gone to the theater without her he would not have been in bed very long.

She hoped he was at least in bed alone.

FitzRoy opened the carriage door and handed both ladies down then paid the driver. She really should apologize for hitting him in the head. He had been nothing but kind to them. At some point, he had retrieved his lantern and lit it from the lantern in the hackney, and now he lifted it to light their way to the door. Setting Ines's valise down, he knocked loudly on the door.

Catarina waited, her heart hammering in her chest. No sound came from within, though the noise of fist hitting wood had seemed loud enough to be heard for miles.

"Should we knock again?" Ines asked.

"Let's give him another moment," FitzRoy said. A few seconds later, they heard the sound of someone moving about and the door swung open.

"Hello, Ward," FitzRoy said brightly. "Is Draven at home?"

"Not to you," the butler muttered. He was a short man of perhaps forty with a bald head and the shadow of stubble on his cheeks. Catarina had met him when she'd come to Draven's flat that first night.

"I bring guests." He moved aside. "Mrs. Draven and her sister, Miss Neves."

Ward looked at the women then at FitzRoy. "I suppose you'd better come in then." They moved along a hallway shared by Draven as well as those living on the upper floors, and Ward opened the door on the ground floor. When they'd all squeezed into the warm receiving room, Ward held up a hand. "Wait here." He disappeared into a side room and Catarina heard him pound on another door. "It's the woman from Portugal, Colonel. She's back with FitzRoy."

She didn't hear Benedict's response, but Ward came back. "He says to show you to the blue room." He led them to a parlor with walls papered in blue, a small desk, a cream-colored couch, and blue-and-white-striped chairs.

"I'll light the fire if you fetch tea, Ward," FitzRoy said.

Ward gave an exaggerated sigh and stomped out of the room.

"Ladies, please sit down. This will only take me a moment."

Catarina sank into one of the chairs. Her entire body felt heavy and sluggish. The lack of sleep was finally catching up to her. Now that she knew she was safe, she could hardly keep her eyes open. It seemed a great deal of time passed before FitzRoy had the fire going, but it was probably very little time at all. Ines was perched on the edge of her chair, looking about with wide eyes. Tigrino meowed and scratched at the basket. "Shall I let him out?" Ines asked.

"What's in there?" FitzRoy asked.

"A cat, if I'm not mistaken."

Catarina's head jerked up at the sound of Benedict's voice. He stepped into the room, dressed in trousers and a white shirt with the sleeves rolled up. He wore no waistcoat or neckcloth, and his hair was sticking up like the red flames in the hearth.

"Sir!" FitzRoy jumped to his feet. "I'm sorry to intrude, but I found them wandering outside Mivart's and thought it best to accompany them here myself."

Benedict waved a hand. "At ease, man. You've gone above and beyond."

"I wish that were so, but I haven't yet spoken with de la Fuente."

"Let's discuss that in private at another time. For now, go home and get some sleep."

"Permission to return to Mivart's, sir. When de la Fuente finds the ladies missing, it might provide an excellent opportunity to engage him."

Benedict looked thoughtful. "Do as you see best, Colin. I owe you for this."

"I didn't think we were counting, Colonel." He gave a slight bow to Catarina and Ines. "Ladies." And then he was gone.

Finally, Benedict's bright blue eyes fell on Catarina. The warmth from the fire had already seeped into her, but the warmth in his eyes made her restless. She felt the need to reach for her collar and unfasten her cloak.

"You look done in, Mrs. Draven."

"I should explain."

"You can explain in the morning. Right now I think you and your sister—it's Ines, yes?—should go to sleep. Let me settle you in my spare room. Ward!"

Ward entered then, carrying the tea tray.

"Leave that, Ward. It's too late for tea. Carry the ladies' valises into the spare room. I'll take Tigrino, so he'll be close to you."

"Thank you," Catarina said, forcing herself to her feet.

With a heavy sigh and no little muttering, Ward set the tray on the table and lifted the valises. She followed Benedict to the room, where Ines immediately entered and began to look around and explore.

"Bank the fire in the parlor, Ward."

The butler glared at her as he walked away.

"I'm so sorry for causing so much trouble," Catarina said, still in the doorway.

"You have a rare talent for it."

"I can explain—"

"I want you to, but not until you've rested. Then you and I shall have a long talk."

She nodded.

"Good night, *meu amor*."

Startled at the endearment, she almost missed his arm when she reached to grasp it. "Thank you, Benedict."

"No, thank *you* for trusting me. I'm aware trust isn't an easy thing for you. Now, sleep."

***

Benedict did not sleep himself. He'd been awake all night, mulling over the note she'd sent cancelling their theater engagement and trying to decide whether to go and bang on her door at Mivart's in the middle of the night or if it would be better to wait until morning.

In the end, Colin had brought her to him. Thank God he'd thought to send Colin. He should have had his men watching the hotel at all times. But Catarina was safe under his roof now, and he couldn't have wished for a better outcome. She'd trusted him enough to come to him. Now he would have to keep her trust.

Since Ward could be quite foul tempered if his sleep was interrupted, Benedict didn't wake him and instead dressed and shaved himself then made his way to the small dining room where Maggie—his maid and cook—had put toast and tea on the sideboard for him. She did not live in the house and didn't know about the guests, so he gave her coin to go to the market so she might return and prepare a heartier meal. Tigrino wandered in while Benedict sipped his tea. He let the cat out into the garden then called him back in after preparing a saucer with food for him. Tigrino ate it all, then jumped on

Benedict's lap and purred, occasionally attempting to swat a piece of toast off his plate.

"Catarina said he likes you," said a quiet voice. Ines came into the room, young and pretty with delicate features and a slim build. "I didn't believe it."

"He's a clever cat. Your sister was clever to bring you here. Sit down, won't you? I would stand, but the cat might take offense."

"Thank you." She sat, and he offered her tea.

"Which sister are you?" he asked. "I think Catarina mentioned she has several."

"I'm in the middle. Catarina is the eldest, then there's Ana and Luisa and Mara. Beatriz is sixteen and Joana twelve."

"And you are?"

She straightened. "Eighteen."

A child for all intents and purposes, Benedict thought. And now he was responsible for her. The idea didn't strike fear into his heart. He'd been responsible for the lives of his soldiers since he was Ines's age. He could protect two women and a cat. "You did not want to marry and have children?"

Ines wrinkled her nose. "The man my father chose for me was not as old or as ugly as the one he chose for Mara or even Luisa, but I did not want to live my whole life in the village, birthing a baby every year. I wanted to see the world. Catarina asked me to come with her, and I did."

"To Barcelona?"

"First to Lisbon then Barcelona."

"And what were you doing in Barcelona? I gather it was something to do with sewing."

Ines's mouth dropped open. "You have not heard of Catarina lace?"

"Should I have?'

Her eyes bulged wide. "I thought everyone had heard of Catarina lace."

Benedict suppressed a smile. He did not spend much time in the company of women, but he knew enough married officers to have sat through more than one conversation about this fashion or that. "Why don't you tell me?"

Ines seemed to warm at that suggestion. She sat forward eagerly. "You have heard of Brussels lace and Chantilly lace?" Her expression was expectant, as though these were items even a small child would know.

Benedict cleared his throat. "Those sound...vaguely familiar. Women wear it?"

She gaped at him—at his ignorance, most likely. "Yes, but the lace is also used to make items like table coverings and bed clothes."

"I see. And how does Catarina lace differ from"—he waved a hand—"the others?"

"Catarina lace is even more coveted. I think, given a few years, it will surpass blonde lace in popularity, and even the English royalty wear blonde lace."

Benedict ran a hand through his hair. Certainly, the name of the lace could not be a coincidence. And yet, how could it be that his young wife would have a lace named after her? "Is Catarina lace is named after your sister?"

"Yes!" The girl all but bounced in her seat. "She is the one who invented it."

Benedict sat back in his chair, forgetting his toast for the moment, which allowed Tigrino to bat a piece off the plate and devour it. His Catarina had really made something of herself. She had said she would, and he hadn't doubted it. But to invent a new type of lace—not that he was any sort of expert—seemed to surpass all expectations. "Is that why you and your sister went to Barcelona? To make lace?"

Ines sighed as though explaining one-plus-one to a child for the twentieth time. "Don't you know that Barcelona is where all of the best blond lace is made? *Señora* Madras took us there because she saw Catarina's talent and wanted her to study with a master. After six months, Catarina knew enough to create her own lace. It was so in demand that she opened her own shop."

This was quite extraordinary. How many women could boast of such success? "What makes this lace so special?"

Ines was quite excited now. Her cheeks were pink and her hands moved animatedly. Obviously, lace was a welcome topic. "Like blonde lace, there is a contrast between the patterns and the ground, but blonde lace was never considered as good as Chantilly lace because the pattern is not as perfect and regular." She gestured with her hand, making motions Benedict could only assume represented lace patterns. "Catarina not only created new patterns, she designed a process to ensure the patterns were as regular or more regular than Chantilly or Lille lace."

Clearly the young woman had a passion for lace, and though Benedict had no idea what she was talking about, he could appreciate her passion. He'd certainly spent a good deal of time discussing battle strategies in his day. And didn't that make him feel old?

"The difference is that the new patterns are so intricate and detailed, so very fine, that they are harder to reproduce on a large garment. They are not as suited for mantillas and such, but they are perfect for handkerchiefs or collars. And because the process is so—what is the word?—it means it hurts and takes time?"

"Painstaking?"

"Yes. The process is painstaking and the silk thread expensive. Most people cannot afford to purchase a large quantity of Catarina lace."

"And you know how to make this lace?"

She seemed to bristle. "Of course! I am the first person she taught. And now we have five other lacemakers working for us. They are sworn to secrecy because Catarina wants to keep her process and patterns exclusive for as long as possible. Of course, anyone with bobbins is hard at work trying to recreate Catarina lace themselves."

"Bobbins?"

Ines frowned at him. "You really do not know anything about lace, do you, sir?"

"I admit I do not. Do you have a sample you could show me?"

"Of course!" She reached into a hidden pocket in her simple gray dress and pulled out a handkerchief, smoothing it on the table for him to inspect. Normally, he would have noted only the material in the middle, the section he would have need of. But now he studied the edges, which were indeed made from a delicate lace with an intricate and quite beautiful pattern. This pattern resembled a flowering vine that began at the corners and crawled to the center then swirled along the edges, bursting into flowers of various shapes and sizes.

But when he looked closer, he saw even the flowers were not simply flowers. Inside the floral design, he spotted letters, animals, and—was that a boat?

"Are you impressed?" Ines asked.

"Very." He looked up. "You made this?"

She nodded. "But I am not nearly as talented as Catarina."

She was a loyal sister. That much was obvious. "And where does Juan Carlos fit into all of this?"

Ines looked away. "That is for Catarina to tell you."

It had been worth a try. Suddenly, Tigrino looked up. With a meow, he jumped down and padded to the doorway. A moment later Catarina herself entered, looking adorably rumpled in a simple cream-colored gown with blue ribbons at the sleeves and a lace shawl about her shoulders. If Benedict was not mistaken, it was Catarina lace.

The cat wound himself around her ankles, and she bent to scratch behind his ears. "What am I to tell you?"

Benedict rose. "We'll discuss that after you have broken your fast." He hadn't meant it to sound like a threat. On the other hand, the time for secrets was over.

Seven

"When the hurly-burly's done,
When the battle's lost and won."
Macbeth, *William Shakespeare*

Catarina was so hungry, she barely said a word during breakfast. She ate everything on her plate and then contemplated filling another. By then Ines had finished and claimed she wanted some air and sunshine. Catarina glared at her sister's back as she retreated to the garden with Tigrino.

But their current predicament could not be blamed on Ines, and if nothing else, Catarina owed Benedict an explanation. She folded her hands in her lap. "I apologize again for intruding last night." She was relieved he hadn't had a woman with him and relieved he hadn't turned her away.

"It wasn't an intrusion. I was glad you came." He looked so handsome sitting across the small rectangular table. The sunlight filtering through the thin lace curtains—Mechlin lace, she thought—flitted over his red hair, making it look fiery. He'd tamed it this morning as well as shaved. She rather liked him a little rough around the edges, but she supposed he was trying to play the gentleman for her. "I was worried about you after I received your note declining my invitation to the theater."

"I tried to keep you from worrying."

"As it turns out, I was right to worry. I take it your sister was not truly ill. What really happened?"

"I had a…" What was an English word she could use that would not alarm him? "A falling out with Juan Carlos and decided to leave." She did not want to trust him with too many of the details. In her experience, men could not be trusted—not her father, not Juan Carlos, and not Benedict Draven. At least not yet.

"In the middle of the night with all of your belongings? That's quite a falling out."

She couldn't say more. If Benedict knew the truth, he'd probably kill Juan Carlos, and Juan Carlos had made it clear that if he died in any suspicious manner, a letter detailing her crimes would be published.

"We argued, and he threatened violence."

Benedict stood. "Did he touch you?"

"I'm fine," she said, evading the question. "But I didn't feel safe."

Benedict's blue eyes seemed to pierce through her. She was certain he knew she was not telling him the whole truth. He glanced toward the garden. "Your sister tells me you have become renowned for your lace. Is Juan Carlos an investor in your business?"

"No." She swallowed. "He's a rival, actually. His family has made Spanish blonde lace for generations." She knew where this conversation would lead, but at this point, she had no choice but to tell Benedict the truth—as ugly as it may be—and face the consequences. If he put her back out on the street, then she would be no worse than she had been last night. Perhaps she could sail for America. Would Juan Carlos's stories about her reach that far?

"So he's not a partner at all." Benedict put his hands on the table and looked down at her.

"He would like to be. That's why he wants me to marry his son. Then he will own me and my business."

"You don't strike me as a woman who likes to be owned."

She couldn't argue with that.

"And despite all your claims to the contrary, am I correct in assuming you don't love this Miguel."

"I don't. But if I do not marry Miguel…"

Benedict's blue eyes were locked on her face.

Her heart galloped in her chest, and she whispered, "Juan Carlos will ruin me."

Benedict didn't move. "How?"

She looked down at her hands.

"Whatever it is, whatever you've done, I won't think less of you."

She swallowed the lump in her throat and closed her eyes against the sting of tears. She had tried so hard to forget what had happened, what she'd done.

"None of us are perfect," Benedict said, stepping back then moving to take the seat next to her. His leg brushed hers, and Catarina was grateful for the comfort of his touch, even if it was inadvertent. Did that make her as pathetic as she feared? "I have done unspeakable things, which I regret to this very day."

She looked up at him. "Those were done in battle. You had to do them."

"Do you think because I ran a man through in battle that I forget the look of pain and horror on his face or the feel of his warm blood on my hands? I will never forget, but that's not the worst of what I've done." He took her hand, linking her fingers with his.

"You don't have to tell me more," she whispered.

"I want to." He took a breath, squeezing her fingers. Her gaze met his and she felt a tremor of longing race through her. "One of my men was a soldier named Peter Collins. He served in a suicide troop. I was charged with recruiting the men, and the troop had one purpose—to defeat Napoleon at any cost. I didn't usually recruit married men. I don't like creating widows. But Peter was so skilled with explosives we needed him. He wanted to join, and I knew when I looked into his eyes that he wouldn't go home to his wife alive. I signed the papers anyway."

"He chose to join," she said. "Surely, he knew the risks."

"He did, and he took every risk. He died in a fire that almost killed two more of my men. It was an ambush, and a horrible way to die."

"How can you blame yourself?"

"Because I knew it was an ambush." A muscle in his jaw clenched. "I couldn't be sure. My best intelligence man had seduced the wife of a French commander and obtained information about the location of a building housing ammunition. He brought me the information and told me he believed it, but he also thought the woman might regret her liaison with him and tell her husband.

"I took a chance and sent those men in anyway. In the end, it was the wrong choice. The husband knew what she'd revealed, and he and his troops were waiting for their chance. When my men were inside, they set the building on fire."

She lifted his hands, holding them tightly. Now, she wanted to offer comfort. "You didn't know it was an ambush. You knew it was a risk. You took the risk."

"I should have trusted Rafe's instincts. I didn't, and because of it, one man died and another was severely scarred for life. I gave the order. No one else. I'm responsible.

"That troop I formed? It was composed of thirty men. Eighteen of them died. Eighteen young men whose lives were ended far too early. Their deaths weigh on my conscience."

She squeezed his hand again. "That sort of responsibility cannot be an easy thing to live with, and yet England needed men like you and your soldiers. All of Europe did."

He gave her a thoughtful look, neither agreeing nor disagreeing. She imagined he would keep his own council as to what the world had needed in that dark time. "Answer me this," he said, his eyes locked with hers. "When you look at me, do you think me a monster? Does my touch sicken you?" He glanced down at their joined hands.

"Of course not!"

"Then don't expect me to look at you that way." He raised her hand to his mouth and brushed his lips over her knuckles. For a long moment, she could hardly breathe. "Tell me what happened, Catarina. You can trust me."

It was time to tell him. She did not know if she could fully trust Benedict, but she could no longer afford not to risk trusting him with some of her problems. He'd given her and Ines sanctuary, and he deserved to know from what he protected her.

"There was a rich, powerful man in Barcelona who often came by my shop," she began. As she spoke, the sights and sounds of Barcelona came back to her. She could feel the warm sun on her face and the breeze from the sea. All around her was the scent of baked bread topped with garlic and tomato or spinach sautéed in olive oil with raisins and pine nuts. She could almost hear the seagulls calling and see the women in their bright dresses and lovely mantillas walking through the markets, often pausing to peruse her shop.

"His name was Don Felipe, and he bought lace for his wife. In fact, he spent a small fortune on lace. I made her a scarf and it cost thousands. I thought him a devoted husband, but one day when I had stayed late to work, he waited for me outside the shop."

Benedict's hand tightened on hers.

"He had a proposition for me, and I think you can guess what it was." Her cheeks heated even thinking about it.

"He wanted you as his mistress."

She was relieved he had said it, sparing her the humiliation. "I said no, and I don't think anyone had ever refused him before. He was so angry. I told him I was married, but he didn't believe me or didn't care. He began to follow me everywhere, sometimes trying to charm me and at other times threatening me."

"How does Juan Carlos fit in?"

"As I said, Juan Carlos was a rival lacemaker. He too was often near my shop. He tried to bribe my lacemakers for information, offered to buy my shop, offered to become my partner. I told him no. I liked my independence." Perhaps that had been her downfall. Her father had always told her that godly women married and submitted to their husbands. But she had liked having no one to answer to. She had wanted to be desired for her, not for her business or her sewing. Her pride was sinful, and she'd paid the price.

"One night I was walking home alone. The king had ordered a cravat of my lace, and I wanted it to be perfect. I stayed late working on it. You must understand, my rooms were not far from the shop. Just across the lane and up a set of stairs. It was a very short distance, and I'd walked it after dark many times. But as soon as I stepped out of the shop a man grabbed me from behind and pushed me back in."

Benedict stood, releasing her hands. He paced away, his breath coming quickly now. "Go on," he said, his voice calm, though it was obvious he was upset, even angry.

"He bent me over a table and started saying *who are you to deny me? You think you are better than Don Felipe?* He was going to rape me, *senhor*."

"Did he?" He knelt in front of her. "It won't change how I see you. I won't blame you. I've been to war. I know what happens, and few women are strong enough to fend off a man. Those who do are often killed for their pains."

She swallowed because she heard in his words that he did understand. And she knew, too, that he was the kind of man who would never take a woman against her will or condone any other man who did so.

"He didn't have the chance. I grabbed a pair of scissors on the table and stabbed him in the leg. I was terrified, and when he fell—" She covered her mouth.

Benedict took her in his arms, holding her tightly. She stiffened with surprise at the unexpected comfort. "I'm here. You're safe now." He stroked her hair, and she let out a breath. Then took another in, inhaling the scent of him—the smell of tea and butter and, more faintly, gunpowder and horse.

"I don't know what happened. He was lying there, injured, and I didn't care. I stabbed him again." She closed her eyes. "And again. And again." She shuddered at the memory of the blood on her scissors, her hands, her face.

"You killed him." His voice was even and matter-of-fact.

She nodded, even though he could not see her face. "I did not mean to."

"It was instinct. Your instinct to protect yourself took over."

She sat back and looked into Benedict's eyes. He was so close to her now, his hands resting on her waist. "When I came back to myself—I suppose you could say—Juan Carlos was there. He had been standing in the doorway the entire time and had seen everything. Or at least enough."

Benedict's lip raised in disgust. To a man like him it must seem inconceivable that another man would stand by and do nothing to help a woman in distress.

"I was weeping and frightened," she continued. "I did not know what to do. Juan Carlos told me to leave everything to him. He went for Ines himself, and she brought clean clothes. In the back room, we burned the blood-soaked clothing and cleaned all the blood from my hands and face. When we came back to the front room, the body of Don

Felipe was gone. Juan Carlos had disposed of it. Ines and I cleaned the blood from the floor, and it was almost as though it had never happened."

"Except Juan Carlos knew."

Benedict hadn't moved away from her. His hands still rested on her waist. Was it possible he really did not see her differently?

"Yes, and he finally had the leverage he needed."

"How long ago did this happen? Did you leave for London to find me right away?"

She knotted her hands in her lap. "Not right away. I knew you did not consider our marriage valid, but I tried to use it to keep from having to marry Miguel. I should not have involved you. You never wanted any of this." She gestured widely to indicate her presence at the house.

He grasped her face lightly in his hands. "Don't apologize. You did the right thing. There's nowhere I'd rather you be than here."

She frowned at him. How could he say that? He hadn't wanted to marry her in the first place. Five years ago, she'd been a thorn in his side. Now she brought him more trouble.

"We will solve this problem." He said it like a soldier riding into battle, as though success was a foregone conclusion.

"How?"

"Not by hiding. Let's see Juan Carlos as soon as possible. I want to know if he intends to carry out his threat against you. If so, I'd like to warn him of the dangers."

She placed her hands over his, lowering them. "I thought of that. If Juan Carlos reveals my crime then he implicates himself as well. But he says no one will believe me, and he is right. Who would take the word of a woman over a powerful man like Juan Carlos? His family is wealthy and respected in Barcelona. I'm an outsider, a provincial from Portugal. I am no one."

"That's not true. You are someone, and your voice matters."

"But I killed a man," she whispered. "Even if I do not hang for it, my business is destroyed. Who would want to wear Catarina lace if it is associated with a murderer?"

"It's a risk we have to take because whatever happens, I won't allow you to marry Miguel. You've faced this alone. Now we face it together."

***

Benedict left Catarina and her sister at his residence with strict instructions to Ward not to admit anyone, and Benedict had complete confidence that if Juan Carlos tried to force his way in, Ward would stop him. He'd offered to pay Maggie extra if she would act as a lady's maid to the women, and she'd happily agreed. An older woman, she had a son with a wife and children, and the additional funds would be appreciated.

At the Draven Club, Benedict handed his coat to Porter in the wood paneled vestibule. "Where is FitzRoy? He sent me a note to meet him here."

"He's in the card room, Colonel. Shall I ask him to go to your parlor?"

"The card room is fine. I know the way." He climbed the winding staircase carpeted in royal blue then made his way past the dining room with its murmur of male voices to the card room. It was empty except for Colin FitzRoy, who sat at a table covered in green baize, a deck of cards in his hand, turning them over onto the table and sorting them into groups. The chairs at the other two tables had been turned upside down and were resting on top of the tables. The scent of lemon oil lingered and the wooden mantel gleamed.

"I hope I didn't keep you waiting." He crossed the small room and sat across from Colin.

"Not at all. I still have half my ale." He lifted his mug. "Should I ring for Porter to fetch you something?"

Benedict flicked his wrist. "No need. Your note indicated you have information for me."

Colin nodded, his green eyes unreadable. "I happened to be loitering in the lobby at Mivart's this morning when an irate *Señor* de la Fuente stormed in and demanded to know where his women had gone."

"That sounds like quite the scene." Benedict reflected that it was fortunate he hadn't come upon de la Fuente. After what Catarina had told him, he wanted to throttle the man.

"It might have been had *Señor* Martinez had not intervened."

Benedict ran his gaze over FitzRoy's coat. It had a distinct Spanish look about it."

"Found it at a pawn shop," Colin said, noticing his gaze. "Paired with this"—he removed what looked like mutton chops and a mustache from his pocket—"I made quite the Spanish gentleman."

"I'm sure."

"*Señor* Martinez offered *Señor* de la Fuente his assistance, which de la Fuente declined until I offered to buy him a glass of Madeira at the tavern across the street. Several glasses later and we are the best of friends. Would you believe we were both born in the small town of Besalú?"

"What a coincidence," Benedict drawled.

"A fortunate one because we could reminisce about our old friends." Which meant Juan Carlos could reminisce and

Colin could pretend he knew the same men. "But then I asked him why he left, and he told me his family was well-known for making lace. They had a shop in Barcelona."

"They have a reputation for Spanish blonde lace, I believe."

Colin raised a brow. "I'm not telling you anything you don't know."

"You're corroborating." And it was good to hear Catarina's story supported. She might be his wife, but he didn't know her well. He wanted to trust her, but as a lifelong soldier he had learned the value of verifying.

"If I only needed to corroborate, then you might have mentioned that so I didn't have to hear about lace for a quarter hour." Colin sipped his ale.

"I assume you heard about de la Fuente's competition."

"Yes, she of the Catarina lace. I had no idea last night that your wife was such an important personage."

Benedict crossed his arms over his chest. "Meaning?"

"I have three sisters, and every single one of them is mad for Catarina lace."

"And here I thought today was the only time you were forced to listen to talk of lace."

"Would that it were. Usually, I can ignore it, but no one could ignore the way my three sisters argue over that lace handkerchief. They have one Catarina lace wipe between them, and every day there's a squabble over who had it yesterday and whose turn it is today."

"You need your own quarters, FitzRoy."

"You are not wrong, sir. However, my living situation proved useful today as I knew exactly what Catarina lace was and how costly it is. It's no wonder de la Fuente wants to marry your wife off to his son."

Benedict tried not to let the casual talk of *his wife* disconcert him. "So you learned that. Did you determine his plan?"

"He knows a secret about her. He was careful with his words but said enough that I gathered she had done something illegal. I can't think murder of her, but he hinted at that possibility." Colin's eyes met Benedict's, but Benedict kept his face expressionless.

"Go on. Will he ruin her or is he all bluster?"

"It's hard to say. He has a high opinion of himself."

"Meaning his pride will be hurt if she doesn't marry his son."

"His business as well. I deduced he's been losing money to her shop for some time now."

"Any suggestion for how I should deal with him?"

"Don't humiliate him publicly. He'll strike back. I don't think he's open to negotiation, either. He's decided he needs Mrs. Draven to save his business and, now that he's made it public she will marry his son, his reputation. I'm not sure he can be disabused of that notion."

"If I offer him money?"

"He'll be insulted. He'll probably take the coin." FitzRoy finished his ale. "But he'll still want your wife."

"If I agree to a business partnership?"

Colin shook his head. "He wants it all, though he might agree initially and then try to swindle you later."

"So basically, he's to be a permanent thorn in my side."

"You could have Mostyn kill him," he said, referring to the soldier who the others in the troop had called the Protector because of his strength and fighting skill.

"I'm not an overly religious man, but I seem to remember an injunction against murder."

Colin shrugged. "Send in the Negotiator then, but I don't think even Phineas will sway de la Fuente. He's made up his mind."

"I'll simply have to unmake it for him." Benedict rose. "Thank you, FitzRoy. I—"

Colin stood abruptly. "With all due respect, Colonel, if you tell me you owe me again, I may lose my temper."

"Understood." And Benedict did understand. His men were brothers-in-arms. They did not keep score. He had never quite felt a part of that brotherhood, but he knew the men considered him one of them. He didn't deserve that position. If nothing else, he deserved their contempt. He'd been the one sending them into battle. He'd been the one asking them to risk their lives while he sat safely in his tent behind friendly lines.

Colin sat again. "I think I'll finish my game." He indicated the cards he'd left on the table. "If I go home now, I'll probably be subjected to more talk of lace."

Benedict understood this reference too. He'd opened this club so his men would have a place to gather. A place to lick their wounds out of the gaze of the public. A place where the brotherhood they'd forged in battle could take root in peace. And Benedict was a part of this place too. He was here to offer advice, lend aid and sometimes blunt, to catch a man veering off course and set him right again.

But he didn't expect any thanks for it. He'd created the Draven Club for himself as much as for his men, because he needed a respite from the outside world too.

Except at the moment, the outside world—or at least one woman in it—was beckoning him home.

Eight

"The play's the thing
Wherein I'll catch the conscience of the king."
Hamlet, *William Shakespeare*

"I wish I could go to the theater," Ines said, her lower lip sticking out in a pout. "You look so elegant. I want to go."

Catarina gave herself one last look in the mirror before giving her sister a sympathetic smile. "This outing is not for pleasure, as you know. When all of this is over, Benedict and I will take you to the theater. It is not as though I go every week and leave you home. I have never been either."

"It is not fair!"

"No, it is not. It is especially not fair that I will not even be able to enjoy the theater because I will be waiting for Juan Carlos to find me and threaten me." Ines was behaving as though this foray to the theater was all for amusement. But it had a much more serious purpose. Benedict had said he'd made his plan to take her to the theater well known. Anyone who wanted the information certainly had it.

"Do not allow Juan Carlos to ruin the whole evening. Try to enjoy all the admirers you collect."

Catarina looked down at the lace on her three-quarter length sleeves and the trimming at her bodice. "We are sure to receive orders for lace trimming after my dress is seen"

Ines rolled her eyes. "I do not mean the people admiring lace. That will be the ladies. I mean the men. They will not be able to take their eyes from you."

"Why?" She glanced in the mirror again. Her gown was not too low-cut, and she'd put on long gloves to cover her bare forearms.

"Because you are beautiful!"

Catarina smiled. "That is very sweet of you." But they both knew Ines was the beautiful one. She was slender and her facial features much finer. Even her hair was a lovely shade of chestnut. Catarina looked like the peasant stock from which she had come. She had wide hips and an ample bust. Her face was full, and her hair coarse and dark, though not so dark as to be considered black. She did like her eyes. They were quite dark and her lashes long, but she did not know how a woman with brown eyes could compete with all the blue-eyed beauties in London.

"So you do not believe me?" Ines put her hands on her hips. "Just you wait until your husband sees you. I have a feeling I will be in this bed alone tonight."

"Ines!"

She blinked in mock innocence at Catarina. "I said nothing improper. He *is* your husband."

"You should not speak of such things." Benedict would certainly have more than enough lovely women to admire tonight. She would try not to be jealous. "Besides, Benedict and I hardly know each other."

"Mama and Papa did not meet until the week before their wedding, and everyone knows you were born almost nine months to the day."

Catarina did not want to discuss bedding her husband any further, so she lifted her reticule from the bed she would *most certainly* share with her sister again tonight and opened the door to their chamber.

Maggie, who had dressed her hair, waited outside. "Colonel Draven is in the parlor, madam."

"Thank you. You didn't have to wait out here for me."

The woman indicated Tigrino, who sat in a corner. "The cat growled every time I tried to walk away."

"Tigrino!" Catarina scolded. In response, Tigrino merely stretched, arching his back. "He will not hurt you," she said.

"As you say, madam. If you don't mind, I'll return to the bed chamber. I thought Miss Ines and I might play a game of cards to pass the time."

"Yes, thank you. I know she will be glad of the company."

Catarina made her way to the parlor, followed by Tigrino. She found Benedict inside, standing by the mantel and staring into the fire. Catarina cleared her throat. He looked over at her and his eyes widened. He stared at her for so long that she smoothed her skirts.

"Is this dress not appropriate?" Perhaps she did not look British enough. Unfortunately, she had little choice when it came to evening gowns.

He stepped forward then paused. "It's appropriate. It's lovely. The lace is yours?"

"I made it, yes."

"I can see why your work is so highly valued."

She smiled. "You are a great connoisseur of lace now."

"No, but I don't need to be a connoisseur to know what I like."

"You like my lace?" She lifted her sleeves to examine her work, though she knew it intimately.

He moved closer. "I like you."

Warmth spread through her at the heat in his voice. Her skin seemed to tingle. "Maggie knows how to dress hair."

"It's more than the hair." He moved so close he was almost touching her. Her head swam and her body swayed closer to his, as though it were drawn by a magnetic force. "It's everything about you," he murmured. "You are impossibly beautiful."

Her breath caught. "You are too kind," she murmured, knowing he did not mean it. And yet...the look in his eyes, the way he stared down at her—it felt as though he might mean it. As though he might see her as something, someone, desirable.

"I'm not being kind." He lifted her gloved hand and kissed it, sending heat radiating through her, even though he hadn't touched her bare skin. "Do you know what I am thinking right now?"

She was afraid to venture a guess. She was afraid she might say something that would shock him—and herself. Something wicked and wanton and something that would reveal how she was feeling. How she wanted him to kiss her again. She swallowed. "Are you thinking that we will be late if we do not leave soon?"

He smiled slightly. "No." He put his hand around her waist and drew her closer. Catarina's breath caught in her throat, and her heart pounded in her chest.

"Then what are you thinking?" she whispered.

"That I am the luckiest man in London to be married to you." He bent and brushed his lips over hers. The world spun and happiness burst inside her. Just as she began to respond to the kiss, he drew back. "Later," he said. His blue eyes glimmered with promise.

Catarina tried to swallow the lump in her throat. What if Ines was not simply being kind? Was she, Catarina, beautiful? Did Benedict think her beautiful? She could hardly feel her feet as Benedict led her out of the door and into the street. Would he truly kiss her later? She wanted that and the thought terrified her all at once.

Outside, a carriage waited, and it took her a moment to realize it was not a hackney. "Is this your carriage?"

"I suppose you could say that. It's my club's carriage. I thought we could use it tonight."

A servant opened the door for her and handed her up. Inside, the carriage was more luxurious than the home she had grown up in. The seats were cushioned and their velvet matched that of the draperies. The wood shone in the lantern light and the brass knobs and ornamentation gleamed. Benedict took a seat across from her.

"This vehicle looks as though it were made for a king."

Benedict smiled. "I recently had it refurbished. I'm glad you approve."

The carriage started away, and Catarina peered out the window, watching as London streamed by. It was almost dark, but the streets were still filled with people. Many of them stopped to peer at the carriage, pointing at her.

"They think I am royalty," she said.

"And why not? You're a beautiful woman passing them by in a carriage. Of course, they wonder who you are." She did not know if he was serious or teasing.

"A few years ago, I would have stood where they do, gazing up at a carriage like this with my mouth hanging open. It is difficult to believe I am the one in the carriage now."

"You don't have a coach in Barcelona?"

She closed the curtains, uncomfortable with all the eyes on her. "I have no need of one on a regular basis. I have thought of buying one, so I could have the opportunity to buy thread from markets other than those in Barcelona. A carriage and horses are so expensive."

"From what I hear, you are doing well for yourself and can afford the expense."

She gave him a long look. So he had investigated her. She could hardly blame him as she did not trust easily—or at all—and now he must know that she had told him the truth.

"But is a carriage necessary? I do not like to be frivolous. I have women counting on me for their livelihoods."

He nodded, and she thought she saw approval in his eyes. "You grew up poor and know the value of money."

"I like to think so. There is no reason to spend money on things I do not need."

"No wonder you've done so well." He studied her for a moment. "Have you ever thought about opening up a shop here in London?"

She had thought about it, but it seemed an impossible dream, even when she did not take Juan Carlos's threats into account. But why would Benedict mention it? Did he want her to open a shop here? Did he want her to stay close to him?

"I think that is a wonderful dream, but I do not know if I could ever make it a reality," she said, finally. Then, because she wanted to change the subject to one more comfortable, she peered out the window again. "Which theater are we attending?"

"Drury Lane," he answered. "Edmund Kean is performing in *A New Way to Pay Old Debts*. It's supposed to be quite an amazing play. I do hope you weren't expecting Shakespeare."

"The only performances I've seen are those on the street, and they are generally puppets hitting each other in the head to make children laugh."

"Then I'll be eager to hear your opinion on this production."

They arrived at the theater, and Benedict escorted her inside. Immediately, she was surrounded by more people than she'd ever seen in her life. She could barely move, but Benedict led her confidently through the crowds and up the stairs to a curtain. He pushed it aside, and Lord Phineas rose.

"Colonel Draven and Mrs. Draven." Lord Phineas bowed. "How good to see you again."

Benedict put his hand on the small of her back and led her inside the box, which overlooked the stage. For a moment, Catarina simply stared at the theater. It was enormous and lit by so very many chandeliers. Across from her, there were four tiers of boxes and below were the floor seats. The theater itself boasted lovely arches soaring high above the patrons. Deep red curtains ornamented the stage.

"Thank you again for the use of your box," Benedict said. Catarina turned back to the conversation.

"I've been offering it for months, but you never agree. Thank you, Mrs. Draven, for finally persuading him."

The box curtain swayed again, and a lovely woman with blond hair and blue eyes entered. "Oh, hello!" she said with a smile.

"Lady Philomena, may I present Colonel Draven and his wife, Mrs. Draven? My sister, Lady Philomena."

Benedict and Catarina bowed and said all the appropriate words, but just as Lord Phineas was offering her a seat, Lady Philomena gasped. "Your lace!"

Catarina glanced down at her sleeves, where Lady Philomena's attention seemed riveted. She feared she had stained or torn it.

"No, no. It's quite fine. But I would swear on my father's grave that is Catarina lace."

"It is," Catarina told her.

The woman was instantly at her side. "May I look more closely?" She gasped again. "You have it on your bodice as well!"

Catarina nodded and held up her sleeve for Lady Philomena's inspection. Lady Philomena turned her arm this way and that. "Oh, my. It's simply exquisite. So delicate and intricate. The workmanship is beyond anything else I have ever seen"

"Thank you," Catarina said. "I do my best."

"You?" Lady Philomena looked away from the lace then back again.

"Mrs. Draven is Catarina," Benedict said. "The woman who designed the lace and creates it."

Lady Philomena looked as though she would stumble backward. "What? Why, I am in the presence of greatness! You cannot know how much I love your lace. It is very difficult to acquire here in London."

Catarina felt her cheeks warm. It always made her both proud and self-conscious when she received praise. "I would be very happy to give you a length or two. Or perhaps you would like me to make you something?"

"Would you?" She clapped her hands together. "I would simply die for a handkerchief."

"Then consider it done." It was the least she could do and something she would enjoy. "What is your favorite color? And I will want to personalize it with your initials as well."

"Oh, you are simply lovely." Then her expression fell. "But I don't know how I will ever pay for it. My brother, the duke, insists on managing my money, and he keeps his purse closed tight."

"No, no. It is a gift. For allowing me to sit in your beautiful box."

"Oh, thank you! You will make me the envy of every woman in London. I cannot wait until the next ball."

"No doubt you'll accidentally drop the handkerchief ten times so it will be seen," Lord Phineas muttered.

His sister smacked him playfully on the shoulder. "Oh, hush!"

"Will you let the woman take her seat now?" Lord Phineas gestured to a cushioned chair. Catarina took it, and Benedict sat beside her. The play had not yet begun, and she surveyed the crowds of people across from and below her. Everyone looked so sophisticated. Fans fluttered and jewels sparkled. More than one lady or gentleman held a small spy glass held to his or her eye to better see the people in the theater.

Her gaze skimmed over most of the people seated on the floor as they were not as elaborately dressed, but then she dragged her eyes back to a man staring at her with so much hatred she could feel it all the way across the theater. Catarina reached over and grasped Benedict's hand.

"What is it?"

"He is here."

He didn't need to ask who. "Where?"

"There." She didn't want to point, so she inclined her head in Juan Carlos's direction., toward the seats near the back of the floor.

"I see him. He can't hurt you." Benedict squeezed her hand. "You're safe with me."

She was safe with him. She knew that, but the way Juan Carlos looked at her made her stomach churn.

"He's seen you. That's what we wanted. Now we have to hope he tries to approach us. We'll leave the box during the intermission."

Catarina wanted to grasp her chair and refuse to go anywhere. Logically, she knew hiding would only prolong the inevitable. She had to face Juan Carlos. But instinctively, she wanted to climb under her chair and cower.

The play began, though it seemed to Catarina no one was watching the actors on stage. She certainly couldn't pay much attention, and although Benedict seemed to watch, Lady Philomena whispered in her ear, pointing out this person or that, throughout the first act. Intermission came too soon, and Benedict rose immediately.

"I want to take Mrs. Draven for some air."

"Oh, but my friends will want to meet her," Lady Philomena protested.

"Some other time, Mena," her brother said. Then turning to Benedict, he warned, "You'd best go now. I can hear the stampede coming this way."

Benedict took Catarina's arm and escorted her out of the box and back down the stairs to the lobby, where refreshments were being sold. He bought her a measure of wine and one for himself, then situated himself with his back to a pillar.

"What are we doing?" she asked.

"Waiting."

They didn't have to wait long. Juan Carlos spotted them not long after Catarina saw him emerge from the theater. He stalked across the lobby, aiming for them like an arrow.

"*Señor* de la Fuente," Benedict said, not giving Juan Carlos the courtesy of a bow.

Juan Carlos glared at Catarina. "What do you think you are doing? We had an agreement."

Benedict angled so his shoulder was slightly in front of Catarina. It was a protective gesture she appreciated. "My wife no longer wants any part of your agreement."

Juan Carlos's face hardened. "I would be careful, if I were you, Colonel. I could ruin your wife with a few words."

"My understanding of the situation is that you would ruin yourself too. Or is burying a body and not reporting a death to the authorities acceptable practice in Spain?"

"You stay out of this," Juan Carlos said, his face turning red. He focused his dark eyes on Catarina again. "Who do you think the judge will believe? My family has owned a business in Barcelona for decades. We are well-respected members of the community."

"And she was a lone woman defending herself," Benedict inserted. "Surely the court will have compassion."

Juan Carlos sneered at him. They both knew courts had little compassion where wealthy men were concerned.

"What occurs to me," Catarina said in Spanish, her voice low, "is that if you report me to the authorities, your reputation will not go untarnished. After all, if you suspected me of a crime, why would you not report it? Instead, you sought to benefit from my misdeed and use it to blackmail me."

"No one will believe that."

Catarina translated for Benedict.

"They will believe it if I stand at her side and make sure they listen." Benedict put his arm about Catarina's waist. "She has a protector now, de la Fuente. She has her husband at her side. I think it's best if you return to Spain and forget all about Mrs. Draven."

Juan Carlos's face was dark crimson, and he shook with anger. "What about your shop? Your business? You will abandon it?"

"That is not your concern," she told him.

"Why not sell it to me?"

"Never. It is mine. You will never have any part of it."

"Go home, de la Fuente," Benedict said.

Juan Carlos looked at both of them in turn, hate burning in his eyes. "This is not over." And he stalked away.

***

"You didn't enjoy the play, did you?" Benedict asked when they were once again inside his flat, cozy and warm in the blue-papered room. She sat on the cream couch and Benedict built up the fire in the hearth. He'd given Ward permission to retire, and since Maggie had reported Ines had gone to sleep early, it was just Benedict, Catarina, and Tigrino in the blue parlor.

"I confess I could hardly pay attention to it. I could feel Juan Carlos staring at me during the first act, and then he was gone after the intermission, and I half feared he would come into the box." She shivered, as though she had been cold and was only now warming up.

"He would have never been allowed in the box. And he will never be allowed near you again."

Her shoulders seemed to relax at those words, and she leaned back against the couch and stroked Tigrino, who closed his eyes as though in bliss. "And what if he tells everyone what I did? No one will buy the lace of a murderer."

Benedict leaned an arm on the mantel, where a fire burned low. "There's nothing we can do to keep Juan Carlos from telling everyone what happened. If he does, then we will counter with the truth—that you were protecting yourself. I will take the blame for you, since I wasn't there to protect you."

She looked up from Tigrino sharply. "You cannot blame yourself, *senhor*."

"*Senhor*?" He gave her an exasperated look. "I thought you were calling me Benedict now."

"Very well. Benedict, you should not blame yourself."

"And yet I do. I should have been there to protect you. I knew when I took my vows they were not legally binding, and yet I still felt bound by them. I couldn't protect you then, but as soon as I was free, that was my chief concern."

"And then you couldn't find me."

Tigrino jumped to the floor and rolled on his back, showing the soft fur of his belly. She stroked him.

"That too was not your fault. Ow!" She yanked her hand away as Tigrino grasped it with his claws and nipped at her fingers.

Benedict shooed the cat away and knelt in front of her. "Are you hurt?" He took her hand in his, examining it.

"No. He is just playing, but I fall for his tricks every time."

"You want to believe everyone is as well-intentioned as you. But sometimes men, like cats, are just waiting for a chance to strike." As he spoke, he rubbed his thumb along her fingers, making her skin tingle. "But Juan Carlos will find that lashing out at you only hurts him."

"Perhaps that is so here, where he has little influence, but in Barcelona, no one would dare go against him."

"You're not in Barcelona now," he said quietly.

"But I will have to return."

"Not necessarily." His thumb roamed in lazy circles on her bare flesh. "I like having you here."

She swallowed and licked her lips as though they were dry. "My sister and I must be an inconvenience."

"Your sister is a sweet girl, and you are surprisingly little trouble."

She smiled. "You mean compared to the way I behaved when we first met."

"You certainly garnered my attention." He took her hand in his. "You still do." He tugged her arm gently, pulling her closer to him. "I'd like to kiss you, wife."

Her breath hitched. Dare he believe she wanted this? That she was attracted to him, even if it was only half as much as he was attracted to her?

"By virtue of our marriage, I do not think you are required to ask, husband."

"And yet I want to ask. I want you to want to kiss me." His hand ran up her bare arm. "Do you?"

She nodded, her face blushing a pretty pink. That was all the encouragement he needed. Since she'd stepped foot into his house—hell, since he'd stood beside her in the rain storm—he'd imagined this moment. He released her arm and took her chin between his thumb and forefinger. Her skin was so soft. He had the urge to cup her face and pull her close, run his fingers over her silky face and thread them through her hair, freeing it. When they'd first met, she worn it long and loose about her shoulders. He missed seeing it that way.

"Then kiss me," he said. He was an old fool to make her prove she wanted him, but he'd always had a little too much pride.

"*I* should kiss you?"

Benedict laughed quietly. "I never knew you to be afraid of a challenge. Where's the girl who pointed a pistol at me and demanded I marry her?"

"She is older and has hopefully outgrown some of her impulsiveness." Her breath was warm where it brushed against his hand. God, how he wanted her.

"That's too bad." He released her chin, but before he could drop his hand, she caught it. His heart raced along with his hopes.

"There are benefits to losing one's impulsiveness."

"Such as?"

"Taking the time to think about what one really wants."

"And what's that?"

"This." She took his face in her hands and pressed her lips to his. It was a soft, sweet kiss. He wanted more, but he was in no mood to rush her. So he would have to content himself with this peck tonight. She drew back, lowered her gaze and, to his surprise, kissed him again.

This time the kiss was longer and warmer. He had time to return it. When she pulled away, her breath came more quickly. He hadn't done this in some time, but he could still recognize the signs of a woman's arousal. Taking a chance, he slid his arms around her waist, pulling her close. Her soft body melted into his. She followed his lead, wrapping her arms around his neck and weaving her hands into his hair. She ran her hands through the wild red sections. "I have been wanting to do this all night," she whispered.

He frowned. "You've been wanting to muss my hair?"

"Exactly. I like it wild and unruly."

"Then I'll never tame it again."

When she kissed him this time it was hot and open-mouthed. His hands tightened on her waist as he tried to control his desire to touch her more intimately. She leaned forward, kissing him deeply, and lost her balance, having reached the edge of the couch. He fell back, and she tumbled on top of him.

She laughed and struggled to right herself. "Are you hurt?" she asked.

"I've felt worse falling into bed." He chuckled, liking the feel of her weight splayed on top of him.

"Then there is no reason to stop." Still on top of him, she kissed him again. He could feel the softness of her breasts against his chest and the warmth of her legs tangled with his. This time he thrust his hands into her hair and pulled at the pins holding it in place. It tumbled down around them, creating a dark curtain.

She rose slightly and pushed it over one shoulder. "Now look what you have done."

"Exactly what I wanted to do. I've missed seeing your hair down."

"You will not miss it when we both have mouthfuls."

"There's a solution for that." He slid her off him and onto the plush blue rug. Then he took her place, levering his hands on either side of her, careful not to crush her.

It had been a long time since he'd been in this position, since he'd had a woman under him. Though he wasn't a youth any longer, he had the urge to toss up her skirts and plunge into her. Thankfully, he was a man of age and experience. He could wait until she wanted him as much as he wanted her. He knew how to stoke her desire.

She looked up at him, her eyes dark and soft with desire. The fire made her skin look dark gold, and he kissed her eyelids, then her cheeks, then made his way slowly to her mouth. She returned his kiss eagerly, her hands on his back, her fingers digging into his shoulders. Her breath came quicker as the kiss continued, as he explored her mouth more thoroughly.

Finally, she broke away. "I cannot breathe."

While she gasped for breath, he touched his lips to her neck and her throat. Her pulse beat fast and her skin tasted slightly of salt and smelled of the rosewater soap she'd used in her bath. His lips trailed lower, to her collarbone, and she moaned softly. It was impossible not to notice the rise and fall of her ample breasts. The gown was cut modestly, but it didn't hide the shape of her.

He kissed the skin just above the plump flesh of her breasts, and her hands dug deeper into his shoulders.

Leaning on one elbow, he brushed a stray lock of hair from her cheek. "You're so beautiful." He didn't know why he said it except that he couldn't *not* say it. He could hardly believe what he saw when he looked at her.

She touched her cheeks. "I must be as red as an apple."

"You look good with color in your cheeks." He paused. He should go on as he had, but it all seemed too good to be true. "You do know, you don't have to do this with me. It's not expected. You can stay here, and I won't expect anything of you."

She blinked at him, seeming confused.

"I must seem an old man to you. I'm not about to take advantage of your situation."

Suddenly, she pushed him off her, and this time his head hit a chair. He saw stars and blinked the pain away.

"Did that hurt?" she asked.

"Yes." He rubbed the growing knot.

"Good."

"Good?" He sat. "What does that mean?"

"It means you insult me. Do you think I am feigning how I feel? I can hardly take a breath for the pounding of my heart. Do you think me an actress like the ones on stage tonight?"

"I didn't mean to imply—"

She waved a hand. "I do not know what that means. You all but said I was pretending. I am not. And if you do not want me, you can just say so."

Benedict wasn't certain how everything had gone so wrong. "I do want you," he protested.

She folded her arms across her bosom—the bosom his hands itched to reveal and touch. "Oh, really?"

"Yes, really."

"Then why are you all coolness and composure while I am hot and striving for breath?"

"I…" Did she want him slobbering over her? This evening had taken a turn he hadn't expected. "I'm trying to keep a sense of control. I don't want to go too far."

"I will tell you what too far is."

He had no doubt of that.

"You have not gone nearly far enough. And another thing."

He raised his brows.

"You are not an old man. You are stronger and fitter than most men half your age. I wanted to marry you because I needed a man, not a boy. That is still the case."

She stood then and swished her skirts so they smacked him in the face. "Good night, *senhor.*"

It was the *senhor* that did it. As she flounced away, Benedict grasped her about the waist and dragged her back.

Nine

"We know what we are, but not what we may be."
Hamlet, *William Shakespeare*

She thought about protesting the way he pulled her back down and onto his lap. But there was nothing to protest when this was exactly what she wanted.

"So I am *senhor* again, am I?"

"Yes." She notched her chin up.

She was still angry that he should think she would ever feel compelled to submit to his advances because she thought he would put her out on the street if she didn't. She knew him better than that. Did he not know her at all? She'd killed a man rather than submit to his advances.

There were many times in the intervening weeks when she'd wondered if it would have been easier to simply allow Don Felipe to have his way with her. But she didn't regret what she'd done. She hadn't wanted that man touching her. She had only ever wanted Benedict.

"I see what you are doing," he said, his lips close to her ear, his breath making her tremble. "I am trying to make certain I don't take advantage of you. That is no reason to treat me coldly."

She turned to face him. "And I see what you are doing, *senhor*."

His blue eyes burned with fire. "And what's that?"

"Making excuses for doing what you really want." She prayed that was true. But she didn't think she'd mistaken the way he looked at her, touched her. "I am no child. I will not allow you to do anything I do not want. I thought you knew me better."

He stared at her for a long moment. Finally, he chuckled and looked away. "You're right. I do know you better than that. You'd have me groveling in pain. Tell me then, Catarina, what *do* you want from me?"

She gave him a saucy look. "Why do you not show me what you can do, and I will tell you whether I like it or not."

His hands tightened on her waist. "Oh, you are playing with fire, little Cat. I'm a soldier, and there's nothing I like better than a challenge."

"If I had a gauntlet—that is the word, yes?—I would throw it at your feet."

He took her face in his hands. "And I'd pick it up." He kissed her, his kiss just as intoxicating as it had been earlier, but this time there was an intensity in the way he moved his mouth over hers, the way his hands held her, the way his body tightened against her. Her heart leapt into her throat, and though she'd never admit it, she was a little frightened. Frightened and thrilled.

He drew her down onto the plush rug and lay down beside her, still kissing her. His hands threaded through her hair, winding it around his hand until he forced her neck gently back. He kissed her arched throat and she murmured her approval. He nipped and licked and teased lower until he reached the bodice of her dress. Her skin pebbled with anticipation as his hand traced the path his mouth had taken. And then moved lower.

His fingers brushed over the silk of her dress, over the material covering her breasts. She shivered as his light caresses drifted over her. He didn't squeeze or grope. She desperately wanted to better feel his touch. It was muted through the layers of material.

"I'd like to take this dress off you."

"I would like that too," she said. She freed her hair from his hand. "But not here. Take me to your bed chamber."

He winced as though in pain. "You don't know how tempting that offer is."

"I have some idea. That is why I made the offer."

"Catarina." He pressed his forehead to hers. "I do like your honesty, even if it surprises me."

"And what is surprising about me being honest that I want to feel your skin on mine?"

"Nothing, except most women do not talk like that." He closed his eyes then opened them. "Listen, before I take you to my chamber, I think we had better make some rules. I don't want to do anything to lose your trust."

She blew out a breath, his mention of breaking the fragile trust she had given him making her belly churn with fear. "Rules? I want to kiss you and touch you. Why do we need rules?"

"Because if you go to my bed chamber, you jeopardize your right to annulment. Right now you can say that we never considered the marriage permanent and never believed it would lead to the creation of children. I only married you to save you from your circumstances at the time. Further, you can argue that at the time of the marriage you lacked the necessary discretion to consent to the marriage. Not that I forced you, but that there were outside factors that made you feel compelled. But if you and I become intimate, I can't, in good conscience, testify to any of that." He gave her a regretful look. "Our situation changes once we agree to act as husband and wife."

"But the annulment is based on what our intentions were before the marriage occurred."

"I think whether or not I consent to the annulment will also bear some weight. And if there's even a remote possibility that you are carrying my child, I won't feel right agreeing to an annulment." His jaw tightened, and she could see he was determined on this point.

"It might not even matter, being that you are Protestant and I am Catholic."

"I'm no religious scholar, but I am a war hero." He smiled as though the sobriquet didn't fit him well. "And if I oppose this annulment, it will be all but impossible to obtain. Which leads to my question, do you want to give up your request for an annulment?"

She opened her mouth to say yes. She'd only wanted the annulment to save herself and her sister from Juan Carlos's threats. Those threats were still very real, but now she'd rather have them come to fruition than be forced to marry Miguel and have to give up her business.

But what if she remained married to Benedict? He might want her, she could believe that now, but he didn't love her.

How would this be any different than a marriage her father arranged for her? She might be desired for her body, but she wanted to be desired for herself—her mind, her talents, her whole being. No man had ever cared for her like that—not her father, not Don Felipe, not Benedict.

And could she trust that if she stayed, she wouldn't lose everything she had worked for? Wouldn't she have to give up her business? Benedict said she should open a shop in London, but did he realize what owing a shop entailed? She worked long hours. She wouldn't be sitting home waiting when he came back from his business for the day. She'd manage the shop, not his household. Her father had thought no sin worse than his wife not giving her attention to every detail of his household.

Perhaps in remaining married to Benedict she would lose what little freedom she still had. But if she survived whatever plans Juan Carlos had made and then obtained an annulment from Benedict, she'd be free to do as she wished. That prospect was quite appealing. She never wanted to go back to the time when she had been forced to submit to her father's whims. And she did not want to submit to a husband's whims either, not even one that fired her blood.

Part of her hoped that Benedict was the sort of man who would never require her to submit, but could she really afford to trust him? If she was wrong about him, she and Ines would suffer.

"I see you are thinking everything through," Benedict said quietly. "Perhaps you need more time to think."

She wanted more time in his arms, but all the passion she had felt a few minutes before had ebbed away as thoughts tumbled about in her head. What did she want? What was her future?

Finally, she said, "I think I should go to my bed chamber for tonight."

She wanted him to argue, wanted him to push her back to the floor and kiss her again. She could make that happen, but he'd made it complicated now. She could not have him *and* her freedom.

He rose and offered a hand, helping her to her feet. "Good night then, Mrs. Draven."

His voice was like a cold rain washing over her. She gritted her teeth and gave him her back. "Good night."

***

But it wasn't a good night. She tossed and turned so much Ines woke near dawn, hit her with a pillow, and begged her to be still. Since Catarina couldn't sleep any longer, she pulled on her dressing robe and went into the blue parlor with her bobbins and pillow.

The small desk in the room was cleared, so she laid her pillow there and took out the piece of Catarina lace she'd been working on. She would finish it and then work on a handkerchief for Lady Philomena. She arranged her pins and her bobbins then began to move the bobbins so that the attached thread formed the intricate patterns she wanted. She worked quickly, lining the bobbins up by pairs, crossing them and then moving to the next group. This work was calming and rote. The click of the wooden bobbins as she lifted them and set them down was only interrupted by her pauses when she inserted the pins to hold the thread in place.

After a while Tigrino settled at her feet as he was apt to do when she worked. He kept her feet warm, and if she worked too long, meowed to be fed and petted.

She didn't know how long she'd worked before Tigrino rose and sauntered away. She expected him to nudge her for attention, but he didn't return. Finally, she looked over her shoulder to see where he'd gone and noticed Benedict sitting in the chair across the room. Tigrino was sprawled on his lap—much as she'd been last night.

She turned back to her work, her cheeks burning.

"I didn't mean to interrupt you," Benedict said. "I couldn't sleep and went to the kitchen for tea. I heard the clicking."

He spoke as though the events of the night before had not occurred. How could he be so formal and polite with her, after the heat that had boiled between them? Had she imagined it? Was it only lust?

Who was she kidding? Of course, it was only lust. And she was in no position to judge. She was not in love with him.

"You are not bothering me," she said without pausing in her work. *Cross-cross-lift-move-cross-pin-cross-cross.*

He traversed the room and stood behind her. "I've never seen anyone make lace before. How do you know which way to move the wooden pegs?"

Fine. If he wanted to speak of banal things instead of what she was certain they were both really thinking about, she would oblige. "They are bobbins. I was taught as a child. As I grew older I learned more intricate patterns, and then *Señora* Madras in Lisbon taught me even more complicated methods." She didn't look at him, merely continued to move the bobbins. *Cross-cross-lift.*

"This is more than rote memory, though. This is art."

That statement startled her. Her fingers fumbled uncharacteristically for a moment. "It is practice and, yes, some skill. I was taught at the knee of my mother. Most lacemakers were taught in this fashion."

"Watching you work is like watching an artist create."

She did pause now and looked up at him. His expression was one of complete sincerity. Catarina had been praised for her work before. She'd heard hundreds if not thousands of compliments. But this was the first time she felt tears sting her eyes.

She hadn't known how much she wanted Benedict to approve of her. It was gratifying when his eyes warmed at seeing her dressed for the theater. It was arousing when his eyes burned as he looked down at her after kissing her half senseless. But it was empowering when he gazed at her with admiration. Because making lace was part of her, an outside expression of her innermost self. And when he saw into that deep part of her and told her it was beautiful—it was art— she felt loved.

It had been so long since she'd felt that way. Her mother had loved her, of course. Her aunt had loved her, and Ines loved her. But that love was the love anyone was obliged to feel for his or her family. Benedict wasn't obligated to love her. Perhaps he never would.

But in that moment, she loved him.

And it terrified her because if she loved him, she would be vulnerable. And she couldn't allow herself to be vulnerable again.

***

Benedict was pleased that she allowed him to watch her for another hour or so. He hadn't paid as much attention as he might have. He couldn't stop thinking about what had almost happened the night before. He had to be the world's biggest idiot to discuss rules before taking a woman to bed. But he hadn't expected her to refuse him. He hadn't expected her to still want the annulment.

But she obviously did.

She didn't want to be married to him. She didn't trust him enough to take that step. Unlike most other women of the day her skill with lace gave her more options and freedom. She needed Benedict to protect her from Juan Carlos, but beyond that, she obviously didn't want Benedict as a husband. She wasn't averse to taking him as a lover. He knew she hadn't been feigning her attraction to him. And he wouldn't pretend her reaction to him didn't make him feel younger and more desirable than he had in years. But he was a man used to being sought as a husband, and her rejection stung. Strange that for years mothers had been trying to marry their daughters to the war hero—daughters barely out of the schoolroom, girls who looked at him as though he was their toothless grandfather—and now he had a wife who looked at him like a man but wanted no part of marriage.

She had almost finished the lace by that time, and, like the creator, the lace was impossibly intricate and beautiful. By this time the household was awake—at least, his maid and Ward were up and about. Benedict left Catarina to her work and went to his bed chamber to dress.

He'd never looked at lace before, not really. He'd never considered how it was made or who sat for hours twisting thread to make the detailed designs. He had a few items with lace ornamentation, not many as he was a former soldier, not a dandy or a peer. But now he took one of his shirts with lace cuffs from its shelf and studied the lacework. It was adequate, but he could see it was nothing compared to what Catarina created.

No wonder her lace fetched such high prices and universal admiration.

"Important business today, Colonel?" Ward asked as he entered and saw Benedict with the shirt in his hands.

Benedict folded the shirt again and replaced it. "I'll be at my club for a few hours."

"Very good. I have the water for your shave."

While Benedict shaved, Ward laid out garments then waited to assist.

"I can do it myself, Ward," Benedict said. "But I do have something I need you to do for me." He lifted a towel to wipe away the last of the water from his face.

"You want me to guard the house while you are away."

Benedict lowered the towel. "How do you know that?"

"I needn't be a master of deduction to assume the lady— Mrs. Draven—is in some sort of trouble and has come to you for help. She arrived with that…animal and her sister quite in the middle of the night. She seems to have a penchant for arriving uninvited."

"Ward." Benedict said it with a tone of warning, but he couldn't really argue with Ward. He'd first met Catarina when she'd arrived uninvited in his tent.

"I have also heard rumors that she was with a Spanish gentleman when she came to London. I assume there was some trouble with that man or another last night."

Benedict lifted his shirt and donned it. "I think you underestimate your powers of deduction. They're quite formidable."

"Hardly, Colonel. Neither you nor Mrs. Draven seem to have slept well. That fact alone hints of some trouble at the theater. Is it the Spaniard I am to watch for?"

"Juan Carlos de la Fuente. Don't open the door to him and keep the ladies home. If they want to go out, I will escort them later."

"I am but a mere servant, Colonel. I cannot keep them here against their will."

Benedict tied his cravat. "You're more than a servant, and you know it. And the day you have to resort to ordering anyone to do your will is the day geese talk and sheep sprout wings and fly."

"I believe you are implying I am manipulative," Ward said, helping Benedict into his coat.

"Don't let it go to your head."

***

At the Draven Club, he found a few of his men scattered about the various rooms. FitzRoy wasn't in, but Porter said he'd been in the night before and said he would return in the afternoon.

While Benedict waited, he dined with Neil Wraxall, who had been his first in command of the Survivors, and Ewan Mostyn, who had been, and most probably still was, one of the strongest and most lethal men alive. Ewan was also his business partner, but Benedict had neglected the boxing studio since Catarina's arrival. Ewan ate heartily but said very little, as was his custom. Neil was in the process of building a new house and bemoaned the cost of supplies as well as the capriciousness of workmen who promised to arrive early to begin work and didn't make an appearance until midday.

It was all so very ordinary that Draven could hardly believe just a little over a year ago they had all been slithering about the Continent, one wrong move away from death, risking their lives in an attempt to thwart Napoleon.

"Want me to kill one of them?" Ewan asked when Neil had gone on a bit long about the lazy workmen.

Draven thought he was joking. It was difficult to tell with Ewan because the promise of violence usually brought a smile to his face. He wasn't smiling now—not very much, at any rate—which mean he wasn't serious.

Or was he?

Neil scowled at him. "If you kill the workers, then the project will never be finished. And don't tell me to hire more"—he pointed his fork at Ewan, who didn't look like he intended to say anything of the sort—"no one will work for me if I have a reputation for killing the builders. However..." He set the fork down with a clink. "If you could come by and perhaps scare them a little."

Ewan was nodding, a bit too enthusiastically in Draven's opinion.

"A *little*, Ewan," Neil repeated. "Just skulk around and look menacing. I'll spread the word that you're displeased at the slow pace and that might motivate the workers." Neil leaned forward. "What time can you come?"

Ewan shrugged, clearly not as interested in the venture now that the fun had been taken out of it.

Porter entered the room and approached with FitzRoy behind him. "Colonel, Mr. FitzRoy has arrived."

Benedict rose. "Let's speak in my parlor." He tossed his napkin on the chair.

Neil rose to greet FitzRoy with a handshake, but Ewan only looked from Benedict and then back to his abandoned plate.

"Are you finished?" he asked.

Benedict had only eaten half of his meal and not tasted any of it. "Yes."

With a nod, Ewan lifted the plate, dumped the food onto his own plate, and continued eating.

"It's a comfort to know that though everything else in the world may change, Mostyn's stomach remains bottomless," FitzRoy remarked as he and Draven walked out of the room.

"How did he manage not to starve in France?" Draven asked.

"That's why he always liked Beaumont so much. Rafe brought him food he pilfered from the tables of the ladies he charmed. Once in a while I was able to do the same, but I think he was still hungry. That's probably why he was in such a bad mood for the duration of the war."

Benedict hadn't seen any change in Ewan's mood, but he hadn't spent as much time with him as FitzRoy. They entered the parlor and Benedict took a seat behind his desk. He pointed to the chair opposite, but FitzRoy shook his head. "I don't have good news."

"I didn't expect you would. Has de la Fuente spread the story about Mrs. Draven yet?"

"No, but I've seen him with his son, their heads together as if they are planning something."

"Tell me about the son."

FitzRoy waved a hand dismissively. "He's nothing to worry about. He drinks so much he's barely conscious most of the time. When he is conscious, he spends all his time at a brothel that caters to men with eclectic tastes."

"How so?"

FitzRoy shook his head in disgust. "Women who have been maimed or were born deformed in some way and have no other recourse but to become prostitutes. I doubt the son ever had any interest in marrying Mrs. Draven. I can't see how she would appeal to him if his tastes are what I think they are."

"It's his father who wants her under his thumb."

"And now you've taken that possibility away."

"Will he knock the entire house of cards down?" Benedict asked.

"I don't think he's that much of a fool. He knows he'd bring himself down as well. But her business is still a threat to him. He won't let her go without a fight. I advise you to keep Mrs. Draven close and to watch your own back as well."

"That's good advice. Has he grown suspicious of you yet?"

"Not yet, but I may change disguises and observe a bit longer."

"I know you don't want me to say that I owe you—"

"Then don't." And FitzRoy bowed and walked out of the room.

Benedict was left wondering what to do. He was safe at his club, but he hardly wanted to spend every day here. He was often called into the Foreign Office to consult or lend the wisdom of his experience to the ministers there. He wasn't afraid to move about London, but neither did he want to tempt fate.

And with his wife at home and his attraction to her growing, going home would also tempt fate. They would end up in bed together if they spent much more time together. He wanted her. He couldn't deny the truth of that to himself. But he would let her go if that was what she wanted. Unless of course, there was the possibility she was carrying his child. How could he grant the annulment then? How could he send her into the world with a sister, a cat, and a child to care for? But how would he ever convince her to stay? Better to keep his hands off her than to risk pregnancy.

Which meant he didn't want to bed her unless she was sure she wanted to remain married to him. Last night she'd clearly had reservations about the idea. And why not? It would mean spending the rest of her youth with an aging former soldier. He might be hale and hearty now, but what about ten years from now or twenty? Why would she want the burden of caring for an old man when she was still in her prime?

But he couldn't leave Ward—capable as he was—all on his own. Benedict would have to go home at some point. And if it was inevitable that he took Catarina to his bed, there were ways they could find pleasure without risking a child.

The thought made his throat go dry. Before he could reconsider, he was on his way down the stairs. In the vestibule, Neil was still trying to convince Ewan to frighten his workmen into doing what he paid them for. But at his approach, Neil broke off. "Is everything all right, sir?"

"Perfectly fine. Why do you ask?" He held out his arms, so Porter could help him into his greatcoat.

"You seem in a hurry."

"No hurry. Good afternoon, Wraxall. Mostyn."

"Enjoy your evening," Ewan said.

The man had so few words that Draven looked back at him and was left with the impression Ewan knew exactly why he was rushing home.

Ten

"You have witchcraft in your lips."
Henry V, *William Shakespeare*

Catarina was in the blue parlor working on Lady Philomena's lace when Benedict burst into the room. She jumped, dropped her bobbins, and stared at him. His face was flushed, his hair tousled—which was not unusual—and he was breathing quickly.

She half-rose from her chair. "What is it? Has something happened?"

He stared at her for a long moment. "Pardon?"

"What happened? You look as though you ran all the way here."

His cheeks colored slightly. "Nothing is the matter. I wanted to...speak with you."

At that moment, Ward came into the parlor, making clucking sounds. "Colonel, you did not give me time to take your coat or hat."

Benedict looked at his servant with annoyance, and Catarina stared at her husband.

"Are you certain you are well? You are acting very strangely."

"I'm fine. I—" But Ward was attempting to assist him out of his outerwear, and he turned to remove the garments himself and shove them at his man.

"Well!" Ward said, leaving the room with a huff.

"I think you've upset him," Catarina said, taking her seat again. She'd thought the awkwardness of the night before had passed, but it seemed to be returning. Now Benedict was simply standing in the middle of the parlor, staring at her. When their eyes met, he quickly looked away.

"I'll speak with him later. I wanted to talk to you."

"What is it?" She folded her hands and gave him her attention, but instead of launching into whatever topic he had in mind, he ran a hand through his already disordered hair. She was still not used to being in such close proximity with him. When she was close to him, she had the constant urge to touch him in some way—smooth his hair or take his hand or kiss his lips…

She was having a more difficult time controlling that urge every day, but she reminded herself men were not to be trusted.

Finally, after looking everywhere in the room but at her, Benedict said, "It's about last night."

Her heart clenched in her chest. She did not want to talk about last night. She didn't know how to feel about all of his rules and her own growing desire for him. She didn't want an annulment, but she didn't want to be forced into a marriage either. She'd married him the first time to avoid just that.

She wanted a choice, and if bedding him removed that choice, she had no option but to refuse him. "You mean, what happened at the theater?" She could hope.

"After the theater."

Her shoulders slumped. That was exactly the subject she'd wanted to avoid.

She pressed her lips together, and focused on a spot to the right of his head so she did not have to look into his beautiful blue eyes. "Has something changed? Have the rules changed?" She darted a look at him as he sat on the couch beside her chair. He leaned close, his voice low.

"No."

Oh, how she wanted to lean closer to him. She managed to restrain herself and give him a perplexed look.

"Yes. Yes and no. I was thinking about you at my club. Imagining…well, I don't need to detail what I was imagining, but it occurred to me that I can still give you"—

now he leaned even closer, so close his breath warmed her cheek—"pleasure without causing a baby. We could—"

Her breath hitched in her throat and heat flooded her...everywhere.

"Oh, Ward said you were home," Ines said, walking into the room and sitting in the chair on Catarina's other side. Benedict moved back and Catarina sprang away from him, as though the two of them were naughty children engaging in mischief. "I asked him to bring tea for us. He will return in a moment." She lifted her bobbins.

"Perfect." Benedict rose and Catarina followed.

"You're not staying for tea?" She knew they couldn't continue their discussion with Ines in the room, but she did not want him to leave in the middle. She wanted him close again, wanted to feel the heat from his body.

"I'm not thirsty at the moment, and perhaps it might be best if I returned to my club."

Ines looked up at him. "You're leaving again?"

"Yes." He looked at Catarina, and she swallowed hard. "But I'll be back, and I'll be here tonight. And every night.." His gaze held hers for a long moment, and she wondered if he could read her thoughts. Then he was gone.

***

Catarina spent the next several days engrossed in lacemaking. She made lace, though her mind continually turned over Benedict's words. He could pleasure her without creating a child. He *wanted* to pleasure her. She was curious and uncertain. She very much wanted him to touch her and to touch him. She wanted to kiss him and explore his body and all manner of wicked things. But if she gave in to her baser instincts, would she be able to leave him when this business with Juan Carlos was at an end? Benedict was polite and solicitous to her when she saw him, but his eyes held a promise. She knew the next move was hers to make.

Ines and she worked seven or eight hours a day, often in the dining room, as it had the best light and opened to the garden, where Tigrino liked to nap if the weather was not too cold or wet. She finished the handkerchief for Lady Philomena and sent it with her compliments as well as a half dozen more handkerchiefs, a fichu, and assorted pieces that could be added to garments for ornamentation.

Ines had done almost as much work, though she hadn't been quite as enthusiastic about staying home and working all day. She was eager to see more of the city, and of course, she had nothing she needed to keep her mind off.

Making lace seemed all Catarina could do to keep her mind off Benedict. He was home most days, although he was occasionally called away. If he was home, he generally stayed out of her way, attending to his correspondence or business matters.

But even if he was in one room and she in another and they didn't see each other for hours, she still knew he was there. She felt his presence. Sometimes at night she would wake and think about the way he'd held her and kissed her. She would imagine him sleeping in his bed chamber and know that she could go to him and be welcomed with open arms. He would give her pleasure, and she desperately wondered what wicked things he would do to her.

But what happened after the pleasure? How could she walk away after sharing intimacies with him? Was she ready to give up her freedom for a few hours of pleasure? Sometimes the answer was yes. She'd half fallen in love with him the morning he'd told her she was an artist. Nothing he'd done in the meantime had diminished that feeling at all. In fact, the more she saw of him, the more she respected him. He was a good man. He treated his servants well. He was indulgent toward her sister. He obviously managed his finances in a manner that left him quite comfortable. And his counsel was sought on a regular basis by those who valued his service to his country.

And that said nothing of the way he looked at her. Sometimes when the three of them—four if one counted Tigrino stalking under the table hoping for a scrap to fall—ate dinner together, she would catch him looking at her, and her own heart reflected the longing she saw in his eyes.

He wanted her to come to his bed. Did that mean he also wanted her for his wife? Could she trust him to cherish her? She'd watched how her father treated her mother. He used her mother in the night when he had need and then treated her like a servant the rest of the time. And her father could be kind and generous to his daughters when he wanted something and then violent and frightening when he did not get his way.

It was during one of these dinners, when she and Benedict were studiously avoiding looking at each other and probably too quiet for Ines's liking, that Ines announced. "I will go shopping tomorrow."

Catarina's spoon clattered to the table. "No, you will not. Benedict thinks it is dangerous for us to go out."

"Juan Carlos is still in London," he said. "I don't know why he's still here, but I can't think it's for any noble purpose. I'd prefer he doesn't give us an illustration."

"But I must go shopping," Ines said. "We are out of thread."

Catarina sat forward. "What? You are mistaken. There is more in my valise."

"I took it out yesterday, and now it is all but gone."

"Why did you not tell me?"

"I did tell you. I do not think you hear half of what I say."

"I will send a servant to buy more thread," Benedict announced.

Ines and Catarina scoffed in unison.

"And what is the matter with that idea?"

"A servant cannot choose the thread," Ines explained. "If we were in Barcelona, we might be able to tell the servant where to go and the proprietor would know what we wanted, but here we do not know the shops or the quality of thread to be found in them."

"We shall have to go ourselves," Catarina said. To her surprise, Benedict agreed. She thought he might argue that they didn't need to make lace and thus didn't need thread.

Instead, he sat back. "We'll go shopping, but not tomorrow. How about the day after?"

Catarina and Ines agreed, but Catarina wondered why he'd wanted to wait. Surely one day wouldn't make any difference. A good wife would not have questioned her husband. She would have passively accepted his decision.

And if he cared for her, why make her wait? Perhaps her request was nothing but an annoyance to him.

After a day of trying not to think about why Benedict had wanted to wait, and failing miserably because she had no lace to keep her occupied, Catarina knew she'd never be a good wife.

After Ines fell asleep, she pulled on her dressing gown and tiptoed into the blue parlor.

But Benedict wasn't at his desk as she'd expected. Which could only mean he'd gone to bed.

She should go back to bed as well. Instead, she found her feet moving in the direction of his bed chamber. She'd expected his candle to be extinguished. She'd expected to turn right back around and go to the chamber she shared with Ines. Instead, she found light flickering under his closed door.

Catarina stood outside it. There was no shame in knocking. She could ask her question and go back to her bed.

There was no shame in staying. He was her husband in the eyes of God. He was her husband in her own eyes as well, and he was a man she respected and even liked. If he would take her in his arms and kiss her as he had the night of the theater, then she might never go back to her own chamber again.

I can still give you pleasure without causing a baby. We could—

She longed to know what words he would have spoken next.

Before she could lose her courage, Catarina tapped on the bed chamber door.

"Come in," he called.

She stared at the latch. She hadn't expected to be invited in. She'd thought he would answer the door. But, of course, he thought it was Ward knocking.

She lifted the latch and stepped inside, closing the door softly behind her. Benedict stood at his wash basin, shirt off, splashing his face with water. She had a moment to admire his broad shoulders and the solid lines of his back. He was no lean boy, but a man of thick muscle and power. He had a smattering of freckles here and there as was typical of people with his coloring.

"What is it?" he asked, fumbling for a towel to dry his face and eyes.

"I had a question," she said, her mouth dry. If her legs were not frozen, she would have crossed to him and run a hand down his bare back.

He spun around, lowering the towel from his eyes and staring at her with shock. "I thought you were Ward."

"I realize that." Now she could see his bare chest, which was wide and lightly covered by hair that matched the ginger on his head. His waist was probably thicker than it had been in his youth, but his belly was still flat. She imagined kissing that belly and heat flamed in her face.

"You *had* a question? Not anymore?" he asked, placing the towel on his washstand and standing before her as though her obvious perusal of his naked flesh did not affect him.

"I-I cannot remember what it was."

"Do you want to come back when you do?"

How could she walk away when he was standing there looking as he did? It was one night. She could trust him for one night.

We could...

Those words taunted her. She wanted to know what they could do together. She wanted him to touch her again. Her heart was beating so hard she could barely hear her own words when she stammered, "I will stay, if that is acceptable to you." Her gaze met his, and she saw in his eyes a flickering of relief. Of course, he'd offered her an exit. That didn't mean he wanted her to take it.

"It's more than acceptable." But now he seemed at a loss for what to do next. "I would offer you some wine or other refreshment, but I have nothing."

"I am not thirsty." She took a step toward him. Moving close to him was more instinct than thought. Her body tingled at the anticipation of his touch.

"I'm not either. Is there something else you want?"

She swallowed. Would he make her say it? She wasn't so proud or so stupid as to deny herself yet again. "You. I have missed you."

He didn't need to ask what she meant. He closed the distance between them with two steps. "I've missed you too." His arm came around her waist, and he tugged her gently to him until their bodies were pressed together. *This.* This was what she'd wanted. How had she survived even a day without his body touching hers?

"I've missed your mouth." He touched her lips with his thumb, still wet from the water he'd used to splash his face. Her head spun with the intensity of need. "I missed kissing it."

"I want you to kiss me again," she managed, her voice raw and desperate in her ears,

He bent to do just that, and she wrapped her arms around his neck. She would not let him go this time. The hair on his chest tickled where bare skin brushed over it, and he was so incredibly warm. She could have made a little burrow in his chest and wintered there.

His lips took hers, gently at first then with more urgency. He tasted clean, like peppermint toothpowder, and smelled faintly of soap. As his tongue stroked hers, she felt her body come truly alive. Like the fire in the hearth, her blood began to simmer low and hot.

His mouth moved to her neck, where he pulled her loose hair to one side to gain better access. She shivered as his hands slid up her body and back down to her waist again. Their hands met together at the tie of her wrapper, and she smiled as their gazes locked.

"We had the same idea," he said.

"It is rather warm in here." She was burning up and nothing would ease that feeling but his hands on her, all over her.

He nodded as she unknotted the tie and slipped the wrapper off. She still wore her chemise, a short garment that didn't even reach her knees and was so thin he could probably see through it. He took the wrapper from her and stepped away to lay it over the foot of the bed. His gaze lowered to her legs. They weren't long or slender, and she felt somewhat self-conscious about them, but the way he looked at them, with heat and desire, made her forget her worries.

In fact, she wondered if he would look at the rest of her with such longing, and she found herself reaching for the hem of her chemise. She began to lift it, and he backed toward the bed.

"I'd better sit down if you're about to do what I think you are."

"You are my husband," she said. "I have nothing to hide from you." She wanted him to look at her with approval and longing. She wanted to see that he wanted her. Needed her as much as she needed him.

"Damn right." His breath hitched as she pulled the garment up her thighs, over her hips, across her waist, and tugged it over her head. She let it drop on the ground then.

"I don't know what I did to deserve this," he murmured, "but I'll thank God until my last breath. Can I—can I touch you?"

She nodded, her voice seeming caught in her throat. He held out a hand and she took it, allowing herself to be pulled between his legs. Then his arms were on her waist again, and his mouth on her lips. But she couldn't concentrate on the kiss. His hands roamed down over her bottom and he groaned softly before tracing the curves of her hips. She shivered when she thought he might touch her belly and dive lower. Instead, he traced a path up her ribs and cupped her breasts.

"Catarina," he whispered as though she'd just revealed some treasure to him. "I know exactly what I want to do with you."

She opened her eyes and looked at him. She wanted to give herself to him completely, but how could she throw everything she'd worked so hard for the past five years away with one act? "You said...the other day in the parlor..."

"I'll make certain we still have the option of annulment."

His words surprised her and not happily. She didn't know what she'd wanted him to say. Wasn't his response what she'd expected?

"It will take some—very well, *all*—of my control, but if I've learned anything in life it's self-control."

The warmth she'd felt before had begun to ebb away. He was content to leave the possibility of annulment open. Did that mean he didn't want her as his wife? Or maybe he didn't think she wanted him?

His mouth was on her shoulder, then her collarbone, and it was impossible to entertain any thought when he kissed her like that. His hands were on her bottom again, stroking and kneading gently. And when his mouth skated over her breast, the warmth she'd thought gone rushed back hotter than before.

Her nipples hardened, and he took one in his mouth, causing her to moan audibly. The way he sucked at her roused urges she'd never felt before. The hand on her bottom slid between her legs, and her knees buckled. She could feel how slick she was as his hands skated over her core.

"You'd better lie down," he said, releasing her and standing. He guided her to the bed, but before she could sit, he turned her, and his hands were on her backside again.

He surprised her again when he knelt and kissed the small of her back. She trembled at the intimacy of such a kiss and the waves of pleasure it sent through her. Then he moved his mouth lower until he'd left a wet trail over one cheek. Lightly, he bit the fleshiest part, and she gasped. She wanted him to reach between her legs again. Her breasts were aching, her nipples so hard they almost hurt. She had the urge to touch them herself while he stroked her.

But he reluctantly turned her around and she toppled onto the bed. He was still on his knees, and he lifted one of her feet and kissed her ankle.

"What are you doing?" she said with a laugh since her feet were ticklish. "You cannot mean to start kissing me there."

"Can't I?" The wicked look in his eyes assured her he knew exactly what he wanted to do. "Watch me." He turned her leg, kissing her calf and then the inside of her knee. She began to tremble as her leg was spread wider, and he brushed his lips over the inside of her thigh. "Your skin is so soft," he murmured, his breath on her flesh making her catch her breath. He parted her legs further, his mouth growing closer to the thatch of dark curls at the juncture of her thighs. When he reached them, he brushed his lips over them, and Catarina bucked.

With a smile, he moved up her body, kissing her lower belly, then her navel, then her abdomen. Finally, he took her breasts in his hands and made circles about them with his thumbs. The circles grew increasingly tighter, but he never seemed to reach her aching nipples.

"Please," she said. His thumb brushed over one then the other and she moaned loudly.

"Lay back," he said, helping her fully onto the bed before coming down beside her. "I must ask you a question now."

She blinked at him, hardly comprehending. Her body was on fire, her mind focused on the feel of him and his touch.

"I'm not asking to judge you but because I need to know how to proceed."

Now she stiffened slightly. "What is it?"

"Are you still a virgin? You can answer truthfully. I won't be angry if you're not."

She sighed. "I am. I never wanted—" She didn't quite know what to say next.

"I have another question. Have you ever touched yourself to bring about orgasm?"

Her face reddened.

"I know you are a religious woman, and the church teaches against such things, but I'm your husband, and I wouldn't censure you."

"I have never done that," she answered truthfully. "I have never wanted to…before."

His lips curled in a smile. "I make you want to touch yourself?"

Her face felt as though it was on fire.

"Good. That's how you're supposed to feel. You'll tell me if I do anything you don't like. You should feel only pleasure." He gathered her in his arms, turning her toward him and kissing her mouth, as his hands roamed about her body. When she was acutely aware of every single part of her, his hand came to rest on the dark curls at her center. He cupped her there, not moving, not doing anything but allowing her to get used to the feel of his hand there.

Gradually, as his kisses became slower and deeper, he slid his fingers into her curls, and then, finding her passage, traced one finger around it.

She could hardly breathe at the feel of him there. She couldn't concentrate on Benedict's kisses, and he drew back, his eyes meeting hers as his finger slowly entered her. He withdrew again, curving his finger upward until she was jolted with sensation. She gasped.

"Again?" he asked.

She made an incoherent sound, and he slid his finger into her again. This time he went a little deeper, but he withdrew as slowly and at that angle that meant he slipped against the most sensitive part of her.

When he entered her again, her hips moved, pushing herself against his hand to gain the most pleasure. Still inside her, he pushed her onto her back and spread her legs. He moved the finger within her slowly, his hand at an angle that caused her to writhe on the mattress and wantonly spread her legs further. This time when he withdrew, she all but screamed in frustration.

"Close your eyes," he said. "Don't think of anything. Just feel."

She felt two fingers at her opening. Carefully, he slid them inside, to the first knuckle. "Yes?" he asked.

"Oh, yes." She moved, taking him deeper. She could feel how wet his hand was, how wet her curls, but she tried to forget that. She felt only the way his fingers arched up, sliding in and out to rub against that tightly coiled part of her.

Everything was bright blue and white as he touched her, and the pleasure mounted. She didn't know what she did, what she said, what she moaned. She only knew that finally all of the sensations coalesced into one tight ball that shattered into a sensation of perfect bliss.

When she finally opened her eyes, he was lying beside her, his hand on her breast. "Catch your breath," he said.

She stretched and smiled at him. "I feel…mmmm."

"Yes. I told you only pleasure tonight." He pulled the sheet back and moved her body until she was underneath it, then he joined her. "I don't want you to feel cold."

How could she with him beside her? He was so deliciously warm. She kissed his chest, her lips trailing up the line of hair, and he pulled her close. "Sleep for a bit. I don't want you to be too weary tomorrow."

"But it's not even eleven."

"I know. Which means in a little while I can pleasure you again."

"Again?"

"And again."

She took a shaky breath, certain she would never be able to sleep with all of that to anticipate. But a few minutes later she was dreaming.

Eleven

"What's past is prologue."
The Tempest, *William Shakespeare*

He had a naked woman sleeping in his bed. She was truly sleeping now. He wasn't so much a brute that he would keep her up all night, though he was certainly tempted. But he'd awakened her twice before, and he didn't have the heart to do it again, even if he still had the urge to touch and explore her body.

It was almost dawn now, and if he laid next to Catarina much longer, he would give in to temptation. Instead, he rose and splashed water on his face then put on clean breeches and found a pressed shirt. He stood in front of his mirror and stared at his chest. He could see the white mixed in with the ginger hair. He found gray hairs in his beard before he shaved and more seemed to crop up on his temples daily. He'd always had wide shoulders and a barrel chest, but he'd lost some of the muscle and definition he'd had ten years ago.

He wondered what Catarina had seen when she'd looked at him last night. Had she noticed all his flaws? She said she didn't think him too old, and he certainly didn't feel old with her body beneath his hands.

He tugged a shirt on over his head. She didn't have to stay married to him, of course. He was still willing to agree to an annulment once he knew she was safe and no longer needed his protection. But if matters progressed beyond what they had last night, he would not be amenable. He didn't want to produce a bastard or saddle her with a child she could not provide for, although truth be told, her lace would probably make her a wealthy woman if Juan Carlos didn't ruin her reputation out of spite. If that happened, it might be better for them to stay married.

And perhaps he was really just looking for a way to keep her. It was ridiculous that he should feel any obligation to her. They were not legally wed, and yet, he'd stood in that church and said vows. And he'd meant them too. Not because he loved her—he'd barely known her. But because he respected her and liked her and wanted to do something to help her. Giving her his name had seemed such a small thing.

He hadn't counted on it meaning anything to him. But it had.

He hadn't seen her for five years, and in that time, he'd met his share of lovely women. The women in brothels across the Continent were easy to ignore. Benedict wasn't interested in paying for a woman. But when he'd come home from the war, he'd been celebrated as a war hero. He'd been asked to every ball and dinner party and celebration London could muster. He had always enjoyed social occasions. He was no recluse who detested dancing or conversation.

What he hadn't expected was the number of women who had openly propositioned him. It was easy to say no to the women who were married. It was more difficult to say no to the widows. At one point, he wondered why the hell he *was* saying no to the widows.

So he said yes, and ended up doing no more than boring the poor woman with old war stories.

He knew why, even before Catarina had been naked in his bed.

Because he felt married. In his heart, Catarina was his wife. And though he'd thought he might never see her again, though she might have had a dozen lovers while they'd been apart, he could not bring himself to be disloyal to her.

And now here she was. And she had kept to her vows as well. He hadn't expected that of her and would not have faulted her if she hadn't. But perhaps it meant something that they'd found each other after years of honoring their vows without knowing if they'd ever be together again.

Or perhaps he wanted it to mean something. She might still want an annulment. He'd been her path to freedom before, and he didn't want to be the one who closed the door on her now.

"You rise early," she murmured from the bed.

He turned, clenching his fists when he saw her rumpled hair and her sleepy eyes. He was testing his self-control mightily these days.

"I suppose it's an old habit. Did I wake you?"

"No. I am also in the habit of waking early." She looked down, her cheeks coloring. "I am at a loss for words this morning. I have never spent the night in the bed of a man before."

He knew what she was wondering—had things changed between them, and if so, how was she to act now?

Things had changed, or so he hoped. "I'd like you to spend the night here again," he said.

"I would like that too." She put her hands to her cheeks. "I do not know if I should even say such things."

"I think you should say them much more often," he teased. But he could see she still felt uncomfortable. "Why don't I leave you to dress and you can join me to break your fast when you are ready?"

He left her and encountered Tigrino sitting outside the door. Tigrino rose and meowed loudly. "I suppose you are hungry and feeling neglected."

The cat bumped his head on Benedict's leg.

"Come on then. I'll see what I can find for you to eat."

A short while later, Ines and Catarina entered the dining room. Catarina's cheeks were still pink, and Ines was smiling. "I asked my sister where she was last night," Ines said. "She will not answer. Do you know, *senhor*?"

"I do," he said, rising and pulling out chairs for both of them.

Ines nodded. "Good. I slept very well without her kicking me and stealing the covers. Perhaps she can sleep wherever she slept last night tonight."

Catarina elbowed her sister. "Ines, you are scandalous. Keep quiet."

Ines stuck her tongue out, and Catarina looked as though she sorely wanted to strike her.

"I thought we would go to Bond Street today," Benedict said, changing the topic. "I have made inquiries and have it on good authority that is the place to buy quality thread."

"Excellent. When can we go?" Catarina asked.

"I've ordered the coach for ten."

***

When the coach arrived, he handed the two ladies up and nodded to the coachman in the box and the footman holding on to the back. The men of his former troop looked very believable—Colin more than Ewan, of course, but then Colin was a master of disguises and Ewan was difficult to ignore. Benedict wasn't taking any chances with Juan Carlos.

They had no trouble en route to Bond Street, and the sisters chattered constantly about the shops they passed and the ladies out walking and the general business of London. Benedict found he enjoyed their talk. It had been years since he'd lived with his family, and he'd missed listening to his two sisters talk.

Finally, the carriage halted, and Benedict led the ladies to a shop he'd been told might have what the women wanted. Ewan trailed them, causing men and women to part like the Red Sea before Moses.

"Are all footmen so large?" Catarina asked when they entered the shop, Ewan standing guard outside.

"Yes," Benedict said without blinking.

He wasn't sure she believed him, but she didn't argue. Instead, she approached a clerk and asked to see their thread. An hour later, Ewan was slouched against the door outside and Benedict wanted to pull his hair out. How the hell difficult was it to buy thread? They didn't even need colored thread, just white. It seemed to him Catarina and her sister had inspected every piece of thread in the shop and dismissed all of them as inferior.

He still harbored a faint hope that the clerk would find something to appease the women, but when he returned with his arms raised as though in surrender, Benedict wanted to groan.

"Thank you, anyway," Catarina said. "We will go elsewhere."

"You may go elsewhere," the man said, "But you won't find any better. We have the best thread in the country. The best modistes in London buy from us."

"Then they are either blind or stupid," Ines said. "Because anyone could see this thread is inferior."

"We should go now." Benedict stepped between the clerk and his charges and offered his arm to Catarina.

"Gladly." Catarina took his arm and marched out the door. Outside, Ewan gave Benedict a baleful look.

"Where shall we go now?" Catarina asked.

"That was the shop everyone recommended," Benedict said. "I don't know any others."

"Surely there must be others." Catarina began to walk, pulling Benedict with her. "Look at all the shops here. We will probably find what we want with a little more effort."

Indeed, there were more shops. Many more. And the women inspected the thread at each one. Benedict gave in to curiosity and listened to their discussion and reasons for dismissing some thread and considering others. Finally, at one shop in the back of an arcade, the women bought a small measure of thread.

Benedict carried it out. "So this is what you want?"

"Yes," Ines said. "Do you see the texture is fine but the thread is sturdy? And the color is quite pure. Not irregular as in some of the other samples we've seen."

"It is too bad this was all she had," Catarina said. "It won't be enough to make more than a few items."

Ewan came to stand behind them, looking hungry and cross.

"She said she would try to acquire more," Benedict said. "We can come back again in a few days."

"Surely, we could look at a few more shops," Catarina said. "There are some we have not yet visited."

Ewan made a sound like a growl behind them.

"Let's stop for tea first," Benedict said. "I'm famished."

"Oh, I am not hungry at all," Catarina argued.

Ines was nodding, though. "I would like that. Catarina, how can you say no? You want to visit an English tea shop, yes?"

***

Once they arrived at the quaint little shop, Catarina was glad she had agreed. The shop had lace curtains—Mechlin lace, she decided—and platters of delicious smelling pastries on display. Throughout the shop, small wooden tables were scattered, surrounded by chairs with soft, colorful cushions.

Benedict directed the ladies to sit and returned shortly with tea and a plate of small cakes. Catarina realized she was actually quite famished, and she and Ines had finished the cakes and a cup of tea in quick order.

"But you did not partake, *senhor*," Ines protested, pointing to Benedict's empty plate.

"My pleasure was all in watching you indulge." He caught Catarina's eye and winked at her. She swallowed. Last night it had seemed all his pleasure was in giving pleasure to her. Did he want none for himself or did he not want to trap himself into marriage with her? Suddenly, she felt quite selfish for dragging him about all morning. Surely, he had better things to do than squire them about.

"You know, I am rather more tired than I thought," she said. "Perhaps we should return home and come back in a few days' time."

"Catarina!" Ines whined as she had when she'd been a child. "Just a few more shops."

"Not today," she said firmly.

"I agree," Benedict said. "I think we have tested our luck long enough. Even with a footman to protect us, I'd rather not meet Juan Carlos."

Ines sighed. "Oh, fine."

"Would you like to take some pastries to our footman?" Benedict asked Ines. "I'll buy a bag, and you can deliver them to him."

Ines face lit up. "Oh, yes, please."

Catarina sipped the rest of her tea then smiled while Ines carried the bag to the footman outside. "I hope she doesn't flirt too outrageously," she said when Benedict reclaimed his seat.

"He's immune to that sort of thing. But she seemed to need something to do."

"I am afraid the last few weeks have been very difficult for her. She is a spirited girl, and she does not want to stay inside day after day and night after night. She wants company and entertainment."

"I'm sure it won't be long now until she's able to return to her regular life." He'd been looking at Ines through the window, where she had obviously given up trying to engage the footman. But now his brow furrowed, and he rose hastily.

"What is wrong?" Catarina asked.

"Stay here," he said. "I'll be back in a moment. Do not move from this seat."

"But what has—"

He was already striding out the door, and now she saw the coachman had arrived. Had something happened to the carriage? She watched the three men speak, heads close together so Ines could not hear, and so intent was her attention on them, she didn't see the man sit down at the chair Benedict had just vacated.

"More tea?" he asked, lifting the pot.

Catarina gasped at Miguel de la Fuente. She hadn't even seen him come in. He looked quite sober. She couldn't remember the last time she'd seen him sober. She might *never* have seen him sober.

"What do you want?" she hissed.

"I have a message for you," he said, sitting back, looking quite comfortable in Benedict's chair.

"What is it?"

"My father says he will give you one last chance. You do not have to marry me. You can have your colonel." He waved to the window where Benedict could still be seen talking with the coachman and footman. "But you must sell him your shop in Barcelona and agree never to make Catarina lace again. He has drawn up papers." He withdrew them from his coat now and placed them on the table between them. "Sign them or you will regret it."

How strange to see Miguel sober and speaking to her so casually, as if he had not tried to rape her the last time they had seen each other.

"What will happen if I do not sign?"

He gave her a regretful look. "I do not know, but I would not defy him. *Buenos tarde.*" And he was up and walking away as the door flung open and three men—Benedict and his servants—sprinted inside.

"Did he hurt you?" Benedict rushed up to her and took her by the shoulders.

"Where did he go?" the footman asked.

"Out the back!" the coachman yelled, gesturing toward the back of the shop.

"I am fine," Catarina said. "He came to deliver a message."

"What's that?" Benedict asked.

"Sell him my business or else." She pointed to the papers on the table, her fingers shaking. "Where is Ines?"

"I am here," she said. "Your husband almost ripped my arm off pulling me inside."

"Good. I want you close to me," Catarina rose and hugged her sister. "Go after him." She waved a hand toward the back of the tea shop. "I know you want to, Benedict. We will wait here."

The two women sat again, Catarina attempting to sip her now cold tea without spilling it all over her bodice. Her hands were shaking badly. The shop was deathly quiet except for the shrill tinkling of the bell over the door. The other patrons were quickly finishing their tea and leaving.

Finally, Benedict returned with the footman and coachman, who she was beginning to suspect were not footmen and coachmen at all. "He's gone," Benedict panted. "He must have had a carriage waiting."

"I saw him walking along the street," the coachman said, "but he went into a tailor's shop. He must have gone out the back and come in here without us seeing."

Catarina narrowed her eyes. "Do I know you?"

He raised his brows. "You might."

"Let's go home," Benedict said. "I want the ladies out of danger."

Everyone in the shop watched them as they exited the building and walked to the carriage. Catarina no longer felt excitement about finding the thread she'd wanted. She'd allowed herself to forget about Juan Carlos, to pretend he wasn't still a threat. But he hadn't forgotten her. And he still wanted to take everything she'd built and worked so hard for.

"While I hesitate to call what happened today a positive sign," Benedict said once they were in the carriage and on the way back to Jermyn Street, "I am not wholly discouraged."

Catarina held up the contract, which she'd refused to relinquish. "He wants me to sign away my business and sole rights to make the lace that bears my name."

"And what will he do if you refuse?"

"I do not know." She and Ines were seated across from him on the front-facing seat. "Something awful, I am sure."

"He'll never get close enough to do something to you, and notice he's no longer threatening to reveal your secret."

"He can't without hurting his own reputation."

Ines leaned forward. "He does not have to say much. A few whispered words are all it takes to damage the good name of a lady."

At any other time, Catarina would have smiled and cheered. She'd been cautioning Ines to curb her behavior for years with that advice. She hadn't thought Ines was listening.

Obviously, she had been, and she was correct. A few hints that Catarina had a scandal she kept hidden and the wealthy would balk at wearing her tainted wares.

"I think you underestimate the power of *my* good name." Benedict tapped his fingers on the seat. "Finally, my reputation as a war hero might do some good."

"More decorated men than you have been taken lower by their wives, *senhor.*" And she did not want to be the woman who caused him scandal or loss of prestige.

But he seemed unfazed. "Not if the only evidence against them is vague rumor." He plucked the contract from Catarina's hand and ripped it in half. "You'd better go home and make more lace, ladies. Once Lady Philomena shows off her handkerchief, you'll be in high demand."

Twelve

"This is the way to kill a wife with kindness."
The Taming of the Shrew, *William Shakespeare*

Benedict couldn't have known how prescient his words would be. Lady Philomena attended an inordinate number of social functions and apparently waved her handkerchief about at all of them. At the Draven Club, Phineas complained that his sister had dropped the wipe on the floor so much people were likely to mistake it for a mop.

But the lady's exhibition of the handkerchief had proved effective. Several gentlemen had come to call on Benedict to order Catarina lace pieces for their wives. Ladies could not call at a gentleman's home alone, especially if they were not acquainted with the man's wife, which meant Benedict also received invitations to several gatherings.

He showed the invitations to Catarina at dinner each night. She took them and perused them slowly, her spoken English being better than her ability to read it.

This evening at dinner, she looked lovely in a dark gold dress with lace at the sleeves and her hair done up in a loose knot at the nape of her neck. She hadn't come to his room in two nights. He wanted to ask her why, but he didn't want her to think he was angry or expected her to come to him. She was obviously a woman used to her independence.

But he missed kissing her, touching her, lying beside her.

"Benedict?"

He blinked. "I'm sorry. Did you say something?"

"I said, do you want to attend any of these?"

He sipped his soup, considering. "I have no objection. They might be good for your business." He glanced at Ines who was practically jumping in her seat. "And I believe Miss Neves might like to get out for an afternoon."

"I would! I would!"

Catarina set the invitations beside her plate. Ines immediately snatched them up. "Do you think it safe?"

"Lady Philomena's garden party will be safe enough."

"Is it not too cold for a garden party?" Catarina asked.

"The duke has an extensive greenhouse as well as braziers that servants will set out to warm the air. With enough money, one can conjure spring even this late into fall."

"I see."

"That event will be on the grounds of the duke's town house, and although it would be difficult for anyone not invited to make his way inside, I can ask Lord Phineas to make sure the servants are vigilant."

"What would I say to a duke and his friends?"

"It's the duke's sister and her friends, and you really only need three topics of conversation."

"What are those?"

"The weather, the food being served, and the Prince Regent's latest scandal."

She looked unconvinced.

"It would certainly make my life easier," Benedict said, taking another sip of soup. "You could meet the ladies and sell to them directly, rather than having to go through their husbands and me."

She sighed. "We should go then. When is it?" She glanced at Ines who still had the stack of invitations.

Ines frowned at the vellum, shifting one sheet on top of the other.

"Tomorrow at three," Benedict answered.

"Tomorrow? I have nothing to wear."

He waved his soup spoon. "Wear the dress you have on now. You look beautiful in it."

Ines covered her mouth, and Catarina looked down at her dress. "This is a dinner dress." From the way she jolted, Ines must have kicked her under the table. "Er—thank you for the compliment."

"We will find something, *senhor*," Ines promised.

After dinner she led Catarina to their bedroom, and he didn't see either of them the rest of the evening. He was surprised when the knock sounded on his bed chamber door. He didn't make the mistake of assuming it was Ward this time. He opened it, hoping against hope it was not Ward, and he wasn't disappointed. Catarina stood before him, her hair loose about her dressing gown. Good God, but she was a vision. She seemed more beautiful every time he saw her.

"Come in."

"I hope I do not bother you." She stepped inside, her gaze going directly to the bed. "I was afraid you would be asleep already."

"Still awake." He'd removed his coat and his cravat hung loose, but he still wore his shirt and breeches. "And you could never be a bother to me. In fact, I'm glad you're here. There's something I want to discuss with you privately." He gestured to the bed. "Sit with me a moment."

She looked at the bed and then him. He wondered if she too was remembering the passion they'd shared there a few nights ago. Slowly, she nodded and sat on the bed. He sat beside her, careful their knees did not brush.

"I don't mind people coming here to buy your lace, and if you are truly uncomfortable with attending Lady Philomena's garden party, I will send our regrets."

"But that is why I came to see you." She put her hand on his knee as though to comfort him, and he almost jumped out of his skin. She didn't seem to notice. "I do want to attend, and I want to thank you for having faith in me. I will do my best not to embarrass you. I know I was born a peasant in a small village in Portugal. I have no pedigree, no illustrious family tree."

"I don't care about that." How could she think that mattered to him?

"There will be people at the garden party who will. But I will not embarrass you. I have lived in cities and dealt with the upper classes enough to know how to behave."

"I never worried about that for a moment. And even if you did say the wrong thing, or ran through the lawn with your shoes off, it wouldn't embarrass me. Nothing about you could ever embarrass me."

"That is kind of you. Why are you so kind to me?" Her hand moved in lazy circles on his knee.

"I'm not being kind—"

"But you are! You have always been kind. From the first time I met you, you were kind. I certainly do not deserve it. I have caused you nothing but trouble."

Because her hand was distracting him, he lifted it and kissed it. "Do you want the truth?"

She nodded.

"I suppose it's because I was drawn to you from the first time I saw you. I probably should be ashamed of myself. I'm far too old to be lusting after a woman of your age."

She brought her hand up and placed two fingers over his lips. "You are not old. And you are not the only one who lusted. One reason I picked you to be my husband was because I thought you quite the most handsome soldier of all of them. You sat so tall on your horse. You were so in command. I wanted you."

"And now?" he asked, his voice hoarse and his lips tingling as they moved against her fingers.

"I still want you. I still lust for you."

"When you didn't come back the last few nights—"

"I did not want to seem greedy or wanton...and there were thoughts in my head I needed to sort."

"Catarina," Benedict said. "I don't mind at all if you're both greedy and wanton." He believed that was part of it, but she was also testing him. She'd wanted to see what would happen if she did not come to him. He must have passed her test.

She smiled back. "Oh, really?" She stood, pulling her hands away. "Then I have something to show you."

His mouth went dry as she reached for his cravat and drew it slowly from his neck. She draped it over her own neck so it slid down the front of her thin robe. Then she reached for the buttons at his throat and undid each.

"You don't have to do this," he said.

"I have been thinking of little else for the past few days. I had to start two pieces over because I was not paying attention."

With the collar of his shirt open, she slid her hand down the V of bared skin, causing his flesh to heat as though fire licked at him.

"I wish you'd come to me sooner."

She reached for the hem of his shirt and pulled it from his breeches then unfastened the cuffs. "I suppose I have also stayed away because I have been afraid that the more we are together in this way, the more I will want to remain married. I will lose my independence. You will want a wife who keeps your home, not works in a shop."

"What the hell gave you that idea?"

She seemed to consider as she pushed his shirt up his chest and then over his head. "I do not know, but I began to realize how foolish that thought was when I saw what you were doing for me. You were selling my lace. You were working to expand my business by gathering invitations." She dropped the shirt on the floor, and her hands rested on his shoulders.

"You're talented," he said, trying not to think about her hands on his bare flesh. "I want you to succeed. But it's more than that."

"Oh?" Her hands ran up and down his biceps casually.

"I don't like seeing someone like Juan Carlos prey on those he considers weaker. I've never liked that. That's one reason I went into the army and fought so hard against Napoleon. I cannot abide the abuse of power." He closed his eyes. "And if you keep doing that to me, I won't be able to form a coherent thought in a minute."

"This?" She slid her hands down his arms again. "Or this?" She slid them over his chest so that his flesh tingled at her warm touch.

"Both."

Her hands continued their exploration of his chest. "What is the other reason?"

"Reason for what?" he managed to grind out between his clenched teeth. It was the only way to keep from grabbing her and kissing her.

"You said that was one reason you joined the army. Are there others?"

"I'm a second son. I'm expected to go into the army. Third sons generally choose the clergy."

Now she stepped closer, so close he could smell cinnamon and he might have brushed his lips across her breasts. Her hands roamed down his shoulders to explore his back. "Your father is a gentleman then?"

"He was. He owned land, which passed to my eldest brother. But there was precious little money to buy me a commission. I had to earn my rank for the most part."

"That makes you all the more admirable."

"I am not feeling admirable at the moment, Mrs. Draven."

She smiled. "I think I can see in your eyes what you have in mind, but you shall have to wait."

"Why?"

"Because I want to explore your body tonight." With a little shove that wouldn't have toppled a kitten, she pushed him back on the bed. He went willingly, and she knelt beside him, running her hands up and down his chest. "You do want me," she said, her hands brushing over his waistband. She couldn't fail to see the evidence of his arousal there.

"I always have." His breath caught as her hand trailed up and then back down, pausing so close to his erection that he almost arched to meet her. And then her hand was back on his abdomen.

"I was so overwhelmed by your attentions the other night, I did not pay any attention to you."

"I didn't have any expectations."

"No, of course you do not. You think yourself old and cannot fathom why a woman of five and twenty would want you. She does." Her hand slid over his erection then and he inhaled sharply. "Tonight you told me I was beautiful." Her hands began to unfasten the fall of his breeches. "I think you are beautiful."

And the way she looked at him, he believed it.

She slid his breeches over his hips and then knelt to do away with the rest of his clothing. As she had been the other night, he was naked on the bed. "Now that you have me at your mercy, what do you plan to do?"

"That is a good question." She looked a bit panicked for a minute. "I liked what you did to me. Should I do the same?"

Only if she wanted to kill him. But Benedict was content to die when she knelt on the floor and kissed his calf. "Your hair is red everywhere," she said as she moved up his leg.

"There's some gray now too," he said. At least he thought that was what he said. He couldn't be certain because he couldn't think of anything but her mouth on his knee and then the inside of his thigh. Dear God, if she took him in his mouth, he would not be able to maintain control.

Her lips moved higher, and her hands followed.

Her hands slid over the tops of his thighs, sifting through the light hair there. Her mouth followed, and she paused when she reached mid-thigh. "What shall I do now?"

"I am completely at your mercy, Mrs. Draven."

"Would you like it if I touched you?" Her hand came to rest beside his erection.

"Yes." His voice was barely more than a whisper.

Her fingers grazed him tentatively, learning the feel of him. He closed his eyes and clenched the bed clothes. It had been so long since any woman had touched him. He had never dared to dream Catarina would want him. She was so beautiful and now so accomplished. He was nothing special—a man who was lucky enough to stay alive during the war with Napoleon. He wasn't tall or particularly slim. His red hair and freckles were less than fashionable. He wasn't wealthy or even all that well connected, though he had a few friends he could call upon if need be.

But when her hand closed on him, small and warm and eager, he felt as though none of that mattered. Catarina wanted him. She thought he was beautiful. She touched him as though he were beautiful.

"Like this?" she asked.

"Yes," he said through clenched teeth. "And like this." He closed his hand over hers and guided her hand to show her what he liked best. She watched his face and learned what pleasured him, managing, within a few minutes, to bring him very close to the edge.

"You should stop now." He closed his hand over hers, stopping her.

"Why? I can see by your breathing and the way your cheeks have reddened that you enjoy this."

"I'm close to climax."

"Is that not the point?"

He shook his head. "I don't want to—" How to say this delicately? "I don't want to stain your dressing robe."

"Oh, I see."

To his great disappointment, she released him. It was for the best, though he wondered if he could convince her to sleep beside him. He didn't want her to go yet. "Catarina, I'd still like—what are you doing?"

She'd reached for the tie on her dressing robe and unknotted it. Then she dropped the garment on the floor, standing before him in her short chemise. She kicked the dressing gown away. "Now that problem is no more. Just in case, shall I remove my shift too?"

He couldn't even manage a response as she drew it over her head and tossed it away.

Then she lowered herself to the floor again, kneeling between his legs. Her bare breasts brushed the inside of his thighs, her dark nipples waiting for him to take them in his mouth and tease them to the ripe cherry color he'd so enjoyed the other night.

Her hand closed on him again, and he groaned. She moved her hand up and down the length of him, stroking him until he was all but panting.

"Faster?" she asked.

"Please. Yes. Please."

The orgasm swept over him before he was prepared for it. It was violent and freeing, and he gave a shout as he came. He fell back on the bed when she finally released him and was vaguely aware that she'd taken a towel and dipped it in the wash basin to use to clean up.

He looked over as she brought the towel back to the basin, admiring her round bottom and the curve of her hips, the perfect place for a man's hands to rest.

"I hope you're not thinking of leaving," he said. "I'd like for you to stay. We can simply sleep."

She turned back to look at him, and he realized she was breathing hard. Her eyes were bright, her nipples hard. She'd been aroused by what she'd done to him. Very aroused.

He sat. "Come here." He held out a hand, and she took a few steps then closed her hand on his. He pulled her between his legs again, hooked one hand around her neck and tugged her mouth down. The kiss was long and hot and left her gasping. She broke free to breathe, and he settled his hands on her hips and placed his mouth in the valley between her breasts. His mouth explored the slope of her flesh, the soft underside, and the taut peak. Her hands were in his hair as he licked and nibbled her. His hands slid over her buttocks, feeling the way she trembled at his every touch.

"I feel like I might fall," she whispered. Benedict pulled her onto the bed and straddled her, taking his time, kissing every inch from her shoulders down to her wrists, from her collarbone to her navel and then lower still.

Her hips arched as he slid a hand between her legs. She was wet for him. When he inserted a finger inside her, she clenched around him immediately. He moved lower, pushing her legs open to reveal the glistening pink of her sex.

She didn't try to close her legs or hide herself. She watched him. Her hands slid over her breasts, rubbing the hard nipples and her hips bucked. He spread her and bent to lick her gently. She gasped then moaned as his tongue found her small nub and he flicked it so very gently.

He liked the taste of her and continued kissing and licking as she moved her hips in a slow rhythm. Then her hands slid down to fist in his hair, and she brought him back to that tender nub.

She knew what she wanted, and he teased and tantalized until her fingers gripped his hair tightly. And then she was bowing, pressing herself hard against him and making small mewling noises. She released his hair, flinging her hands outward as she rode the pleasure he gave her.

Finally, she was still, and he lay beside her. She was gloriously naked, her body begging him to touch it again. He didn't know if he would ever have enough of her. He could have touched her all night and never tired of the feel of her skin under his fingers.

She turned her head and looked at him. "I did not know about that."

"I was happy to show you."

"It was better than—than anything, I think."

"Rest for a little while, and I'll do it again." He pulled her under the covers with him and held her for a long time. He thought she might be asleep, but then she looked up at him.

"What do you think will happen with Juan Carlos if I do not sign those papers? Will he come after me or Ines?"

"I won't let him hurt you."

"That is not what I asked. Do not try and shield me. Will he come for us?"

He looked up at the ceiling. "I don't know the man as well as you, and I think it's futile to try and predict a man's actions. That said, I made something of a career out of doing just that. I watched and studied and predicted troop movements, battle strategy, and likely points of attack. I think our Juan Carlos is not done yet."

"So he will make good on his threat if I do not sell him my business."

"Unfortunately, we've not given him many options. We've taken away the leverage he had when he held your secret, though I suppose he may have a self-destructive bent. He may still decide he has less to lose by revealing it. But I worry more about the threat he made through Miguel."

"Perhaps it was an empty threat. Miguel said only that I would regret it if I did not sell."

"You won't sell, which means he has no choice but to retreat. I hope he's the sort that walks away when the odds are against him, but men like that are forged out of the knowledge of what it means to face defeat. I don't think Juan Carlos or his son have ever been told *no*. He'll make good on his threat."

She took a shaky breath. "What do we do?"

"We take no chances, and when he attacks, we strike him down. For good."

She tightened her hold on him. He pulled her closer, offering her comfort. And then he did the next best thing— offered her distraction.

Thirteen

"My bounty is as boundless as the sea,
My love as deep; the more I give to thee,
The more I have, for both are infinite."
Romeo and Juliet, *William Shakespeare*

Catarina had her arm linked with Benedict's on one side while Ines was stationed on his other side. He joked he was the luckiest man at the garden party, but she couldn't help but think it was she who was the fortunate one.

"Colonel!" Lady Philomena greeted them as soon as they stepped onto the lawn. "Mrs. Draven. Miss Neves. How wonderful of you to come to my little gathering."

It was far from *little*. There must have been over a hundred guests on the expansive lawn. The day had proved sunny and mild for this time of year, but braziers had been set up to make certain the guests were kept warm. Large white umbrellas dotted the edges of the lawn, and guests reclined on rugs stacked with pillows as they sipped tea or champagne and nibbled the delicacies served.

"We're honored to be invited," Benedict said. "Especially when we came with so many addendums."

Lady Philomena, who looked lovely in a Grecian-style white gown, shook her head. Her curls, intertwined with gold ribbon and jewels, bounced. "Don't be silly. My brother lives for any sort of danger or excitement. He's dreadfully bored when there's not some threat at his door." She turned to Catarina. "Enough of that sort of talk. You will steal all my admirers. Look at you!"

By this time Catarina had observed that all the women wore light-colored dresses, like Lady Philomena's. Whites and pastels were obviously the appropriate dress. But she and Ines had chosen bold colors. She wore a bright pink with green accents and Ines wore a sapphire blue. "I fear Colonel Draven did not tell us to wear white."

"Why would he? You stand out. I like people who stand out—for their dress or their ideas or"—she put a hand on Catarina's arm—"their skills." She pulled her handkerchief from her bosom. "I do adore my handkerchief. I give you fair warning, you shall soon be overwhelmed by ladies who want an introduction and their own Catarina lace." She held out a hand to Ines. "Miss Neves, may I introduce you to a few of my friends?"

Ines, eyes wide and hopeful, looked at Catarina. Catarina nodded. Lady Philomena led Ines away, chatting amiably with her and drawing every eye.

"I'm afraid my lack of attention to fashion has not served you well," Benedict said. "But for what it's worth, I much prefer you to any of these women. Lady Philomena is correct that you stand out." He nodded to someone and Catarina spotted Lord Phineas making his way across the lawn with glasses of champagne in hand.

"Colonel and Mrs. Draven." He gave a fashionable bow, not seeming hindered at all by the glasses in his hands. "Refreshment?"

Catarina took a glass and sipped it.

"I have followed your orders to the letter. No one comes in or out without an invitation, and every servant here is one I know or who has worked for the family before."

"I had no doubt you'd do as I asked." Benedict sipped his own champagne.

"But what you did not realize was that I have a surprise guest for you."

Catarina stiffened. She liked surprises less and less of late.

"The Duke of Wellington has graced us with his presence. If you'll allow me to escort your wife, you will find him over there. I'll bring her to you in a few minutes."

Benedict looked at Catarina, who took Lord Phineas's arm. Benedict nodded. "I will see you in a few moments." He began walking across the lawn, stopping under an umbrella and enthusiastically shaking the hand of the man beneath it.

Lord Phineas began to walk slowly. "I hope you are not cold."

"Not at all." She adjusted her wrapper, which was thin but warm enough for the unusually mild day.

"Your husband thinks I am sparing you all the initial nonsense between him and Wellington."

"Initial nonsense?"

He rolled his eyes. "The two will go on for ten minutes about this campaign or that. It will bore you to tears."

"But he only thinks you spare me?"

"Yes, in truth I want to tell you a secret."

She drew back slightly. She'd known the sort of man who wanted to tell her secrets before. She hadn't thought Lord Phineas that kind.

"I can see I've begun poorly," Lord Phineas said as they walked past a group of ladies who stared at them with undisguised hope of being encouraged to join them. Catarina assumed it was because Lord Phineas was so handsome, but they might have been eager to place orders for lace as well. Wasn't that why Benedict had brought her? So ladies might meet her and be able to call on her to order lace?

"What I mean," Lord Phineas said, "is that I have never seen Draven like this."

"Like what?" she asked.

"In love."

She furrowed her brow, and Lord Phineas nodded. "I didn't think he had said anything to you. That's why I called it a secret."

"I think, my lord, what you believe is love might just be a feeling of obligation." And lust, she thought, remembering with a quick blush that he'd spent much of last night between her legs.

"He's a man with many obligations, Mrs. Draven. But he doesn't look at any of us that way." He nodded discreetly at Benedict, and she glanced over and saw Benedict watching her. "Do you mind if I ask you a personal question?" Lord Phineas paused and turned to her.

Catarina stiffened. "I suppose it depends what the question might be."

"Fair enough. Are you in love with Colonel Draven?"

Catarina inhaled. "That *is* a personal question."

"I don't ask for my own curiosity, you understand. I ask because I—we, the soldiers who have served with him—have an interest in his well-being. I've known him for years, and I have never seen him look at a woman the way he looks at you. I have never seen him do anything more *than* look at a woman, if truth be told. I don't know what vows you made or when, but I would stake my best horse that he's honored them."

"So have I."

"That's not my question or my concern."

"You want to know if I love him?"

He inclined his head, clearly waiting. One of the women from the small group who'd been watching them broke free and began to approach, but Lord Phineas, his gaze never leaving Catarina, held up one finger, and she slunk back.

"What if I told you that I don't know? There are moments when I think I do, when I feel…something I cannot define. But am I in love with him? I am not certain. I think to love him would be dangerous."

Lord Phineas looked startled at this. "Why?"

"Because when the problem—my problem—is dealt with, I will go back to Barcelona, and he will be here."

"Why not stay here?"

"My shop and all my lacemakers are in Barcelona."

"Why not bring them here?"

She bit her lip. Lord Phineas seemed to think Benedict loved her, but he hadn't told her that himself. She was beginning to trust Benedict, but to take such a monumental step seemed premature. What if she changed her whole life for him, moved countries and her business, and then when he realized how much time and effort her business really entailed, he ordered her to give it up?

Lord Phineas rubbed his chin, as though in consideration. "What if I told you—"

"I thought you would join us in a moment," Benedict said as he crossed the lawn with large strides. "I want to introduce my wife to the duke."

"Far be it from me to keep the two of you apart," Lord Phineas said. Benedict took her arm and led her to meet the former general.

She tried to behave as she imagined ladies of Benedict's class might, but she worried constantly she would embarrass him. She was a lacemaker, not the daughter of a gentleman. But seeing her surrounded by the daughters of nobility did not seem to change how Benedict treated her. He looked at her as though he was proud of her, as though he thought her the most desirable woman in the world. She found herself falling a little more in love with him.

She met many others at the party, but Wellington was the only personage she had heard of previously. Mostly, she spoke with women who were eager to purchase her lace. She invited them all to Benedict's home and promised to make them something original and beautiful.

When the afternoon was over, Lord Phineas gave Benedict his coach to take them home. Ines and Catarina were so entranced by the lavish interior that it wasn't until the coach came to a halt and they peered through the windows that Catarina realized they were not at Benedict's flat.

"Where are we?" Ines asked.

A footman opened the door, and Benedict stepped out. Holding a hand out, he said, "Come and see for yourself."

He led Catarina, with Ines following, into an empty shop. It was bare of furnishings and a bit dusty, but the window was large and caught the last of the afternoon light.

"What do you think?" Benedict asked.

Catarina looked about, uncertain why he should ask her opinion or even take her to an empty shop. And then her eyes widened. "You don't mean to say this is to be my shop?"

Ines gasped.

"If you like it," Benedict said. He gestured expansively. "I know it's small, and if it's too small, I can keep looking.

But let me show you the back. It's quite spacious, and I believe four or five ladies could work there without being crowded."

He started for the back room, and Catarina stumbled after him, too shocked to remember to lift her skirts. There was only a small window back here, and the light was coming from the front of the store now, so she could not see very much of the space.

"Hold on a moment," Benedict said as he withdrew a tinder box and lit a candle. He held it up and Catarina looked about the workroom in amazement. It was just as he'd said, quite spacious. Several tables would fit as well as supplies. She and Ines and several other lacemakers could be quite comfortable here. And in the morning, it would be bright and sunny.

She turned to Benedict. "It is as you say and would be perfect for a lace shop, but I cannot accept it. In Barcelona, my shop was little more than a stall with a small enclosure in the back. This"—she gestured to the windows and the shelves—"is too much. Do you not agree, Ines?"

"She didn't accompany us," Benedict said. "I think she waited in the front to give us privacy to discuss."

Catarina nodded. Ines could be thoughtful when she wanted. "Is it that we have taken over your house? Our pillow and thread are spread out in your parlor and people will soon come to call in the afternoons—"

Benedict took her hands. "I don't mind that at all. You can have the whole house if this shop doesn't suit. But I thought you deserved a place of your own."

"In London?"

He closed his eyes. "I am an idiot. I'm doing this all wrong." He sank to his knees before her. "Catarina Ana Marciá Neves Draven, would you stay married to me? Will you marry me again? Here, in London?"

How could she say no to this? But saying yes to Benedict, giving in to what she wanted, would be to risk more than she ever had. For so long, she'd had no one but herself to rely on. She'd never trusted a man because no man had ever showed her he was worthy of trust.

She wanted to trust Benedict. She wanted to give him her trust along with her heart. She could make a small start by telling him yes now.

Tears swam in her eyes, so many that she couldn't see his face. Then she sank to her knees. "Yes, I will."

He took her face in his hands, kissing her gently. She moved closer, pressing her body against his, wanting to show him how full her heart was. Finally, he broke the kiss. "Your sister," he said quietly.

She nodded. "Later then."

He smiled. "I'd like that. But do not keep me in suspense. Will this suit or shall I continue looking? Rather, I've sent Lord Phineas out to look as he is better with that sort of thing. But when he showed me this one, I knew you had to see it."

Her heart clenched at the knowledge Benedict had been looking for shops for her. "This will suit perfectly," she said.

"Then we'll purchase it. It will take a few months before we can have it furnished and ready. You can send for your lacemakers in Barcelona, if you like. We can find them rooms to rent. And, of course, you'll need a steady supply of thread. Perhaps they could bring a quantity with them while we search for an importer or someone to buy in bulk."

Catarina put her finger over his lips. "You have thought of everything. My head is spinning. Tomorrow we will make lists and write letters. Right now, let me go and tell my sister."

He helped her up and led her back into the front room, slipping out the door with the excuse of checking on the horses.

"Well?" Ines asked. "Is this what I think it is?"

"If you think he is buying this shop for me, then you are correct."

Ines squealed and embraced Catarina. "Our own shop! Not a stall! Not a corner of someone else's shop, but ours! This is what we dreamed!"

"I know. I can hardly think how to thank him. Ines, he asked me to stay married to him, to marry him again in London."

"He did?"

"He knelt down and took my hands. It was a real proposal, although we are already married in the eyes of God."

"And now you will be married in the eyes of the world. Oh, Catarina, he must love you so much."

Catarina began to reply and then realized Benedict had not said anything at all about love. She *thought* he loved her. The way he treated her was evidence of his feelings, certainly. But she was still reluctant to trust in this new relationship completely. Men changed their minds. They were kind one day and abusive the next. She wanted so much to give this new life a chance, but she would keep some part of herself back. She must be cautious about trusting too easily.

"—and find new lacemakers," Ines was saying.

"Benedict said we can bring ours from Barcelona."

Ines gave a little skip of joy. The lacemakers had been their best friends, and Catarina assumed Ines missed them more than ever. Catarina knew not all of them would want to leave their home, but she hoped a few would consent. She could train others if she had enough business.

Benedict opened the door and cleared his throat. "Is it all settled then?"

Ines ran to him and hugged him. He gave Catarina a desperate look. These English were so uncomfortable with open affection. Catarina took Ines's arm. "Let us return to the coach. We can discuss all our plans on the way home."

***

Draven took dinner at his club in the paneled wood dining room with its large hearth and thick wooden beams running across the low, white washed ceiling. He'd met Phineas there to discuss purchasing the shop. "It's a good price," Phineas was saying from across the table covered in white linen. "But I could try and get it for less. The owner opened a bigger shop in Mayfair. She's not in any sort of a desperate situation."

"I'm sure you'll negotiate the price down to a pittance," Draven said. He had been right to propose to Catarina. Though they were already married, the expression on her face had told him that the gesture had meant everything to her. He hoped that she believed that he wanted to be with her no matter what. "Just bring me the papers, and I'll sign. Then I must face the prospect of shopping for furnishings."

"I can send my sister with Mrs. Draven, if you like. She's good at that sort of thing."

"And she has expensive tastes. I'd better go along." Benedict didn't want to admit it wasn't so much Lady Philomena's expensive tastes as the fact that he wanted to be part of every aspect of the experience. He was enjoying his new wife and this part of her life. If he could be helpful to her, he wanted to be there.

"I hope you're not planning to go too soon," Colin FitzRoy said, taking the chair beside Phineas. "De la Fuente is still in Town, and while I haven't managed to convince him to confide in me, I would bet my right thumb he is making plans."

"Your right thumb?" Phineas wrinkled his nose. "That's an odd expression."

FitzRoy shrugged, lifting a silver fork and examining it. "Here's another for you. He's drinking like a fish, but the man can hold his liquor. If anything, the drink makes him more stoic."

"And more dangerous too, I'd wager," Phineas added. "Not that I'd bet my thumb or any other body part."

"Keep me informed," Benedict said. "I imagine it will take time to finalize the contracts and I can use that as an excuse to put off going out too much."

"There is a problem," FitzRoy said. "I think he's growing suspicious of me. It might be better if you sent someone else in. I can still keep an eye on him, but I will have to do so from a distance."

"I should have pulled you sooner," Benedict said. "But I don't have anyone else to send in."

"What about Jasper? He's good at slinking about," Phineas offered.

"He's getting married," Colin said.

Phineas straightened. "I didn't get an invitation!"

"Neither did I," FitzRoy said. They both looked at Draven.

"Jasper prefers small, intimate affairs. There'll be less than a dozen guests."

"You'll be one of them?" Phineas raised a brow.

"You are welcome to take my place. You know I don't enjoy that sort of thing. Can we return to the matter at hand?" He looked at FitzRoy. "Is there any way to persuade de la Fuente to leave the country? Preferably before he realizes my wife is opening a lace shop here?"

"I'll take a look at the letters he receives," FitzRoy said. "There may be family business that will call him back. If that doesn't work, we may have to resort to something less…above board."

"That sounds interesting." Phineas sat forward. "You can count me in for that. It's been too long since I wore my dancing shoes."

Draven's men had a common saying during the war. When they were embarking on a particularly perilous mission, the commanding officer would say, *Put on your dancing shoes, lads. It's time to dance with the devil.* They'd known they might end up in hell that night, but they'd gone in and completed the mission anyway. Eighteen of the thirty had died in the line of duty, and not a day passed that Draven didn't think of each and every one of them.

It was a good idea to have Phineas involved in this. The more men watching Juan Carlos, the better. FitzRoy had all but smelled the desperation on the Spaniard. Benedict knew he would have to be more vigilant than ever to keep Catarina safe.

Phineas rose. "Excuse me, I see Stratford and have a matter to discuss with him."

"One would think that as the son of a duke, Phineas would have more to do than plot to send Spaniards back home," Benedict said, though he appreciated the assistance.

"We might need his assistance," FitzRoy said, echoing Benedict's thoughts. "He has more blunt and better connections. In the meantime, be careful."

"I will," Benedict said, reminded that no one ever told him to put his dancing shoes on. He was not expected to take the risks his men did. But he was home now and he would take responsibility for Catarina and all connected to her. FitzRoy and Phineas would do their best, but Benedict would be damned if he allowed Juan Carlos near his wife. She was really his now, and he'd keep her safe.

***

Benedict arrived home later than he'd anticipated, and the house was quiet. Ward greeted him, which was surprising as Ward did not like to wait up and it was past the time he usually retired.

As Ward took his coat, Benedict asked after everyone.

"The ladies have retired," Ward told him. "I think they wore themselves out with their chattering. The cat, however, has taken up position in front of your bed chamber door. I could not get in to stoke the fire or turn down the bed."

"Tigrino still doesn't like you, eh?"

"That cat is evil, and one day I will catch him in the act of scratching the furniture and see if I don't douse him with water for doing it."

"Ward, you've done all you can today. I can turn my own bed down. Good night."

Ward sniffed and headed for his room. Benedict headed for his own, pausing as he passed Catarina and Ines's door. He'd been looking forward to fulfilling the promise she'd made him earlier, but it was his own fault for staying out so late. He thought about knocking on her door but didn't want to disturb her sleep or wake Ines.

But it would be a long night without her. He'd grown used to holding her in his arms.

Tigrino was indeed sleeping in front of his door. Benedict knelt down and stroked the cat, who turned lazily onto his back and yawned widely. Benedict petted him for a few minutes. "Leave my furnishings alone," he told the feline. "There's nothing more miserable than a wet cat." Stepping over the cat, he entered his room and immediately wondered if Ward's memory was failing him. The fire was stoked and the bed was turned down.

And then he realized the bed was not empty.

Fourteen

"What, with my tongue in your tail? nay, come again,
Good Kate; I am a gentleman."
The Taming of the Shrew, *William Shakespeare*

"I hope you don't mind that I am here," Catarina said, sitting up in Benedict's bed. He stood in the doorway for a moment, looking absolutely shocked. In fact, he stood for so long, Tigrino wandered inside. Finally, when the cat rubbed on his leg, Benedict bent down, shooed the cat back outside and closed the door.

"Mind? Whatever is the opposite of *to mind* is what I feel right now." He took a step closer. "Are you—" He gestured toward her.

She looked down at the sheet covering her. "Naked? I thought I would save you time."

"God help me." He sat heavily in a chair. "Give me a moment to remove my boots."

"Take all the time you want. I was lying here thinking about the shop and the best way to arrange it. Ines thinks we should have a little table to consult with customers wanting lace designed especially for them near the window so customers passing by can see them, but I think it would be cozier and more intimate in a back corner. What do you think?"

"I think cozy and intimate is what I'd prefer." He stood and pulled off his coat, still wearing his waistcoat, shirt, cravat, and trousers.

"So would I." She licked her lips, thinking of the body under all the layers of clothing. She had not been entirely truthful when she'd implied she'd been thinking all evening about the lace shop—well, she'd been thinking about it a little. But as soon as she heard him come in and heard the low rumble of his voice as he spoke to Ward, she'd been imagining touching him and kissing him and having him do all that and more to her.

"Let me help you with the rest of that clothing." She drew the sheet down, watching the way his bright blue eyes darkened as she revealed her body to him. She loved the way he looked at her. She rose and walked slowly to him, reaching up to loosen his cravat.

"I thought you were sleeping. I didn't want to wake you," he said as she slid his cravat from his neck and began unbuttoning his shirt. He hadn't touched her yet, and she wished he would put his hands on her.

"Ines went to bed, but I waited up for you." She pulled the shirt from his trousers.

"I didn't mean to stay at my club so la—so late." His speech stumbled as she tugged the shirt up and slid her hands under it.

"Can you see to the sleeves?" She pulled the shirt over his head. "What were you discussing?"

"The man I have watching de la Fuente has to take a step back. Juan Carlos is becoming suspicious."

"He's the sort of man who has always been given everything he wants. In Barcelona the only friends he had were those he bought with expensive gifts or influence. He wouldn't understand a man who did not want something in return."

Draven's eyes narrowed. "Good point. I'll tell my man to change his strategy."

She ran her fingers up and down his chest, her hands tangling in the red hair. "I take it there is no sign of him leaving."

"Not yet. But he will either grow tired of his game or do something for which we can have him arrested. Time is on our side."

"I wish I had your confidence."

"I've kept you safe, and I *will* keep you safe."

She put her arms around him. "I know." And she did. She believed he would keep her and her sister safe.

The kiss was soft and slow, but as he'd said, they had time on their side. She explored his mouth leisurely, and when he reciprocated, her heart began to pound. She felt for the placket of his trousers, but he caught her hands.

"What is wrong?" She pulled back, her head spinning and the blood pumping in her ears.

"What do you want tonight, Catarina? I don't want any confusion between us."

She understood the question, and she knew her answer. She loved him and she wanted a true marriage with him. That meant she had to let her guard down. She had to stop holding back and give him her trust and her heart. She took a deep breath. "I want you. All of you. I want you to be my husband in every way."

"Are you certain? You know I don't want an annulment. When you said yes at the shop, does that mean you no longer want one either?"

"I want to be your wife."

He cupped her face, his desire evident in the way his hands shook slightly. "Catarina, I don't care what the church or the law says. If we do this, you are mine."

She squeezed his hands. "That is what I want. I want you to be mine, and I will be yours."

Their eyes met and held for a long moment, and then his mouth came down on hers with a passion she hadn't expected. It was as though he was a rushing river, held back by a dam and now set free. He lifted her as though she weighed nothing more than Tigrino and carried her across the room.

"Benedict! You will hurt yourself."

"I'm not that old yet." He set her on the bed and came down on top of her, his body covering hers in the most delicious way. Her breasts rubbed against his chest, and she wrapped her legs around his waist, looking for friction there too.

"Take off your trousers," she murmured.

He stood and removed them quickly then when she held her arms out to him, came down on top of her, his weight braced by his muscled arms. "I am ready," she said, closing her eyes. She'd heard there would be pain, and she was prepared to endure it.

But nothing happened. Benedict didn't move, though she could feel his hard member against her thigh. She opened her eyes. "Do you not have to…do something?"

He arched his brows. "If I were twenty, I might take that approach, but I hope I have a little more patience. Not much, mind you. It's been a long time since I've done this."

"How long?"

"Over five years."

She heard him, but it took several seconds before she could comprehend. "Then it's true. All this time, you have been faithful to me. I never asked it of you."

"Nor I you, and yet we've both kept our vow."

"But…" She had been about to say that he was a man, but why should that matter? God did not have different expectations of men than he did of women.

"To tell you the truth, it hasn't been all that difficult. No woman I met after you could even tempt me."

She swallowed. "I believe you tried to tell me this before."

He gave her a rueful look. "You're ready to hear it now. There's been no one else, and there will never be anyone else."

Her heart swelled with love for him. This was right. Tonight, here in his arms, was right.

"I feel the same, Benedict. There is only you for me." She kissed him, and the kiss grew deeper and hotter. "Take me now," she whispered.

"As much as I would like to do that, I don't want to hurt you."

"I am ready for the pain." She braced herself, closing her eyes.

"Yes, you look like you are ready to have a limb amputated. Why don't I start like this?" His mouth brushed across her chin then down her neck. He teased the sensitive skin there with his lips and his stubble then kissed her collarbone. His hands, meanwhile, stroked her breasts down to her belly, her hips, and then back again. Her whole body was on fire from his touch.

While his mouth found and exploited the sensitive spots behind her ear and in the hollow of her throat, his hands finally drifted to her center, where he gently opened her legs and stroked her. His touch was light and fleeting, his hands returning to her quivering belly and her aching breasts and then back again to the place between her legs that had begun to throb. His fingers parted her, and one dipped into the slick wetness there. She moaned as that same finger circled the nub where the most need was centered. And she clenched his shoulders when one of his fingers entered her.

He knew what gave her pleasure now, and he slid in and out, deeper and harder, pressing against that nub that cried out for more. "I-I cannot wait any longer," she said on a gasp.

"I don't want you to wait." And he moved his hand in such a way that a thousand tiny explosions erupted inside her, causing her to buck against him and gasp in ragged breaths. Just as the pleasure climaxed, he moved between her legs, his hard member sliding against that still convulsing part of her.

She jumped and moaned as he rocked against her, entering her slightly, the feeling not so different from that of his fingers. She was still limp with pleasure as he slid deeper, spreading her uncomfortably wider. She tensed slightly, and his finger was on that little button again, gently brushing over it, making her arch her hips.

"That's it. Relax." With infinite patience and slowness, he sheathed himself inside her. Every time she felt a twinge of pain, he found a way to give her pleasure—touching her, kissing her, caressing her, until she was welcoming him deeper. Finally, he braced himself on his elbows and looked down at her. "Not quite so bad as an amputation, is it?" he asked.

"Are you…is that…?"

"Yes. And now what I really want to do is move. I'll go slowly." He withdrew slightly then returned. She felt uncomfortable, a slight sting, but it was nothing unbearable. The feelings of pleasure from before were still coursing through her, and when he pressed in the right spot, she felt the promise of more. He moved again, this time withdrawing farther, then pressing up and causing her to moan. The pain and pleasure mixed together until she could not concentrate fully on either feeling. She looked into his eyes, focusing on the bright blue of them instead. His gaze was intense on her as he found a slow, but steady rhythm. He twined his fingers with hers, and she couldn't help but think that she might enjoy this next time, when the discomfort was not so distracting.

His breath hitched, and he thrust deep inside her. She winced then watched his face with interest. His gaze was still on her, but she could see the pleasure in the flush of his cheeks and the hoarse growl in the back of his throat. She could feel him pulse inside her. His hands tightened on hers, and he finally lowered himself to press a kiss on her shoulder.

When he finally raised his head, she smoothed his unruly hair. "Definitely better than amputation."

He laughed. "I'll make it better for you next time."

And she knew he would. She knew he could. She could see long years ahead, filled with nights like this, his body slowly filling hers, both of them taking pleasure and giving it.

If only Juan Carlos would leave them alone.

***

She slept late the next day, not waking until she could no longer ignore Tigrino's yowling outside the bed chamber door. She'd felt Benedict rise an hour or so before, had wanted to pull him back to the warmth under the bed clothes, but she didn't have the energy.

Now she sat, flinching a bit at the soreness between her legs and the dried blood on the sheets. She was no longer a virgin. She was a married woman, in truth. She donned her wrapper and stood before Benedict's shaving mirror. She didn't look any different.

She tried to make herself presentable and finally made her way to the dining room to break her fast. She wore her chemise and dressing robe, suitably covered from neck to toe. Ines was sitting alone, looking at one of the fashion magazines Benedict had bought for them. She glanced up at Catarina, back at the magazine, then up again. She stood and gasped.

"What is it?" Catarina asked, looking about for a rat or a spider.

"Finally!" Ines grabbed her hands. "You consummated the marriage!"

"Shh!" Catarina looked about and saw Ward disappearing through the door, obviously no keener to hear the conversation than Catarina was to have it. "What are you talking about?"

"I am your sister. I can tell."

"That is nonsense. I looked in the mirror this morning. I look the same."

"But you are not the same, are you? What was it like? Was it horribly painful?" She pulled Catarina down into a chair and sat on the edge of the one beside it.

"No. It was uncomfortable, but not painful. Do you think I might at least have coffee if I am to have this conversation so early?"

"Early? It is almost eleven."

"I slept that late?"

Ines nodded, fetching Catarina a cup of coffee, which she set before her sister. To her credit, Ines waited until Catarina had a sip before asking more questions. "Was he a brute?"

Catarina understood the question. The men they'd known treated women as objects. "No. He was…very considerate. He made certain we both enjoyed the experience."

"Did he—"

"Ines! I am not saying any more. Not even to my sister."

"I am eighteen. Hardly a baby."

"Some things are personal."

Ins raised a thin brow. "Did he tell you he loved you? Was it romantic?"

Catarina opened her mouth to reply then closed it again. "No more questions."

The truth was, he hadn't told her. Not when he'd pleasured her, not when he'd been inside her, not afterward when he'd held her. But that was between Benedict and herself. Ines thought love was all that mattered. Catarina now knew a marriage was more than that.

But it would have been nice if love were part of it.

She had told Lord Phineas yesterday—had it only been yesterday?—she didn't know if she loved Benedict. But how could she not love him after last night, after the loving way he had treated her? And after the way he had shown he supported her. He'd bought her a shop—her own shop!

"I have bad news," Ines said, snapping Catarina out of her reverie.

"What do you mean?"

"I did not want to tell you right away, but we are out of thread again."

Of course they were. They had not been able to find nearly enough of the quality they needed, and every day new orders came in. "I told Benedict this morning, and he said he would take us to the shops this afternoon."

Catarina nodded. "We will have to wait then."

"You promised the pinch-faced woman—what is her name?"

"Viscountess something. I wrote it down."

"I remember her as the pinch-faced woman."

Tigrino jumped on the table, and Catarina had to scoop him off and into her lap before Ward saw it and suffered an apoplexy.

Ines waited until Tigrino was removed then continued. "Her lace collar is to be ready today. She will send for it at two."

"I have it done."

"And last night I finished the border on the lace for the lady with the red hair that is not truly red."

Catarina had to think a moment. She could not remember the woman's name either, but she knew her sister meant the woman with hair far too bright to be her natural color. "What about the handkerchief for Lady Knollwood?"

Ines frowned.

"She wore an orange and green dress, and her hair was piled quite high."

"Oh, yes! We do not have the thread to start it."

Catarina rubbed the bridge of her nose, where a headache was beginning to form. "We have a little time on that, but we will surely receive new orders today. After all, five or six ladies told me at the garden party they would call on me."

"Several told me as well."

Catarina finished her coffee. "We had better not promise anything too soon. We will not be able to start anything until this evening, and we still have lace to make for past orders. And one of us may have to stay behind and take orders while the other goes with Benedict to pick out thread."

"I want to go!"

"Very well but be ready. I want you two to leave as soon as he returns home."

But he didn't return home by the time callers began arriving to place new orders. They had a steady stream of ladies from the garden party, and though Catarina and Ines tried to put them off, every lady wanted something urgently for this ball or that musicale.

Ines was agitated by the time Benedict arrived home, which was well after six, when the shops were closed for the day. Catarina tried to remain calm. She could work quickly when necessary, and she couldn't expect Benedict to set aside his business to take her shopping. But how happy she would be when Juan Carlos was out of her life, and she could go freely about London.

When she heard him come in, Catarina rose from her chair in the parlor and waved at Ines to stay where she was. She met Benedict in the receiving room. As soon as he saw her, his blue eyes warmed. She was reminded of all they had shared last night. He took her hand.

Ward cleared his throat and announced he would see that all was as it should be for dinner.

"How are you?" Benedict asked as Ward walked away. "I didn't want to leave without saying good-bye, but you were sleeping so peacefully."

"I slept very late and feel extremely lazy."

He gave her a chiding look. "I'm sure you had an afternoon filled with callers and didn't have a moment's peace. You are the furthest thing from lazy."

"The garden party did seem to have the desired effect."

"Good." He took her hands. "And how are you? I didn't...hurt you, did I?"

She felt her cheeks heat. "I am well. You were very gentle," she said quietly.

"I'll have Maggie prepare a bath for you tonight."

The idea of a warm bath was appealing. "Thank you. And how was your day?"

"I was called into the Foreign Office on a matter I cannot discuss. I was there most of the day, reading documents. I'm hungry and tired."

"Then I will see what's keeping dinner."

She gave Ines several warning looks before they went into dinner, but she still scowled and stabbed at her food with her fork.

"Is something wrong?" Benedict looked from Catarina to Ines.

"No," Catarina said at the same time Ines said, "Yes."

He set his wine glass down. "What is it?"

"We were supposed to go to buy thread today. Catarina and I have no thread to make lace. I told you this morning."

He nodded. "I said I would take you if I could get away. I couldn't."

"You can go tomorrow, Ines."

"But what about all the orders due?"

"There is nothing due tomorrow. I can finish everything if you two go early."

Benedict shook his head. "That's not possible. I'm wanted at the Foreign Office again first thing in the morning."

Now Catarina's stomach cramped, and she set down her fork. "When will you be back?"

"By midday, I hope."

"And if you are not?" Ines asked.

"Then you will have to tell your customers their orders will be late." He gave Catarina an apologetic look. "I'm sorry, but there's nothing for it."

"It seems a very bad way to start a business in a new city—late orders," Ines announced.

Catarina agreed. "Is there no one else who could go with us? I've never promised to have a piece ready and then not fulfilled my promise."

"I'll be back as soon as I can."

"What about Lord Phineas? Could he go with us?" Ines asked.

Benedict scowled. "Lord Phineas may have served under me, but he's the son of a duke. I can't ask him to shepherd you about on Bond Street."

Catarina sighed. "I am sure if you are home by three tomorrow we will manage."

But he was not home by three and as the afternoon grew later, Catarina knew the shops would close soon. If she did not have the thread, she would not be able to complete the pieces she'd promised. Worse still was that she had nothing to do. She had always been able to fill idle hours with lacemaking. Now that she had no thread, she'd instructed Ward to tell anyone calling on her that she was not at home. She couldn't take more orders with no way to fill those she had.

She tried to take an interest in the household affairs. She remembered her mother cooking and cleaning and mending almost every waking hour, but there was a cook to prepare meals, a maid to clean, and she and Ines could do their own mending.

In short, she found herself staring at the bracket clock on the mantel and wondering how Benedict could neglect her two days in a row.

"If we don't go now, the shops will have closed," Ines said, speaking out loud what Catarina was thinking.

"I know."

Ines rose, her pink skirts swishing angrily as she paced the small parlor. Tigrino, who had been sleeping under Ines's chair, lifted his head and opened one eye. "And you do not care?"

"Of course, I care. But what can I do?"

"What can you *not* do? We can go ourselves. We are perfectly capable. We did not have a man to accompany us in Barcelona."

"We did not have Juan Carlos trying to hurt us then." Catarina stood now too, tiring of looking up at Ines. "And Barcelona was smaller than London. We were known. Here I feel as though we could disappear, and no one would know what had happened or who we were."

"But that is exactly my point. It is easy to disappear. We wave down one of the coaches for hire and no one would be able to distinguish us from any other coach for hire. We will go to the shop and then come right back."

"And if Juan Carlos sees us?"

Ines gave her a dubious look. "How will he see us? Unless he is watching the house, he will never know we have left. We will be in and out of the coach in a few minutes' time. We know just where to go for the thread."

"But what if he is watching the house?"

"Your Benedict has men watching him. They would have told us if Juan Carlos was watching."

"You are right," Catarina said. Moreover, if they did encounter trouble, she was no fainting miss. She could use a knife and had her grandfather's pistol for show.

"Then we go."

Catarina hesitated for a moment. Benedict would not want her to go, but she had not made her way in the world up until now by being timid and staying hidden. Not to mention, she'd taken care of herself for years without Benedict. If they were quick and careful, there was no danger.

"We go," she said, rising and pulling on her gloves.

Fifteen

"I will be master of what is mine own:
She is my goods, my chattels; she is my house,
My household stuff, my field, my barn,
My horse, my ox, my ass, my any thing."
The Taming of the Shrew, *William Shakespeare*

Benedict rushed into the door, apologies on his tongue. "Catarina! I know I am late, but I have something for you. Catarina?"

Ward appeared, holding out a hand for Benedict's hat and gloves. "She is not here, sir."

"What do you mean?"

Ward assisted him in removing his great coat.

"Mrs. Draven is not in residence at the moment."

Benedict froze and then tore through the flat, his coat still hanging off one arm. "Catarina! Ines!" But the flat was empty except for Tigrino, who was curled up in the center if Ines's bed. Benedict rounded on Ward. "Where are they?"

"They went out to buy thread."

"What?" Benedict roared. "And you allowed this?"

Ward straightened his already stiff shoulders. "I am at a loss as to how I was to stop them. They were determined to go."

"Bloody hell. Why would they act so stupidly?"

"They are but mere women, sir."

Benedict gave his butler a disgusted look. "And why did you not go with them?"

"I?" Ward lifted his bony chin. "I am not a footman."

Benedict closed his eyes and tried to remember how faithfully Ward had served him over the years. He told himself he would be sorry tomorrow if he strangled the man tonight. "How long have they been gone? How did they go, and so help me God, Ward, if you say on foot, I will have your head."

Ward swallowed. "I acquired a hackney for them and put them in it myself. No one was watching. Not that I saw, at any rate."

Ward had traveled with Benedict all over the Continent as they fought Napoleon's forces. His instinct for danger and for traps was as good as any man's.

"They have been gone about an hour," his butler added. "I expect them to return any minute now."

Which meant it would not be prudent for Benedict himself to go chasing after them. He'd probably pass them coming back as he drove away. Nothing to do but wait then. He sat in his favorite chair in the parlor. Looking around the room, he hardly recognized it now. It was still painted blue and square in shape. He'd chosen the furnishings, but an India shawl was draped over on chair and several pieces of lace lay on a table. A pair of women's slippers were tucked under another chair, and a pillow with an unfinished lace design sat on the couch. Tigrino lay on the carpet near the low burning fire. He stretched and yawned when he saw Benedict looking at him, seeming quite unconcerned with all the yelling.

"Shall I take your coat, sir?"

"What?" Benedict looked up a Ward, holding out a hand, and realized his coat was still hanging off one shoulder. He rose and slipped out of the coat, shoving it at Ward.

"Will that be all, sir?"

Benedict slumped back in the chair. "Actually, I feel rather like throttling someone at the moment. Your neck looks as good as any."

Ward huffed and marched away, the great coat hung over his arm.

Benedict could recall feeling this helpless many times in his life. The night before a battle there was often nothing to do but wait for the sun to rise and see what waited. Then there was the helplessness of charging across a battlefield, facing a seemingly insurmountable wall of the enemy and hacking and fighting one's way through it, knowing that one wrong turn, one slow reflex, and he would be dead. Worse had been the years when his troop had prowled the Continent. Benedict would open an order from Wellington and know it would mean certain death for some, if not all, of his men. He'd spent many nights like this one, sitting and waiting for news. And when the missive came from Wraxall, the troop's leader, his fingers would shake to open it and read the names of the dead.

But nothing struck terror into the very core of him like the thought of losing Catarina. He should never have left her alone today. He should have hired ten men to surround her and keep her safe. He should have held her last night instead of trying to be a gentleman and giving her time to recover from their lovemaking the night before.

If Juan Carlos touched her, Benedict would kill the man with his own bare hands. The thought didn't ease the terror coursing through him. And even the act of murdering Juan Carlos wouldn't fill the hole Catarina left in his life if something were to happen to her.

For years, Benedict hadn't known if she'd been alive or dead. He had lived his life, thinking of her but not frantic at her whereabouts. Now she had been out of his protection for an hour and he felt panic welling inside him. He remained seated, remained outwardly calm. Pacing the room and tearing his chairs apart would solve nothing. He was Lieutenant Colonel Benedict Draven. He was calm and controlled. A seasoned soldier.

He would bloody well act like one.

Another quarter hour passed, the hands on the bracket clock, moving excruciatingly slowly before he heard the sound of horse hooves outside the house. He did not rise from his seat. He was not the only one who lived at this address. The upper floors were also taken. It might have been one of his neighbors returning home.

But he knew it was Catarina. His neighbors had their own routines that did not include returning home in a hackney. He heard her voice, then that of her sister, and something inside him broke. Part of him wanted to rise, meet her at the door, and take her into his arms.

But another part wanted to yell at her and shake her until she realized what a risk she had taken. Knowing this last option would cause more harm than good to their fledgling marriage, but feeling the strong pull of it nevertheless, he sat in the chair, his hands gripping the arms as he tried to leash his temper. Tigrino rose at the sound of the door and the ladies' voices. The cat jumped on Benedict's lap, but

Benedict brushed him off. With a flick of his tail, Tigrino sauntered to the parlor door, managing to walk past it just as it opened, admitting Catarina and Ines.

"Benedict, you are home!" Catarina said, her lovely face, red with cold, breaking into a smile. "I am so glad. It is just now starting to rain."

Ines took one look at him and halted in the doorway. "I forgot something in my room. Excuse me, Catarina. Colonel Draven." She left, closing the door so Catarina and Benedict were alone.

"Where were you?" he asked, his voice flat. "At the shops, I suppose."

"We needed thread, and it was obvious you would not be home in time to take us." She moved near the fire, warming herself. She must have seen he was angry, but she didn't seem overly worried about it. She moved gracefully and spoke calmly. "We took a hackney because we knew that was an easy way to blend in. We went straight to the shop where we acquired the thread before and back again. We took no chances."

"You took a chance just by leaving this house." He didn't turn his head, merely moved his eyes.

"I realize that, but we were as careful as we could be. We are not prisoners. We cannot say locked up forever."

"Is that how you feel? Locked up?" He rose now, but she didn't shrink away. Instead, her chin notched up.

"I do not feel that way, but Ines is only eighteen. We cannot expect her to stay inside all the time."

"I took her to a garden party. No one expects either of you to stay inside all the time. But I do expect you to use common sense. I do expect you to stay where I put you." It was a bad choice of words. He knew it as soon as the phrase spilled out of him, but he couldn't think of another, and he was angry enough not to try.

She stiffened. "Where you put me? As though I am a clock or a lamp? I am not just another thing you own. I do not have to stay put."

"And so you risk your life for thread. Were you a least successful?" He already knew the answer.

Her shoulders sagged. "No. The woman we bought from before was not at her stall. I suppose we were too late. And we did not want to risk being seen and going to other shops."

"I'll save you the trouble." He withdrew a package from his coat and dropped it on the chair.

"What is that?"

"Open it."

She lifted the package, untied the string, and unwrapped the paper. Her gaze rose to meet his. "The thread. How did you—"

"You seem to think I forgot about you, but when I realized I would be late, I stopped at the stall and bought you all the thread the seller had. She must have gone home after that sale."

"And then you came home, and we were not here." She sat on the chair. "I am sorry I did not trust in you. I suppose I am not used to having to rely on others."

Her admission and her obvious contriteness should have mollified him. It didn't. He'd spent the longest half hour of his life, worrying he would never see her again. He'd been scared and vulnerable, and no sword or rifle could protect him. If something had happened to her...

"And I am not used to having my directives disobeyed. You knew the danger and you knew my wishes, and you went anyway. From this moment on, I order you confined to this house. You are not to leave unless I give you strict permission."

She blinked up at him, her remorseful expression slowly hardening into anger. "Are you saying I am a prisoner here?"

"Do not be ridiculous. I am trying to keep you safe."

"By making me a prisoner."

"You are overreacting. This is only until Juan Carlos is no longer a threat."

She rose. "Or until you find a new threat. I am not a convict. I will not be imprisoned." She stood, gazing up at him, face pink with anger. "I knew I could not trust you! I knew marriage would mean the end of my freedom."

"Don't be ridiculous. You trust me to keep you safe, and I will. If that means confining you here, then that is my decision."

For a long moment, she said nothing. Finally, she shook her head. "You may keep me here for a few weeks until Juan Carlos travels back to Spain, but you cannot force me to marry you. Once he is gone, I will be too."

And she swept out of the room with her words hanging in the air between them.

***

"I cannot believe I ever thought I would marry him," she told Ines, pacing back and forth in their small bed chamber. Tigrino looked up from the bath he was giving himself to watch her march in one direction and turn. It had been two days since she and Benedict had fought, and neither had spoken more than a word or two to each other in that time.

"You *are* married to him," Ines said, barely looking up from the pillow she was using to make lace.

"Not according to English law." She'd been such a fool. How could she have believed he was different than other men? As soon as she had given herself to him, he'd taken advantage and began to try and control her. She never should have trusted him to treat her as an equal.

"But you care about the law of God. You said he will not grant you an annulment now that you lay with him."

"I do not need an annulment. I do not plan to ever marry. For twenty years I lived under the thumb of Papa. I had no choice in even the most mundane details of my life. He told me what to wear, what to eat, and where I could go."

"Which was nowhere."

She stopped and pointed a finger at Ines. "Exactly. Now here is another man who wants to control me, to keep me from going where I want and doing what I want."

Ines set her bobbins down. "Surely it is not the same. Papa was cruel. He loved to have power over us and made ridiculous demands just to exercise that power. Draven is not like that. He only wants to protect you. He bought you a shop. Surely, he does not intend for you never to visit it."

Ines was right. Draven was not like her father, but neither was he treating her as his equal. How could she marry a man who might, on a whim, demand she stop making lace or no longer see her sister? And he could demand whatever he wanted of her. Because the truth was that once she was married to him under English law, she was his property. He could do whatever he wanted to her.

"I still think it's best if we go."

"Where? We cannot go back to Barcelona."

"Perhaps France or Belgium? When our lacemakers arrive, I will tell them the situation and ask where they want to go."

Someone tapped on the door, and Tigrino growled. That meant it was not Benedict. Tigrino still liked him, despite Catarina's anger with him. But the cat steadfastly disliked everyone else.

"Mrs. Draven?" Ward said on the other side of the door. "The colonel would like you to come into the parlor."

"And now he thinks to summon me?"

Ines bit her lip thoughtfully. "Perhaps he wants to apologize." She clasped her hands together. "Oh, would it not be romantic if he begged your forgiveness and proclaimed his undying love?"

Catarina sighed. She would respond to the summons simply to escape Ines's hopeless romanticism for a few minutes.

"Tell him I am coming, Ward."

She smoothed her hair and dress and thought about making Benedict wait. Her hair was tied back in a simple tail, and her dress was a work dress of dark blue. But what did she care how she looked for him? She made her way to the parlor, stopping just outside the door as she heard two voices speaking. One was Benedict but the other belonged to another man.

She opened the door and gave a small curtsy, immediately spotting her husband standing with one arm on the mantel. Across the room was Mr. FitzRoy. She gave FitzRoy a genuine smile. She had not seen him since the night he'd escorted her and Ines from Mivart's.

"Mr. Draven," she said coolly. "And Mr. FitzRoy. I did not know you would be calling."

He bowed. "I have news to share."

Catarina looked from Draven to FitzRoy. Draven nodded at his friend. "Go ahead."

"As you know, I have been watching Mivart's and keeping tabs on Miguel and Juan Carlos de la Fuente. I've been able to persuade them to trust me and have made them several business propositions." He looked at Draven. "All of them completely fabricated, of course. But de la Fuente was gratified to be asked and fawned over." He looked at Catarina again. "He has been delaying accepting any of my offers, but this afternoon he finally refused me."

She nodded, not surprised. Juan Carlos's business had not been as profitable the last year or so because of her own thriving success with lace. She did not think he had unlimited funds for investment. Curious as to the reason Juan Carlos would give, she asked.

"He told me he is returning to Barcelona in the morning."

"And Mr. FitzRoy has evidence of the truth of that statement," Benedict added.

"I do. He has paid his bill at Mivart's and bought tickets on a ship bound for Spain. The staff at Mivart's told me he has packed his luggage."

Catarina clasped her hands. "So he is truly leaving."

"It would appear so. I'll watch to make sure of it in the morning, but I think we can all rest easier tomorrow night."

"Thank you, FitzRoy," Benedict said, gesturing toward the door. FitzRoy gave her a nod and followed Draven out of the parlor. Catarina might have used the time to sneak back to her bed chamber. Instead, she stayed in the parlor, interested to see if Benedict would return and what he would say. Surely he would not apologize and declare his love, but she at least wanted to give him the opportunity.

"There, you see," Benedict said, coming in a few moments later.

Catarina cut her eyes to him. "What am I supposed to see?"

"That I was right to insist you stay here. De la Fuente cannot get to you and is leaving. You suffered no inconvenience."

"On the contrary, it is quite inconvenient to be treated like a prisoner."

He sighed. "If you felt like a prisoner, it is your own doing. You have kept to your room and avoided me."

"I suppose you think I should go to your bed each night and thank you for my captivity."

His face darkened into a scowl. "Catarina, tomorrow you will be free to go and do as you wish. I recommend you take Ward or Maggie with you, of course, but there should be no danger in you going to the shops or even to your own shop to begin to ready it to open."

"And how long will this freedom last?" She put her hands on her hips. "How long until you find some other way to cage me?"

"Why can't you see that I don't want to cage you?" His voice rose, and she could see he was struggling to control his temper.

"What happens when I work too late at the shop or go out without Maggie or Ward? Then will I be confined to my room again?"

"I don't expect you'll be so stupid as to make a mistake like that," he said. "I thought you could use common sense."

"I am but a mere woman. I am not certain I can be trusted to make my own decisions."

He stepped closer to me. "You are putting words in my mouth and picking a fight with me. I am trying to put things right."

"If I put words in your mouth, it is because I have not heard the ones I deserve."

He took her shoulders gently, and she struggled not to lean into him. "What words do you want from me?" His voice was quiet and tender, and she was reminded of the way he kissed her and held her.

"I want an apology," she murmured. "I want you to make me believe I can trust you. I want you to promise never to tell me where I can go or when or with whom."

His hands tightened on her shoulders, not enough to hurt but enough for her to know he was upset. "And if the choice you are making is poor?"

"Then it is my mistake."

He shook his head. "I'd be a fool to agree to that."

She stepped back. "I will begin to pack then. Ines and I will leave once we have finished the pieces we promised."

"If that's what you want"—he called after her as she walked away—"then give me the annulment papers. I'll sign them. We might as well make it a clean break."

She swiped the tears from her eyes and continued walking.

Sixteen

"The course of true love never did run smooth."
A Midsummer Night's Dream, *William Shakespeare*

"Go away, Porter," Benedict said. "I do not want soup or a mincemeat pie or any other goddamn thing you want to offer me."

Benedict stared at the closed door of his personal parlor at the Draven Club. This was the third time in as many hours that Porter had knocked.

"But Colonel, surely you might like a brandy. It's French."

The last thing Benedict wanted was to drink himself into a stupor. He was old and wise enough to know drinking only numbed the pain temporarily and led to a new pain the next morning. He wanted no brandy. "Porter, do not make me come out there and pour that brandy over your head."

A long silence ensued, followed by the *step-thump* of Porter walking away.

Benedict put his head down on his desk. He couldn't go home. There was too much of *her* there. She hadn't made good on her threat to leave yet, but she would. She would go, and this time he really never would see her again.

And he had no one to blame but himself.

He'd forgotten the one most important rule every soldier must learn. Never act out of fear. Fear wasn't rational, and it wasn't logical. Decisions should be made with a cool head and not deviated from just because conditions on the battlefield induced terror. But he'd acted out of fear with Catarina. He'd walked onto the battlefield and slashed uselessly, hurting no one but himself.

That wasn't quite true. He'd hurt her too. He could see the pain behind her frosty demeanor. She'd told him she needed to trust him. She'd told him she didn't want to be treated like a convict. How could he blame her when she'd escaped a father who'd tried to marry her to a violent man? And after that narrow escape she'd made a life for herself as a renowned lacemaker. Who was he to tell her that she must hide away in his little flat? She'd taken care of herself for years. And when she'd needed help, she'd been smart enough to ask for it.

Why hadn't he told her he was sorry? Why hadn't he begged her forgiveness? Why had he given her more orders and all but promised to curb her freedom in the future?

Because he was afraid.

That was the naked truth of it. He was afraid of losing her. He'd never been so terrified of anything in his life. But in trying to keep her safe, he'd lost her.

The answer seemed simple enough. Swallow his pride and hide his fear and give her his word she'd have her freedom. It would be worth it to have her back in his arms, back in his bed. The problem was he couldn't trust himself to keep his word. He wanted to hold her loosely, but everything in him urged him to clamp on to her, grip her tightly, hide her away.

Porter knocked at the door again. Benedict lifted the blotter from his desk and threw it at the door. "Go away!" he roared.

"Colonel!" Porter's voice was different, high and agitated. "I think you had better come out here."

Benedict looked up. "What's wrong?"

"Ward is here, Colonel. He's bleeding."

***

Catarina had instructed Ward to tell anyone with a new order for lace that she was not at home. She wanted to finish her current orders and prepare to leave. She'd already spent some of the afternoon catering to the customers she had, showing them the lace items she'd finished or the progress she had made.

She hadn't seen Benedict since the evening before. She didn't even know where he was. He was obviously through with her, and she supposed if she didn't see him again it would make leaving all the easier.

So she was somewhat distracted when Ward showed a woman she had not met before inside. Tigrino growled from under her chair, but he growled at everyone.

"Mrs. Reynolds," Ward said, sweeping a hand toward the empty chair across from Catarina. Catarina gave him a look, then rose.

"Madam." She extended her hand. "How good to meet you. Please sit down. Will you excuse me for a moment?"

She followed Ward out of the parlor. "Why have you shown her in?" she whispered. "I told you I want no new customers."

Ward sighed and dabbed a handkerchief at his bald head, though it was quite a chilly day. "I told her, Mrs. Draven. She—er—she—"

Catarina leaned closer. Ward was only an inch or two taller than she, and his eyes kept darting away from hers.

"She began to cry," Ward finally managed. "She begged me to let her in."

Catarina stepped back, staring at him in disbelief. "You are only pretending to be rough and unfeeling." She put a hand on his shoulder. "Is that not right, Ward? On the inside, you have a tender heart."

Ward straightened. "I don't know what you mean, madam. I am simply not feeling well today. I think it has something to do with that cat. He makes my nose itch and my eyes water."

"Does he? Is that why you put down little dishes of savory morsels for him?"

Ward stiffened and put his nose in the air. "I have no idea what you are referring to."

Catarina almost laughed. She'd seen the little dishes and saucers licked clean, but she'd assumed Benedict or Ines had left them for Tigrino. But Ward obviously cared for the cat. It made Catarina sad to think that just as she was beginning to build a home here, she would be leaving.

"If you'll excuse me." Ward turned on his heel and marched away. She wouldn't exactly miss him, but she might think of him now and again.

Catarina could hear Ines speaking with Madam Reynolds, and she turned to go back into the parlor, putting a patient smile on her face. Tears might succeed with Ward, but Catarina was not taking any new orders.

"Ah, here she is now," Ines said as Catarina entered. "Catarina, I was just about to offer to show Mrs. Reynolds the ready-made pieces we have for sale."

Catarina sat in the chair opposite the woman. "I do hope you find something you like. I am afraid I cannot agree to make any new pieces at the moment."

"I'd like to see them." Her gaze flicked to the bracket clock on the mantel. "I'm sure there will be something I fancy."

Ines rose to fetch the pieces and Catarina studied the woman in front of her. She spoke three languages and read four, but she had very little sense of the nuance of any language except her native Portuguese and to some extent Spanish, as she'd lived in Spain for several years. But to her ear, this woman's way of speaking sounded very different from Benedict's or that of his friends. She might be dressed well, but Catarina did not think she was of the upper classes. It made no difference to her. A merchant's wife had as much right to wear beautiful lace as a duke's daughter.

Ines laid the pieces on the table, spreading them out. Mrs. Reynolds studied them, but as Ines detailed the merits of each piece, the woman's gaze seemed to wander—to the clock, to the door, and back to the clock.

"Are you feeling well?" Ines finally asked.

"Actually, no."

Catarina felt shame that she hadn't thought to ask how the woman felt or even to offer her refreshment. "Can I send for some tea?" she asked.

"That would be lovely, but I think a step in the garden might 'elp me more."

"Of course. I will be happy to show you." Catarina escorted the woman to the garden, opening the door so she might go out and take a few deep breaths of air. Tigrino followed, but merely stared at the garden, not taking the opportunity to go out as he usually did. Catarina looked about for a bird or hedgehog, but she saw nothing that could account for his rapt attention out the door.

"I'll take that tea now, if you don't mind," Mrs. Reynolds said, still taking deep breaths.

"Of course." Catarina walked toward the kitchen to ask Maggie to prepare a tea tray. She found Maggie at a table slicing apples.

"What can I help you with, Mrs. Draven?"

"Would you bring some tea—"

The sound of Tigrino howling cut her off.

Maggie jumped up. "What the devil is that?"

"It sounds as though Tigrino is hurt." Catarina raced back toward the garden door, but it was closed now and Mrs. Reynolds was nowhere to be seen. "What—?" She heard a sound and turned, spotting Tigrino crouched under a chair, licking his fur.

Ward marched in from his room. "What is the meaning of all of this noise?" he demanded.

"I do not know. Mrs. Reynolds stepped out and then Tigrino howled, and I cannot find Mrs. Reynolds anywhere. Ines!" Catarina called. "Ines?"

The parlor door opened, and Ines stood in the doorway, pale and visibly trembling.

"What happened?" Catarina rushed toward her.

"No!" Ines cried, holding a hand up.

Catarina froze, and watched as the form of Juan Carlos de la Fuente came into view behind her sister. "*Buenas tardes, Señora* Draven."

Catarina felt her own skin turn cold and clammy. Her belly tightened until she could barely keep from doubling over. "What do you want?" she whispered.

"I think you know the answer to that."

"Now see here!" Ward said, moving forward and acting as something of a shield for Catarina. "I don't know who you are, but you will have to leave."

Juan Carlos held up a sharp blade, pressing the flat of it against Ines's cheek. "Not just yet. If you do not want *Señorita* Neves cut into small pieces, I suggest both of you step into the parlor."

Catarina exchanged a look with Ward, whose face was flushed and whose eyes were bright. He looked angry rather than frightened, and that gave her courage. She moved forward, following Ward. Ines took slow steps backward until they were all inside the blue parlor.

"Close the door, will you?" Juan Carlos said sweetly.

Catarina closed the door but not before Tigrino streaked inside, darting under one of the chairs.

Juan Carlos gestured to the chairs with his knife. "Sit, please."

Catarina and Ines sat. Ward stood, defiant. "Who are you? You have no right to be here."

"I may have no right, but I am holding the knife. Sit."

Ward sat in the chair beside her, perched on the edge of his seat.

"Who else is here?" Juan Carlos asked. "What other servants?"

"No one," Ward said. "I'm the only servant."

Catarina thought of Maggie in the kitchen and hoped she did not come to investigate.

"Good."

"Juan Carlos, it is me who has angered you. Let the servant and Ines go."

"I could do that," he said with a smile. "But then they might fetch someone to help you before my plan is complete." He'd moved closer, standing over her with the knife angled toward her.

Catarina swallowed. "And what is your plan?" she asked, though she thought she knew.

"I am leaving England," he said. "But first I will kill you." He raised the knife, and Catarina let out a gasp. But before he could strike her with it, Ward leapt from his chair and plowed hard into Juan Carlos's exposed belly. Juan Carlos stumbled back, Ines screamed, and Catarina saw blood. Ward pushed forward, and Juan Carlos fell, but he must have sunk his knife into Ward before he fell, because the servant's arm was bleeding as he staggered away from Juan Carlos.

"Ward!" Catarina screamed.

"It's only my arm, madam." He weaved toward the door.

"Run, Ward!"

"Yes, run," Juan Carlos said, standing again. "Go fetch your master so he can see the blood I spill while it's still fresh."

"No!" Ward made to attack Juan Carlos again, but Juan Carlos charged him, this time grasping him by the back of the neck and propelling him toward the door. He opened it and tossed the bleeding servant into the receiving room.

"Go fetch your master." Juan Carlos slammed the door closed and moved a table in front of it. He tossed the knife from one hand to the other. "Now that it's just the three of us, I can get to work."

***

Benedict ran down the winding staircase, almost tripping on the royal blue carpet. He took the last few steps two at a time until he was in the wood-paneled vestibule where Ward sat in a chair, Neil Wraxall on one side, tying a piece of cloth around his arm, and Duncan—he hadn't even known Duncan was in Town—telling Ward, "Dinnae fash. It's the man hisself."

"What the hell happened?" Benedict roared.

"Don't worry about me. It's your wife."

The room seemed to spin. The lights from the chandelier winked out for a moment before Benedict grasped the banister and took a deep breath. "What about her?"

"He's come for her. The Spaniard."

"Where are they?"

"Jermyn Street."

"I'll kill him," Benedict said, starting for the door.

"I'll go with you," Duncan announced. "It's been an age since I killed a man."

Benedict didn't protest. Duncan had been known as The Lunatic among the men of his troop, and if there was ever a time Benedict needed a madman at his side, it was now.

***

Once Ward was locked out, Catarina began to shake. But losing her head would not keep her alive. She grabbed Ines, who sat motionless on the couch and yanked her up and behind her. "If you get the chance, run."

"I am not leaving you."

Juan Carlos turned back to them. "Let her go. I am not interested in your little sister."

Catarina didn't wait for another chance. She shoved Ines toward the door leading to the dining room. Ines shook her head, but Catarina glared at her. "Get out now. I do not want you here."

"I cannot leave you."

"Get out!" she yelled in a tone she'd never used with her sister, or with anyone, before.

Shocked, Ines opened the door. Catarina held her breath until Ines closed it again.

"This is your fault, you know," Juan Carlos said, moving toward her. "If you had just done what I asked. What we *agreed* upon."

"You mean if I had just married Miguel and given up everything I had ever worked for." She slid along the side of the room, not wanting to allow Juan Carlos to corner her. "I did not want to give it up. I created Catarina lace."

"You do not deserve it," he sneered as he attempted to close in on her. "My family has been making lace for centuries. We have lived and worked in Barcelona for hundreds of years. Who are you? No one. Some little Portuguese peasant girl who should know her place!" He lunged at her, the knife clutched tightly in his hand. Catarina flung herself to the side, tripping on her skirts, but jumping to her feet in time to round the couch in the center of the room.

"I am in London now. Go back to Spain and make your lace. No one will remember me."

But he was too angry to listen to reason. He was breathing hard, circling the couch as she circled on the other side. She doubted he had even heard her. He wanted vengeance and would not stop until he had it. She'd hurt his pride. Juan Carlos had been a spoiled and pampered child, just as he had spoiled and pampered his son. He felt entitled to her shop and her lace, and like a child who has had the thing he wants taken away, Juan Carlos was striking out in anger.

"You think you can keep away from me forever?" He was breathing hard now as he chased her around the couch, reversing directions and lunging over the top. "I will catch you."

He would. It was only a matter of time. She would move too slowly or trip on her skirts or one of his wild lunges would succeed. She needed a weapon, but as she looked about the square room, she saw nothing. The room was bare of anything not related to her lace. Even the top of the desk was clean. The clock on the mantel was the only embellishment, and she could grab it, but it was heavy and would be of little use if she tried to throw it. She would have to be very close to Juan Carlos in order to slam him over the head with it.

She jumped back as Juan Carlos slashed his knife over the top of the couch and almost caught her arm. Without warning, he stepped on the couch and leaped over the back, landing in front of her.

She screamed and scrambled around the side, but not before he caught her skirts with the knife. The fabric rent as she tore away, leaving her panicked at the close call and Juan Carlos even more confident than before. He ran after her and she ran too, pushing a chair over to slow his progress. The door was so close, but he'd moved the table in front of it, and it would take too much time to move it. She ran on, pushing a blue-and-white-striped chair between them.

They faced each other, she breathing hard, her heart pounding with fear. He was red-faced and sweating, his teeth showing in a feral smile.

"*Adios, señora.*"

That was when Tigrino pounced.

Seventeen

"A harmless necessary cat."
The Merchant of Venice, *William Shakespeare*

Benedict hadn't waited for a hackney. Duncan had paused to hail one, but Benedict had not even looked back. The afternoon was cold and gray, and he wore no greatcoat or hat, but he didn't feel the bite of the wind. He felt nothing but the slam of his heart against his chest.

She could not die. He could lose everyone, had lost so many, but he could not lose her.

He rounded a corner, running as fast as he could, shoving men and women out of his way, and still he knew he would not be fast enough. She might be dead already. Images of Juan Carlos sanding over her body, bloody knife in his hand, flashed in Benedict's mind. He heard the commotion behind him, the screams and curses, but didn't turn until a hackney coach came up alongside him, careening wildly as the driver barely managed to avoid hitting a fruit stall.

"Hop on, will ye?" a Scotsman called.

Benedict looked up at the wild-eyed, long haired man in the box. The jarvey was nowhere to be seen, but when Duncan held his hand out, Benedict took it and climbed up.

"Hold on tae yer hat!" Duncan warned.

"I'm not wearing a hat," Benedict said as Duncan called to the horse and the beast lurched forward, the force of which almost knocked Benedict out of the seat.

"Then just hold on!"

Duncan was as much a lunatic in the driver's seat as he was on the battlefield. He took no prisoners, endangering the lives of passersby, whether they be old or young, male or female, human or canine. How he managed to avoid injuring anyone or anything was beyond Benedict's understanding.

He lifted his hands from his eyes just as the stolen hackney arrived at his front door. And it was literally at his front door—one wheel having come to rest on the lowest step. With a war cry that all but stunned Benedict, Duncan jumped down and raced for the door. Benedict recovered and was right behind him. They burst into the shared hallway, which was eerily quiet. Duncan reached behind his back and pulled a sword—dear God, was that a claymore?—from what must have been a sheath hidden under his coat. "Which door?" he asked.

"This one." Benedict fumbled for his key, heart pounding as fear at what he would see on the other side of the door made his hands shake.

"Move aside, Colonel." Duncan gave Benedict about a half second to comply then lifted a leg and kicked the door in.

Benedict rushed inside the receiving room just as a woman screamed.

***

The cat landed on the back of Juan Carlos's neck, claws extended, hissing and growling. Juan Carlos let out a howl and reached back to free himself from the cat's sharp talons. Catarina took her chance, shoving the chair forward hard and slamming it into Juan Carlos's legs. He growled at her, still grappling with Tigrino, and then time seemed to halt when the knife he'd held slipped from his fingers and clunked on the floor.

Juan Carlos freed himself from Tigrino and tossed the cat against the wall like a rag doll then went for the knife. But he was too late. Catarina closed on it first, their hands brushing against each other. She stood, knife outstretched, and Juan Carlos lunged for it. Catarina's hand jerked up and she felt warm, sticky blood ooze over her hand as she pulled it away from Juan Carlos's coat.

His face was too close to hers, so close his breath puffed against her cheek. And then he fell forward, and she jumped aside to avoid being trapped under him. He fell on his side, moaning, then turned and looked up at her. The knife was still embedded in his belly, a ring of red surrounding the black hilt.

Catarina screamed. Juan Carlos gurgled then reached for her. She stepped back and screamed again, just as the door crashed open, half off its hinges, and a large man with long hair and an enormous sword burst into the parlor.

Catarina was too stunned to scream. She scampered backward as the man moved to the side and Benedict rushed in. "Catarina!" He seemed to leap over furnishings to be at her side in a moment. He pulled her into his arms then up and away from Juan Carlos's body. Carrying her across the room, he reached the door before she realized what was happening.

"Wait. Tigrino."

"You're not safe in there."

She struggled and he set her down just outside the parlor door. "I am not hurt. Tigrino is injured. He saved me."

"Stay here," Benedict ordered, clearly not listening to her. "I'll kill that Spaniard." He rushed back into the room, and Catarina followed. The large man had lowered his broadsword and stared down at Juan Carlos's body.

"I'd say he's just aboot deid." The man looked at her. "Did you do this lass?"

"H-he fell forward. I did not mean to."

Benedict knelt next to Juan Carlos's body. "He's still alive. Call for a surgeon, Duncan."

"Aye." He stomped out, and Catarina snapped out of her stupor. She gazed around the room, spotted Tigrino laying in a heap of fur on the floor.

"No!" Rushing to him, she knelt beside him and took his limp body in her arms. "No." She buried her face in his soft fur, feeling the warmth of his little body. Benedict knelt next to her. She didn't see him so much as feel him beside her.

"Let me see him."

She sobbed and held Tigrino tighter. "He saved me. He leapt on his back and gave me a distraction."

Benedict rubbed her back. "Listen for his heartbeat. I don't see any blood. He may just be stunned."

But she was sobbing too much to hear anything, and Benedict gently took the cat from her arms. He bent his head and pressed it to the animal's chest. He was perfectly still for three heartbeats, and then he smiled up at her. "He's still alive. His heartbeat is strong. Let's keep him warm and see if he won't wake on his own." He took off his own coat and wrapped the cat in it, still holding Tigrino in his arms. "Come with me. I want you out of this room. Where is Ines?" he asked as he led her into the receiving room.

"I do not know. I told her to run."

"Safe then."

"Ward was injured. I do not know what happened—"

"He came for me. He'll be fine."

Catarina's legs couldn't support her any longer, and without warning, she crumpled to the ground and burst into sobs.

Benedict knelt before her, still holding the cat. "What's all this?"

"I do not know," she sobbed. "I cannot stop shaking."

He pulled her into his arms, the cat between them. "It's shock. Cry it out. It's the best thing. I've cried plenty of times after a battle."

She looked up at him, finding it difficult to imagine him crying.

"I killed him. I killed Juan Carlos."

"He's not dead yet."

She gave him a look.

"It was self-defense. He would have killed you." His voice faltered. "And now I want to start crying. God, Catarina, I was so afraid I would lose you."

"You came for me."

"And you didn't need me after all."

"Of course, I need you!"

"And I need you. I love you."

The words startled her, and she stared up at him. This man with shining eyes and her injured cat in his arms, looking down at her with an expression of love so clear she didn't know how she couldn't have seen it before.

"I love you too."

"I was wrong to try and keep you locked up. That's not what I want."

"I know."

"I want you to be free and independent."

"I know."

"I bought you that shop and then I was an idiot and tried to take it all away."

"You were an idiot, yes."

That shut him up. "You're not supposed to agree with that."

"I will agree to anything if you will only kiss me."

"Catarina," he whispered and pulled her against him, kissing her deeply and tenderly.

Tigrino let out an annoyed sound and they both laughed and moved apart. The cat wriggled, trying to free himself from the coat.

"Slowly now," Benedict said, unwrapping the coat. Tigrino squirmed out, limping slightly when he put weight on his back leg. "We'll have the surgeon look at him too."

The big man clomped back into the receiving room, his steps making the floor shake. "The surgeon is coming, and I found a maid and another lass huddling together in the back."

"Maggie and Ines! Bring them in, please."

"Come in!" he called, and the two women rushed inside, Maggie clutching her skirts and asking about Ward and Ines throwing herself against Catarina. She held her sister, crying with her then shaking when the surgeon arrived and announced there was nothing he could do. Her teeth chattered when, several hours later, some men came and took the body out.

Benedict was at her side the entire time. He answered questions and held her hand as she answered them. Others came and went. Some she recognized and others she didn't. Finally, everyone except Ines, Benedict, and Catarina were gone. Catarina, who had finally been moved to a chair in the dining room, leaned her head back and closed her eyes. Just for a moment.

When she began to fall, Benedict caught her.

***

Sometime after midnight her eyes fluttered open. Benedict lay beside her on his bed, and he brushed her hair back from her forehead as she opened her eyes and looked about in confusion.

"I'm here," he said. "You're safe."

"Ines?"

"Is sleeping in her bed chamber. And"—anticipating her next question—"Tigrino is sleeping by the fire. The surgeon splinted that back leg, and he's finally given up trying to tear the wrapping off and fallen asleep."

Her dark eyes focused on him. "And you?"

"I'm watching over you." Of course, he was. Why had she ever doubted him?

"What time is it?" She struggled to sit, but he pulled her back down.

"It's a little after midnight. Go back to sleep, my love. You need to rest. Tomorrow will bring more questions, more inquiry."

She gripped his hand tightly. "I want to stay with you."

She'd been strong today, answering the magistrate's questions with surprising brevity and clarity. She'd been so strong, and she must be exhausted now. "I won't leave your side. I'll be right there."

"That is not what I mean. Benedict, when I said I would not marry you—"

"We don't have to speak of that now. I know I was an idiot. I want you to give me another chance, but if you can't, if I've lost your trust forever, I won't try to keep you from leaving."

She raised a brow. "You will let me walk out of your life?"

The idea made him feel ill. "I didn't say I wouldn't follow you." He'd been a fool once and let her go. Age had given him wisdom, and he wouldn't make the same mistake again.

"You will not have to follow me." She put her arms around his neck. "I am not leaving you. You are not the only one who was an idiot. I should have known you were acting out of fear."

He pulled back. "Me, afraid?"

She laughed. "Then maybe I was acting out of fear."

He cupped her face. "Or we both were. I need to ask you. Will you marry me? Again? Forever—until death do us part?"

"Forever? That sounds wonderful to me." And she kissed him.

He didn't want to take her then. It hadn't been his intention. He'd wanted her to sleep and regain her strength, but her hands slid under his shirt, pulling it over his head. And when he protested, she told him she needed to touch him, to be close to him. He tried to object when she slid out of her chemise, but the sight of her body made his mouth go dry. By the time she reached for the fall of his trousers, he was in no mood to argue with her. In fact, Benedict would argue that the lady should have whatever it was she wanted.

Right now she wanted him.

He stroked her body with a fervor he could hardly contain. Her skin was so warm, so silky, so soft and full. She moaned and arched and responded to every caress, every touch until they were both out of breath and struggling to keep control.

She wrapped her legs around him. "Show me again how much you love me."

He slid into her, slowly, his eyes locked on hers, giving her all of himself—his every emotion. They moved together as though they had done this hundreds of times before. The way she looked at him filled him with warmth and gave him as much pleasure as the feel of her body wrapped around him. When she finally closed her eyes and whispered, "Yes," he watched the orgasm ripple through her, lighting her face until it was shining in the dim light of the bed chamber. His own release followed, so strong he could barely keep from collapsing on top of her when it was over. Instead, he rested his head on her shoulder, closed his eyes, and breathed in the scent of her.

"You have to marry me now," she murmured, her voice sleepy.

"I always had to marry you," he answered. "You were meant for me."

"And you for me."

He would not argue with that.

Eighteen

"Thou art sad; get thee a wife, get thee a wife!"
Much Ado about Nothing, *William Shakespeare*

The wedding was at eight o'clock in the morning in the church Benedict had attended as a child, the one that bore a pew with the Draven family name on it. His younger brother officiated, and his older brother served as one of the witnesses. The breakfast was held at Somerford Lodge, the Draven family home in Bedfordshire. It sounded rather grand but was small and dark and rather damp and cold in winter.

Still, it was his family home, and he wanted Catarina to see it. "I'll bring you back in spring," he said as they sat down to breakfast with Ines, his family, and a few of his men. "It's too cold to show you anything now."

"I would like that," she said, smiling up at him.

His breath caught when she did that. She always looked lovely, but today in her pale-yellow gown with sleeves and a collar of white Catarina lace, she looked absolutely breathtaking. He must have looked at her too long, because her brow furrowed.

"Is something the matter?"

"No." Everything in his life was absolutely perfect. "I was only admiring your lace. I hope you did not have to make your own wedding lace."

She shook her head. "Now that my lacemakers have arrived from Spain, Ines has put them all to work. She surprised me with the lace for the dress." She looked down the table. "I did think Lady Philomena would attend. She was one of my first customers when the shop opened."

Mr. FitzRoy leaned over. "Forgive me for eavesdropping, but you may not have heard that Lady Philomena's brother, the Duke of Mayne, has passed away. She and Lord Phineas are in mourning and sent their best wishes."

Benedict had known this, but in the pre-wedding frenzy had forgotten to mention it to Catarina.

"I am so sorry to hear that. I will send my condolences."

Benedict put his hand on her arm. "After we return from our trip." He didn't want her writing letters on their honeymoon. He wanted her all to himself.

"That will be soon enough," FitzRoy said. "Poor Phin is accustomed to losing brothers. Three of his four siblings have died. I think he's rather concerned. If the next one goes, the dukedom passes to Phin. He thought as the fifth son, he was safe."

So had his family, else they wouldn't have sent him to France under Draven's command.

"But we have much happier news to celebrate."

Benedict knew he meant the wedding and also the fact that the inquest into Juan Carlos de la Fuente's death had been concluded and found no wrongdoing. Miguel de la Fuente had not been implicated and had returned to Spain. That part of Catarina's life was truly over. Their life together was just starting.

"Hear, hear!" Neil Wraxall said, standing at the other end of the table. "Let's raise a glass to Colonel Draven and his bride."

The other guests lifted their wine glasses as did Catarina and Benedict. Neil lifted his own glass high. "I offer a wedding blessing from all of the Survivors.

May musket balls miss him,

May his bride always kiss him.

May no Frenchies (or Spaniards) give chase,

May she always be pretty in lace.

Colonel, you were always our bellwether,

We hope you enjoy your new tether!"

Everyone laughed and drank deeply. Benedict drank too, and when he looked at Catarina, she leaned over and kissed him.

He kissed her back, happy to be *tethered*, if that was what his men wanted to call it. He had his life and his love. He cupped her face, kissing her deeply as cheers erupted around them, filling all the room with happiness and warmth.

Keep reading for an excerpt from Ines's story. The Highlander's Excellent Adventure is on sale September 8, 2020!

Ines

"She is an unmarried young lady," her brother-in-law said. "It's absolutely out of the question."

Ines narrowed her eyes in annoyance, even though neither Benedict Draven nor her sister, Catarina, could see her. She was eavesdropping. Again. She hadn't meant to—not this time. She'd been passing by the drawing room and heard her name. She'd promised herself she wouldn't eavesdrop on her sister and brother-in-law. They were married and deserved their privacy. But that promise did not apply in case of emergency. And this obviously qualified as an emergency as their discussion pertained to her future.

"We cannot keep her here, under lock and key, forever," Catarina said calmly. "She is young and wants some independence. It is not as though she is one of your fine Society ladies. She is a lacemaker."

"She's part of my family now, and I won't have her living alone above the shop. Even if I thought it was safe, you know her temperament."

Ines bristled but restrained herself from interjecting as that would only prove Draven's point.

"I was a bit wild at her age too," Catarina said, a smile in her voice. "If you remember."

Draven made a sound of dismissal. "That was war, and you were desperate."

"Yes, desperate to escape an arranged marriage to a cruel old man."

Ines nodded her head—she'd been facing a similar fate at one time. She'd run away with Catarina when, at the tender age of fourteen, their father had tried to marry her to one of his friends. She didn't like to think of how close she'd come to being trapped forever. Of course, when she'd escaped, she'd thought she was embarking on an exhilarating adventure. The reality was hours of detailed work in the back of a shop with other lacemakers. Her only excitement had been attending mass on Sundays. Ines ran a finger over a rough piece of paint on the wall and scratched at it as Draven spoke again.

"Why don't we see how things progress with Mr. Podmore?"

Podmore. Ines almost retched aloud. Mr. Podmore must be the most tedious person in London, if not the whole of England. Probably the entire world. He was forever going on about carriages. He was a successful cartwright, and his conveyances were known for their sturdiness and reliability. He'd once spoken for a quarter hour, uninterrupted, on the importance of wheel spokes. Ines had almost fallen asleep. She would never allow herself to be pushed into a marriage with a man like Podmore. She wanted passion, excitement...danger.

"I am afraid the interest there is all on one side," Catarina said. "But perhaps if they pursue an enjoyable activity together, it might help. I will suggest a ride in the park when he arrives today."

Ines started. Podmore was to call on her today? *Caramba!* She had to escape before he arrived or she might be trapped with him for hours, and she simply could not listen to another monologue on wheel spokes.

Ines stepped back and bumped into someone. She spun around and stared into the face of Ward, Draven's butler. He was only a little taller than she. His head was bald, but a shadow of stubble darkened his cheeks. "Ward!" she hissed. "What are you doing there?"

It was a ridiculous question. Ward was everywhere. One never knew when or where he would turn up.

The butler raised a brow. "I might ask you the same question, Miss Neves."

She blew out a breath. This was why she wanted to live above the shop. There was no privacy here. Her color rose as she realized how hypocritical that thought was considering she was the one eavesdropping.

On the other hand, Ward was eavesdropping as well... Ines straightened her shoulders. "I will pretend I did not see you, if you pretend you did not see me."

"Happily, miss."

Ines started for the front door, but Ward cleared his throat. She turned back. "What is it now?"

"Mr. Murray will arrive and knock on the door any moment. I suggest you exit another way."

Ines had no idea how Ward always knew who was coming and who was going and when they would appear, but she was too stunned by the mention of Duncan Murray to say anything.

The image of the Scotsman immediately flashed into her mind. All she had was his image as she had never been introduced to him. Ines had only glimpsed him through cracks in doorways. But those quick peeks had shown her quite enough to arouse her interest. He was tall, oh so wonderfully tall, and big and strong. She liked big men, men who had to turn to the side to fit their shoulders through the door and duck under the lintel to avoid banging their head. Mr. Murray had thick arms and legs—she'd seen his legs because he often wore a kilt. They were muscled and covered by brown hair. He had quite a lot of hair. The hair on his head was long enough to pull back in a queue, which was how he wore it when he visited. But she imagined untying the piece of leather securing his hair and running her hands through the freed locks. Then maybe he'd kiss her with those lips that always seemed to give everyone a mocking half smile. She'd feel the bristle of his two days' worth of stubble.

She didn't need to have met him to know he was a man of passion, excitement, and danger.

"Are you well, Miss Neves?" Ward asked.

Ines realized she'd been standing still, staring off into space. "Yes, why?" she asked quickly.

"Your face has gone red and your breathing has quickened."

"I am thirsty," she said, putting her hands to her hot cheeks. "I think I shall go to the kitchens and ask for a cup of tea." She walked away as rapidly as she could, certain Ward had known exactly what was causing her cheeks to color.

Once in the kitchen, she didn't see the cook, and she set about heating water to make her own cup of tea. She didn't really want any tea, but she needed something to do while she calmed her thoughts.

She had to hide somewhere until Podmore had gone. But if she left, she would miss the chance to spy on Mr. Murray's arrival. She would have to sneak around because Benedict always met with the Scot in private. Ines had once overheard—very well, *listened in*—when Catarina told Draven that Murray was wild and would be a bad influence on Ines. Benedict had said that of course he was. That was why the troop had called him the Lunatic. A description like that only made Duncan Murray more intriguing.

She *had* to find a way to meet him one day.

Ines heard a carriage stop outside the house and groaned aloud. Today would not be that day, obviously. Murray always came on a horse. Podmore always came in a carriage. He had several—a gig, a curricle, a barouche. She knew all about them. She had to escape now or she'd be forced to spend the afternoon with him, and it was such a lovely afternoon—warm and sunny and far too pretty to spend with dull Mr. Podmore. If she could avoid him today, she would be spared his company for the next few days as tomorrow her family was to travel to the country for the wedding of the sister of the Duke of Mayne.

Ines left the cup of tea brewing on the table, wiped her hands on the apron, and crossed the room to the courtyard door. She opened it, peeked out, and when she didn't see any of the servants about, stepped outside and closed the door behind her. Sheets and table linens hung on a line to dry and a half-painted chair had been abandoned in a corner. She could hide here for a little while, but a few sheets would not provide much cover. She had to find somewhere Catarina wouldn't think to look.

She heard a coachman speak to the horses out on the street, and an idea came to her. She would hide in Podmore's carriage. No one would look for her there. She could hide inside until Podmore came back, then slip out the opposite side when he returned. She would miss his visit completely.

Pleased with her plan, Ines opened the courtyard gate, slipped outside, and went around the side of the house, where she spotted the carriage. It didn't look exactly like the one Podmore had showed her last time. It wasn't as shiny and didn't have gold accents. This was much plainer, though she was certain he could make it sound like the most amazing carriage ever constructed.

The coachman had left his box and was speaking with a deliveryman nearby. His absence made Ines's task easier. She walked to the door of the coach, careful to stay low so the coachman would not see her through the windows. But even that was not a worry as the coach's curtains were closed. She opened one door, slipped inside, and closed it again. In the darkness, she couldn't help but smile at her own cunning.

She sat back, prepared to wait until she heard Podmore returning. The squabs were comfortable but not as luxurious as she'd anticipated. Where was the velvet Podmore insisted upon? Perhaps he had realized that velvet seats in summer were far too warm. The heat in the closed space was already making her uncomfortable and sleepy.

A few minutes passed, and then a few more, and she heard the coachman climb back on his box. The coach started moving a few minutes later, which was to be expected. They were looking for her inside the house, and Podmore would not want his horses to stand for too long.

Ines was rather used to riding in coaches now, though she had never even seen a coach in the tiny village where she'd grown up. But even after having ridden in coaches dozens of times the past five years, she still enjoyed the feeling of being carried by a momentum not her own. She closed her heavy eyes and waited for the horses to come to a stop outside Draven's house again. She should probably hop out as soon as the coach stopped. Podmore would have given up on her by now and might be waiting for his coach to carry him home. She would exit on the street and try to sneak back into the house via the courtyard.

Catarina would scold her, but Ines was not sorry. She had told her sister she did not care for Mr. Podmore and that she did not wish to marry any man that she didn't love. She wanted a man who could offer passion, excitement, and— Catarina usually cut her off by then. Her sister treated Ines's pronouncement the same way she treated Ines's requests to move to the little room above the lace shop: with a big sigh. Her older sister seemed to forget that when she had been only a little older than Ines, she had run off on her own and tried to find a husband to save her from the marriage her father had arranged. Not long after, Catarina had swooped in the night before Ines was to be married and offered to take Ines with her to Spain. Ines had agreed, eager to escape a life she hadn't wanted. But now, when Ines craved a little freedom of her own, Catarina still treated her like the girl of only fourteen.

The way Catarina babied her infuriated Ines, but emotional scenes did not sway Catarina. They'd grown up with a violent father who often screamed and yelled for hours. That was before he used his fists. Catarina was not impressed if Ines yelled or stamped her foot or even if she cried. Ines was not ashamed to admit she'd tried all three tactics. Now she would have to think of something else. Perhaps if she took on more responsibility at the lace shop. She could prove that she could be trusted with greater obligations. She pondered that idea for a little while.

She must have fallen asleep because when she jerked awake, she was surprised to find her muscles stiff, as though she had been in the same position for some time. Then she noticed the heat of the day had faded and the noise of London, a noise she had become so accustomed to, had quieted. At the same time, she realized the carriage was still moving. Why was it still moving? Wouldn't the coachman have just made a circle or two and returned to her home to collect Podmore? Ines snatched open the curtains closest to her and stared out into a field dotted with sheep. She opened the curtains on the other side, heart pounding, and stared at a small cottage.

This was not London.

This was not Podmore's coach.

Buy now!

About Shana Galen

Shana Galen is three-time Rita award nominee and the bestselling author of passionate Regency romps. "The road to happily-ever-after is intense, conflicted, suspenseful and fun," and *RT Bookreviews* calls her books "lighthearted yet poignant, humorous yet touching." She taught English at the middle and high school level off and on for eleven years. Most of those years were spent working in Houston's inner city. Now she writes full time, surrounded by three cats and one spoiled dog. She's happily married and has a daughter who is most definitely a romance heroine in the making.

Would you like exclusive content, book news, and a chance to win early copies of Shana's books? You can sign up on her website www.shanagalen.com for exclusive news and giveaways.

Made in the USA
Coppell, TX
14 September 2022

83137298R00213